# THE
# MAGES
## OF
# STARSEA

### THE STARSEA CYCLE BOOK ONE

## KYLE WEST

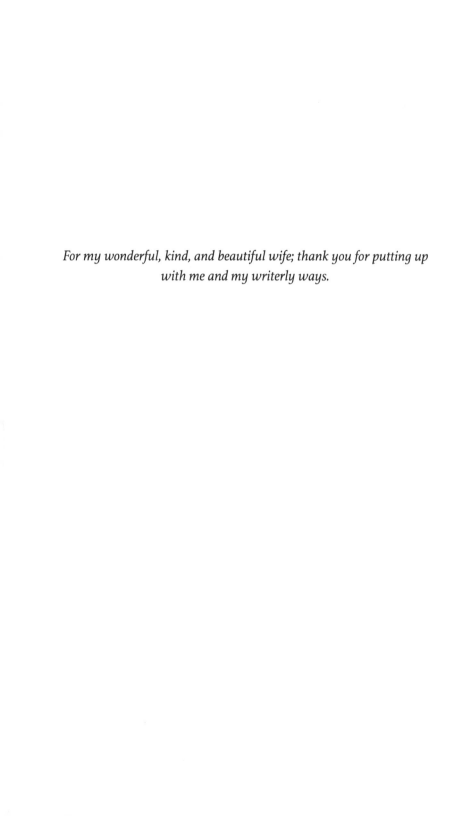

*For my wonderful, kind, and beautiful wife; thank you for putting up with me and my writerly ways.*

# 1

"LUCIAN ABRANTES? The doctors will see you now."

Everyone in the waiting room watched Lucian as if he were a sheep for the slaughter. When he stood, his legs were leaden weights. The tawny-haired nurse beamed a plastic smile as he approached.

"How are we doing today, Lucian?"

Was there even a point to that question? "I've been better."

She frowned, seeming to think for a moment, before defaulting to a wan smile.

"This way, Mr. Abrantes."

She led him through the open doorway down a short corridor. Everything was gray. Walls, carpet, ceiling. Whoever had designed this place hadn't wanted it to inspire any sort of feeling. It was bureaucratic to the core, but that was the League of Worlds for you.

The nurse led him into a small room bordering on claustrophobic. It contained a plastic table and four chairs – three on one side, one on the other. Other than that, it was utterly featureless, without so much as a window to break the monotony. It seemed impossible that the bright sun and white sands of South Shoal were just a couple of kilometers away.

During what should have been Lucian's only metaphysical last week, all they had done was scan his head and send him on his way. He'd read that the follow-up metaphysical exam was worse – so much worse. This room looked like an interrogation chamber from a crime holo.

"Are you sure this isn't all some mistake?" he asked. "I've already been tested this year."

She gave a saccharine smile. "Of course this isn't a mistake, Mr. Abrantes. Please have a seat. The doctors will be with you shortly."

Lucian wanted to tell her that if the doctors had done their job the first time, he wouldn't *be* back. But it would be a waste of breath. It was like dealing with a droid; she could only say what she was supposed to say.

The nurse went off, and Lucian took the single chair facing away from the door. And he waited.

He was left with nothing but his unsettled stomach. At least it wasn't freezing in here, unlike the waiting room outside. His hands and feet were still numb, and probably wouldn't thaw until he was out in the sun again. Judging from this office's inefficiency, that might take a while longer.

That thought was dashed when footsteps approached from the hallway. He drew a deep breath, and exhaled slowly in a vain attempt to calm himself.

Three doctors in white lab coats entered the room and took up the chairs opposite him. The leftmost doctor might have been in his fifties. He was pale, bald, and sporting retro black-rimmed glasses. The middle doctor was a young woman with perfect features that could have only come from gene-tailoring or wallet-crushing surgery. She had blonde hair, blue eyes, and a face too beautiful to be believed. The blue eyes watching

Lucian were too wise for her age. Longevity treatments too, then? Only the obscenely rich could afford that.

The rightmost doctor was a thickset black man with a grandfatherly face. His salt-and-pepper goatee lent him an air of dignity.

All three watched Lucian with the same controlled, neutral mask. As if he were a snake that might bite them any minute.

Yes, this metaphysical would definitely be different.

Whatever news they had, it wasn't good.

# 2

"Mr. Abrantes," the blonde doctor said, "I'm Dr. Ross. These are Dr. Nowak and Dr. Wallace."

The two men nodded in turn at the mention of their names. Lucian looked at each of them warily, but didn't say a word.

"Lucian's fine," he said.

"Lucian, then. We've called you here today to go over the results of your first metaphysical, as I'm sure you know."

He swallowed the lump in his throat. "I thought those were emailed."

Dr. Ross ignored that point. "We'll get you out of here as soon as we can, I assure you. Cutting right to the chase, the exam you already took can't predict magical emergence. It merely flags potential. The next step is to do a sleep lab to confirm if anything's there."

*Sleep* lab? "I don't have time for that, Dr. Ross. Can't you just take my blood or something?"

"It doesn't work that way. The procedure is noninvasive, if a bit inconvenient."

Lucian couldn't wait to hear what *that* meant.

"It should be over in a couple of hours. You'll fall asleep in an MMI vat. The interface fluid will convert the imagery of your dreams into video and emotional feedback for analysis. Dream signatures of mages are different from that of a typical person."

MMI. Mind/machine interface. What the doctor was describing sounded only possible with cybernetic implants. Those were banned for most civilians on most worlds, though there were exceptions. "Sounds pretty invasive to me."

"I'm sorry. We wouldn't be doing this if there were any other way. Unfortunately, it's the law. Usually, the results come back negative. In the entire Tri-County area, we only find a mage every year or two. The odds are one in twenty million, after all. The exam you already did gives a lot of false positives. Especially if you are under stress. So, this is normal, and there's no need for concern."

Her face seemed to say this was anything *but* normal. If so few mages were found, they couldn't have performed this test a lot.

"Do you have any questions before we begin?" she asked. "We'll walk you through each stage of the process."

Lucian had a lot of questions, but for some reason, he couldn't voice a single one of them. "No. Let's get this over with."

He was about to stand, when Dr. Wallace cleared his throat. "Lucian, we have a few questions we need to ask first, if you have none for us."

"Sure. What do you want to know?"

"First," Dr. Wallace continued, in his deep baritone, "I want to ask about your mother. What's your relationship like with her?"

What kind of question was *that*? "Good. How's that relevant?"

"Good?" Dr. Wallace asked, ignoring the question.

"Yes," Lucian said, annoyed. "Good. You didn't answer *my*

question."

Dr. Wallace made a note on his electronic slate. Why was *that* important enough to make a note of?

"And your father?"

"You already have my file," Lucian said, unable to control his tone. "Why are you asking me this, anyway? Just read my mind with your MMI test."

Dr. Wallace's brown eyes were no longer as kindly. "It's important that you answer, Lucian. We need to establish a baseline."

Lucian wasn't going to get out of these questions. The faster he answered, the faster he could leave. "He died in the war when I was five. I don't remember him much."

"You live alone, then?" Dr. Ross's tone held an infuriating note of pity. "That must be difficult."

"It's *not*," Lucian said. "Why's it your business, anyway? I've been taking care of myself for as long as I remember. I've had a job since I was fifteen. I'm studying for the civil exam. I don't need *anybody's* help. I've been doing fine on my own. Would you be asking all these questions if I was forty?"

"Do you experience déjà vu or vivid dreams?" Dr. Nowak asked, in a nasally tone.

The question made Lucian freeze, but he recovered. "No. I mean, *sometimes* I do, but not any more than other people."

"Approximately how often would you say?" Dr. Nowak pressed.

"The déjà vu or the dreams?"

"Both."

"I don't know. Déjà vu once every couple of weeks. Vivid dreams, about the same amount."

"Hmm." He made a note. Lucian almost rolled his eyes.

"Do you have an active imagination, or do you imagine things that often end up happening?" Dr. Ross asked.

He suppressed a shiver. "No to both."

"Do you ever get the feeling that something bad is about to happen, and it comes true?" Dr. Nowak asked.

"Never."

"Have you ever considered suicide?" Dr. Wallace asked.

"As a concept, sure. In reality, no."

He looked at Lucian in a no-nonsense way. "Lucian, have you ever thought of killing yourself?"

"I just answered that."

Dr. Wallace raised an eyebrow.

Lucian sighed. "No."

He made yet another note.

"Do you think you display antisocial tendencies?" Dr. Ross asked. "Have those tendencies grown stronger over the past few years?"

"I'm independent," Lucian said. "I wouldn't say I'm antisocial, though."

They stared at Lucian hard, as if willing him to lie. What did it matter if he *did* have weird dreams, if he *did* have déjà vu? Why would it matter, even if it had happened once a day, or even more? Maybe he just had an active imagination. He didn't buy it. Not for one minute.

"All right," Dr. Ross said. "That'll do for questions. If you would follow us, Lucian, we'll take you to the MMI lab now."

All three stood at the same time. Had they rehearsed that? Lucian followed them out into the short hallway, his pulse quickening. The second test was about to happen. A part of him wanted to run, as futile as that was.

They led him into a large room, in the center of which stood a vertical vat. It was about three meters tall by one meter wide, filled with a viscous pink fluid. A breathing mask hung suspended in the liquid, connected to a breathing tube and a jumble of wires.

"I have to get in *that*?" Lucian asked. "No way!"

"It'll only take an hour," Dr. Ross said. "We've done this test many times before. It's safe."

Lucian had so many questions, but he was already at their mercy. He couldn't show any more weakness. None. If they wanted him to hop in that pink bath, then why not? It wasn't like he could get out of this. "Just tell me what I need to do."

The vat whirred as it rotated downward, until it lay horizontal. The glass door on top slid open with a hiss, revealing the eerie pink liquid within. Both Dr. Wallace and Dr. Nowak stood beside the vat.

"This is the MMI vat," Dr. Wallace explained. "You'll wear the mask and fall asleep inside, taking deep and controlled breaths. The fluid will access your brain, allowing us to see what's going on without the need for cybernetics."

"Don't you have pills for this?" Lucian asked.

"Standard sim pills don't project thoughts outside the brain," Dr. Ross said. "Not in any meaningful way. They are totally insular."

"I assure you, the vat is comfortable," Dr. Wallace said, with a chuckle. "I've been inside one myself. Very warm and cozy. Some people use them for therapy, with promising results."

"I have no problem getting in," Lucian said. "Am I supposed to strip down, or something?"

"We'll provide you a change of clothes," Dr. Wallace said.

Dr. Ross returned from a cabinet, handing Lucian a set of beige scrubs. They looked exceedingly uncomfortable. "Go ahead and put this on. There's a changing room over there. We'll be back in a few minutes."

"Where do I put the clothes I'm wearing?"

"Leave them in the changing room. That's where the shower is, too."

"Do I have to shower first or something?"

She shook her head, her expression terse and annoyed. So, a human person lurked under that beautiful, professional mask after all. "That's not necessary. The shower is for after."

Once they'd left, Lucian didn't waste time. He changed in less than a minute. While he waited in the cold room barefoot, his stomach churned. He tried not to look at that vat. Whatever that pink stuff inside was, it didn't look natural.

He wanted out of here. But how? The League mandated the exam. Getting a pass was out of the question.

One in twenty million. He wasn't one of them. He wasn't a mage.

A minute later, the doctors reentered.

"Okay," Dr. Ross said, forcing a smile. "Step into the vat and sit in the fluid. We'll help you with the mask. Once you're comfortable, go ahead and lie on your back, and submerge yourself."

Hesitation would only make him look weak, so Lucian stepped into the vat. The liquid was warm and syrupy, seeming to congeal around his foot. The warm feeling wasn't unpleasant. That was hard to admit. It was like a bath, but stickier.

He immersed himself up to his torso. Both Dr. Wallace and Dr. Nowak held him by the shoulders, while Dr. Ross stood next to him, slate out.

"Don't force me under," Lucian said.

"We won't," Dr. Nowak replied.

Dr. Ross handed him a pill and a paper cup filled with water. "Here."

"What's this?"

"It'll help you sleep. The whole test is pointless without it."

Lucian stared at it a moment, before popping the pill and washing it down.

"Now," she said, "let me help you with the mask . . ."

"I've got it," Lucian said.

The mask was floating in the middle of the vat. When Lucian picked it up, pink fluid dripped off it in long, snotty streams. The fluid even covered the inside.

"Hold your horses," Dr. Ross said. "Will you let us *help* you?"

Lucian was forced to oblige. A moment later, a disgusting sucking sound emanated from the breathing tube. Once the inside of the mask was clean, the suction stopped.

"I hope you don't do that to me while I'm wearing it."

"There are safety features that prevent that from happening," Dr. Ross said in a world-weary way. "It's to clean the mask before you put it on."

She helped Lucian with the mask, and he let her clamp it on. A steady supply of air entered. The mask covered the entirety of his face. At least he wouldn't have to worry about the fluid getting into his eyes. It was the small things.

"Okay," she said. "Ready?"

Lucian nodded. "I guess." The mask made his voice garbled and robotic.

Dr. Wallace and Dr. Nowak guided him down. Actually, they were *pushing* him down. So much for not forcing things. Lucian fought the urge to free himself, but that would have been pointless.

Before he knew it, he was completely submerged. When the glass door clicked shut, panic seized his chest. His breaths came out rapidly while his heart slammed against his chest.

The vat rotated until it was completely upright. Lucian tried not to think of how exposed and idiotic he looked. But before his thoughts could race out of control, a sudden wave of drowsiness overcame him. It was too powerful to ignore. His heartbeat slowed, and he could barely keep his eyes open.

His last view through the pink haze was of a video screen. The three doctors crowded around it.

The image on the screen was startling. It was of the world through *his* eyes, of him watching the doctors watching the screen, ad infinitum.

It was the last thing before darkness took him.

# 3

THE PRESSURE of the water was crushing, and the darkness near complete. And it was cold. So terribly cold.

Panic seized him, and he swam upward, fighting the freezing, dark water. Stroke after stroke, he clawed upward, his muscles burning. Even as the coldness sapped his heat and strength, his lungs were afire. Where was the surface? How far to go?

He was going to die here.

Through his blurry vision, Lucian saw something floating above. What was it? He swam toward it. It might be his only chance to survive . . .

As the shape of the object materialized before him, he realized it was a rope.

*Let me help you.*

His mother's voice. How was she here?

*Grab the rope, Lucian. I can save you.*

An unseen force stayed his hand. He wanted nothing more than to grab it, but all he could do was stare at it in paralysis.

*Reach for the rope!*

The line was slipping away into the darkness. Lucian's

muscles exploded into action as he swam toward it. But it was withdrawing faster than he could swim.

*Reach, Lucian!*

It was too far. Lucian couldn't hold his breath any longer. He sucked frigid salt water into his lungs. In and out, in and out, in and out. It entered and left cold, stinging, and harsh.

But also . . . life-giving. Oxygen infused into his blood. How could this be? The blackness of his vision receded, until only coldness remained.

Lucian didn't question it. He was breathing, and he would live. He didn't need the rope, nor the salvation it offered.

This was a dream. It could be nothing else.

Upon that realization, the scene shifted.

He was somewhere else . . .

————

HE NOW SAT at a table next to one of Miami's canals. Lucian recognized the place immediately. It was an outdoor restaurant he sometimes went to by his condo. The sultry and humid air stuck to his skin. The fact that it was night didn't make it cool, though. It was a place of comfort, but tonight, he felt as if someone were watching him. The hairs on his neck stood on end. He took a sip of the cold beer on the table in front of him to steady his nerves.

He was meeting someone, he remembered that, but who? It was so hard to remember why he was doing things anymore. His hand clamped around the beer can, slightly crushing it.

"Careful there."

That voice. Lucian turned, and remembered who he was supposed to meet. And why he had been so afraid.

"Luisa," he managed.

His heart ached at seeing her face. How he *hated* that. The woman had taken him for a ride that had nearly killed him.

Her looks made it hard to regret his past bad decisions too much, though.

"May I sit?"

Lucian cleared his throat, and gestured toward the empty seat.

"Once, you would have stood and pulled out my chair," she observed, a bit icily.

Her black dress accentuated her curvy figure. That had to have been a strategic choice on her part. Anything to give her an edge in conversation. Her full lips became pouty as she stared at him across the table. Her shoulder-length black hair fell upon pale shoulders. Those dark brown eyes smoldered with anger and barely suppressed hurt. Still prickly over the breakup, then. This conversation would not be pleasant.

"So, what did you want to talk to me about? If it's about getting back together, well, you can shove it."

"Not that," Lucian said, a little too quickly. Her eyes narrowed further. "There was something I needed to tell you."

"Well, don't leave me in suspense."

"I'm leaving, Luisa. For good."

The sternness of her expression faltered, if only for a moment. So, her harshness was a mask. Lucian wasn't sure how to feel about that.

"What do you mean, *leaving*?"

"I got a job off-world. Tonight's my last night."

"Off-world, where?"

"Cislunar. On a small orbital."

Her face became dangerous. "You can't deal with me, so your solution is to *leave*?"

He couldn't meet her eyes. "I'm sorry. It's not about that, really."

"Then what *is* it about?"

Silence stretched between them. His mind fought for ways

to smooth things over. Why had he even met her here in the first place?

"You lied to me," she said, finally. "I'm *tired* of your lies. Tired of being strung along and toyed with. You're . . . one of *them*, aren't you? Don't deny it!"

Of course. That was why he wanted to meet her here. To tell her the truth about what he was. The idea of it was surreal. What had he been thinking?

"I am," he admitted. "I just . . . thought you should know."

"And ruin everything I ever thought about you?"

She stood suddenly, and reached for something in her purse. Lucian's heart almost stopped when she pulled out an old-fashioned handgun, the kind that used bullets, and pointed it right at him.

Everything went still at that moment. All sound stopped. There was only the gun, the fear, and Luisa's crazed expression. Lucian opened his mouth to speak, but no words came.

"What I do in the next moment depends on you."

The gun shook in her hand. Around them, random passers-by continued to walk, oblivious to the drama playing out. Why was no one stopping? Where were the police drones?

"Luisa, please put the gun away," Lucian said, finally finding his voice. "I'll answer anything you like."

"It's too late for that." The gun rose from his chest to his face. "You're one of them. A . . . *mage*. And you kept it from me. You made me believe like nothing was wrong."

Tears streamed down her face. The gun fell to her side, and she raised a hand to stifle her cries. Lucian was torn between trying to comfort her and running away. What kind of insane reaction was that? His feet remained in place.

He would have to be careful.

"Luisa . . . I'm sorry. I should have told you before. I don't know what I was thinking."

He was thinking she might react like *this*. But even this was too much for Luisa. He had misjudged her. And now, he might die for it.

"You said you loved me. But you threw me aside like I'm trash."

"You're not trash," Lucian said. He held up his hands, and stepped forward. "Luisa..."

She did not raise the gun again. Her face filled with tears, her shoulders shaking. As she fell into his arms, seeking his comfort, he went for the gun.

And was surprised when Luisa pushed him away, her face a mask of betrayal. She raised the gun again, her expression cold.

"Admit it. Admit it, and I'll put it away."

Admit what? That he was one of *them*?

"Luisa..."

*"Tell me!"*

He could never do that. If he did, it meant it was true. He felt that to the core of his being.

"I'm not a mage, Luisa."

Of course. This was only a dream. A test.

He turned and walked away, his heart pounding madly. Any moment now, she might shoot him. One step. Another. He could hear her ragged breaths. Just the slightest exertion, and he'd have a bullet in his back. But only if he was wrong.

In the building ahead was an elevator that would take him up to his apartment. He was steps away when the gunshot rang out. He felt no pain, no hot blood, no darkness, or loss of consciousness. Had she missed?

He turned, and the answer lay a few steps away. Luisa lay in her black dress in a pool of blood, her pale face a mask of death.

Lucian ran toward her, but the space between seemed to stretch. He couldn't reach her. He would *never* reach her. He let out a scream, but it was cut off.

The dream faded, as if it had never been.

———

THE DARKNESS PRESSED in around him. It wasn't water this time, but it was heavy, encasing him like a coffin. The gunshot reverberated in his mind, shocking him inside and out.

Wherever this place was, Lucian didn't have a body. He was a consciousness floating in a void. Was this death? Maybe. And maybe it was even worse than death.

He wasn't alone. He couldn't have said *how* he knew that, but he did. All he wanted was to escape.

But just as he knew he wasn't alone, he knew escape was impossible.

*You are the one.*

Who was that? With every word, Lucian suffered a peal of dread. All he wanted was to wake up. All he wanted was to deafen himself to that horrible voice.

This time, Lucian knew it was a dream. But the realization wasn't enough. He wouldn't leave until the voice had gotten what it wanted. But what could that be?

*What are you?* Lucian wondered at that question. Why had he asked *what*, and not *who*? It had seemed natural, though.

*I am your calling,* the voice responded. *Find the Aspects. Bring them to me. Only by so doing can we prevent the cycle from repeating.*

*What do you mean?*

*No. Listen to me. There isn't time. Only you can do this. Only you have the strength.*

*I want out.*

*Promise me. Swear you'll find them. Swear you'll bring them to me.*

*I want out of here.* For some reason, it was getting harder to find the strength to resist . . .

*Not until you promise me.*

Lucian tried to resist that horrible voice, but it was breaking down every mental barrier he had. The horror needed to end. If that required him to say a few inconsequential words, then he would say them.

*I will. I will find the Aspects.*

*And bring them to me.*

Lucian hesitated. *Yes. I will bring them to you.*

The intense pressure ended, and Lucian felt as if he could breathe again.

*You've done well,* the voice said. *Go. And never forget.*

Darkness swirled around him, forming images. Faces materialized in the maelstrom, apparitions birthed from the dark void. His mother, her face tired and bearing new lines. His father, barely remembered, standing at the boarding gate for his shuttle. The last time Lucian ever saw him. Luisa, her tears black as ink, her expression mournful. There were new faces, too: new faces that were somehow familiar. A tall and regal young woman with soft brown eyes. An old crone of a woman, wearing a dark gray cloak. Two disheveled men, huddling about a fire in a dank cave.

*Remember . . .*

The voice faded, and Lucian was shocked to wakefulness.

# 4

A SCREAM TORE from Lucian's throat as the vat rotated horizontal and the glass door hissed open, admitting the cool air of the lab.

He had to get out. He had to escape. The only thing that kept him from running from the room was Dr. Nowak and Dr. Wallace restraining him.

"Sit still," Dr. Ross said firmly.

She helped Lucian out of the mask and he gasped as if he'd never breathed in his life.

"Easy there," she said. "You had a bit of a nightmare with that last one ..."

Lucian ignored the understatement. His mind reeled with the horrifying images, his heart pounding like mad.

"*Breathe*," Dr. Ross instructed in a calm, collected voice. "In for four, out for eight."

It took a moment for Lucian to follow her instructions. He sat there for a good minute or two, going through the same breathing technique. By the time he'd calmed, Dr. Wallace and Dr. Nowak helped him to stand. A bout of dizziness almost made him collapse, but the two male doctors were there to support him.

"Stay still," Dr. Wallace ordered. "Get your bearings."

It was another minute before Lucian felt calm enough to think straight. The images of that last dream still swirled in his head, inducing a sense of vertigo.

What could it mean? Had the doctors seen all that? But before he could embrace the reality of it, he freed himself from the doctors' collective grip. He had to get out of here.

"Where's the shower?" he asked.

Dr. Ross's expression was a mask of concern. Lucian could only imagine the figure he cut in his pink-soaked scrubs.

"That way," she said, nodding toward the door across the lab. "We'll give you ten minutes to get situated."

The doctors left, leaving Lucian to shower in peace. The globs of pink interface fluid slid off his body and down the drain. Despite the heat of the water, he was shaking as if it were freezing.

By the time he stepped into the air dryer, he had relaxed a bit, but his hands were still trembling. That *voice*. What had *that* been about? The doctors had said *nothing* to prepare him for that.

He tried to push the dreams from his mind. What did they all mean? If anything, it wasn't his problem anymore. All he could do was leave this place and forget this day for the rest of his life.

As Dr. Ross said, the odds of him being a mage were low. What did she say they found, about two a year? Lucian couldn't remember.

Then again, he could be the one. And with a dream like that last one . . .

Lucian shook his head and dressed in his street clothes. He stepped back into the lab, to find Dr. Nowak waiting for him.

"Your paperwork is done," he said. "You should have your results soon."

"Am I good to go?"

He gave a cursory nod. "We'll send them by email. If there's anything of concern, we'll let you know."

"What are the odds of that happening?"

Dr. Nowak hesitated a bit before answering, pushing his glasses back up his nose. "Well, the odds *are* low. Roughly one in a thousand once you get to this point."

For some reason, that didn't make Lucian feel much better. He had the feeling Nowak knew something. But he didn't want to find out what that was.

"Okay. Guess I'll head out, then."

"Drink plenty of fluids and take it easy."

Lucian couldn't get out of the building fast enough. The elevator ride down from the fiftieth floor took an eternity. Once Lucian stepped outside under the sweltering sun, he hurried to the Lev station.

He clenched his fists as he took the steps up to the Lev platform. He couldn't help but look over his shoulder, at the curving façade of the League Health Authority gleaming in front of Biscayne Bay. Before, Lucian had been ambivalent about the League of Worlds, like most of its citizens. Its inefficiency was a nuisance that hardly touched him outside the random inconvenience. Looking at that building now, though, Lucian's mouth twisted in disgust.

A magnetic Lev train pulled soundlessly into the station. A pass cost a small fortune, but they were the most convenient way of getting around the city. Thankfully, Lucian's pass was free due to his internship with the League. Otherwise, he would have had to travel by boat through one of Miami's hundreds of sprawling canals. The city had mostly sunk beneath the Atlantic by the 23$^{rd}$ century, over a hundred years before Lucian's time. He couldn't imagine what the city had been like before. Now, the city was a patchwork of artificial islands, floating high-rises, and multitiered boardwalks interconnected by canals and Lev trains.

He stepped inside the Lev, trying to formulate a reason for his absence that his mother would accept.

If she found out the truth, she'd have an aneurism.

———

"MOM, I'M HOME."

That clatter of pots and pans told him she was cooking. What was she doing in there? They had a meal plan.

She looked over her shoulder, revealing a short woman with shoulder-length brown hair, brown eyes, and a round face. "You mind helping me with this, son?"

Lucian dropped his backpack and walked into the kitchen, to the sight of an open cabinet.

She sighed with exasperation. "Why do you keep things so high? Get that blender for me, will you?"

Lucian got it down for her. "I barely even use it. Forgot I had it, to be honest. Might be dusty."

"I've been away too long," she grumbled. A strand of hair fell across her face, which was pockmarked with several moles. She brushed it aside in agitation. "You don't eat enough fruits and vegetables, Lucian. It's a wonder you grew so tall."

Lucian could only shake his head. "Good to have you back, Mom."

She'd been back three days from her fleet furlough, and it already felt like three months. After living on his own for months, it was hard getting used to her being back. Technically, the condo was hers, but to Lucian it didn't feel that way. She spent months at a time stationed with the Fleet, mostly at Sol Citadel, the League military starbase about half a million klicks from Mars.

His mother placed some banana, pineapple, and blueberries in a blender, along with milk and vitamin powder. After a few seconds of whirring, it came out perfectly smooth.

"Drink this," she commanded, handing him the glass.

He drank. When his mother told him to do something, it was far easier to comply than argue.

"Why do you look like that, son?" she asked, her left eyebrow arched in suspicion.

"Like what?"

"Like you swallowed a frog. And before you say anything, I know it's not the smoothie."

Did he really look that sick? "I'm fine."

"No. Something's happened. Tell me."

"Nothing's happened. I had to stay late to study for the civil exam."

"Uh-huh. Sure. You're worrying me sick." As Lucian struggled for what to say, her face lit up, as if in realization. "Ah, I know what it is. You're hungry, that's it. No worries. I'll make you something more substantial."

Lucian held back his sigh of relief as he watched his mother rummage through the fridge. She took out a few eggs and butter, and started frying them.

"Why're you cooking, Mom? We've got a meal plan. We can have a full dinner delivered in less than five minutes."

She shrugged. "Out there, eating the slop they serve us, I miss cooking. I miss real gravity, too." She flipped an egg, as if in demonstration of her point, and it sizzled on the skillet. "Where have you been? Are you back with that girl? I forget her name."

The mere reminder of Luisa was almost enough to make him shudder. "No, I'm not. I haven't talked to her in a while."

"That's good. She liked to party too much. You need a nice girl, Lucian. Someone a bit older, someone who can take care of you . . ." She frowned, considering. "Yeah, that would be perfect for you."

His mother was going to act like a mother, and there was nothing he could do about that. She wasn't so bad when she *wasn't* sticking her nose into his business, but that was what she did ninety percent of the time. And he had to deal with it for the next six weeks. Lucian got the feeling they would be the longest six weeks of his life.

"So, where were you, son?" She could be so *insufferable*. "And don't tell me you were studying. I can always tell when you're lying."

Lucian heaved a sigh. "I'm *not* lying. Why do you always treat me like I'm half my age?"

"Because you're *acting* half your age." He hadn't counted on her tenacity, so he hadn't thought of any more details to make his story more convincing.

"The civil exam is coming up," he said. "What's so hard to believe about that?"

She shook her head. "Okay, fine." She waved him over. "Eggs are done. You're too thin. How'll you *ever* find a decent girl looking like that? You like all those fake girls who starve themselves and mod their faces. That might be why the last one looked a little funny. Those lips made her look like a trout."

"You're being annoying, Mom."

"If you're going to mod your face, at least pay the money to get it done right," she went on. "Lord knows we have enough face surgeons here in Miami." She shook her head, signaling the end of her rant. "Whatever. Grab a plate."

"I should study."

"You look like something washed up on the side of the canal. *Eat*, and spend some time with your dear old mom before she gets shipped back out. Is that too much to ask?"

Lucian sighed. "Of course not."

"Eat, then."

If there was anything Lucian could count on from his mother, it was brutal honesty. Three days of this, and it was driving him up the wall. He grabbed a plate, putting two eggs with hot sauce over a large spoonful of black beans. His mother made her own plate, with a cup of dark black coffee to go with it. The aroma was so strong it tingled his nostrils. She could chug that stuff all day and not so much as twitch.

Once seated at the table, they started eating.

"So good to be home," she said. "Though it doesn't feel much like home, anymore. Your junk is *everywhere*. You need to find a home for it, or get rid of it." She scrutinized him. "Are you taller? I swear, you keep growing. I don't know who you get it from. Not my side, that's for sure."

"I've grown a centimeter, at most," Lucian said, trying to keep the weariness from his voice.

She waved her hand. "Centimeter? When I was your age, we used inches. I guess they finally drilled out the old measurements from the younger generation."

"Metric makes more sense, Mom. Multiples of ten. Easy to remember."

"I know how it works. But for height, it always makes sense to use feet. Saying you're six feet sounds far more impressive. I don't even know what that is in metric."

"One hundred and eighty three centimeters."

She laughed. "See? You've made my point. Who has the time to say that?" Her demeanor became more serious. "There's something I wanted to talk to you about, and don't think you're getting out of it." She retrieved her slate from her purse, and slid it across the table, screen up, toward Lucian. The screen was open to the family inbox.

There was an email, already opened, from the League Health Authority. It was Lucian's appointment reminder from today.

Lucian hadn't considered that the doctors would send it to

the family inbox as well as his personal one. There was no readymade excuse to spew out. He'd been caught in the lie. *That* was why she had been so insistent, giving him three chances to come clean.

Well, shit.

"Why didn't you tell me about this?" his mother asked.

"Why were you trying to catch me in a lie in the first place, Mom?" he asked. "I'm allowed to keep parts of my life to myself."

"But *this*?" She pointed to the slate. There wasn't anger there anymore. There was fear. "Lucian, you need to tell me about stuff like this. This is very serious!"

"You think *I* don't know that?" Lucian asked. "That's where I was today. I said it was a test, and that's the truth. It *was* a test. It's not even a big deal."

"But you've already taken your metaphysical. Why would they do it again?"

He needed to control himself, but that was difficult to do around her. Lucian drew a deep breath and closed his eyes for a moment before responding. "I don't know. They said my original exam was flagged, and they had to do a follow-up. It took about an hour, maybe two. But it's going to be fine. They let me go, right?"

For once, she was quiet, probably thinking of the ramifications. When she looked at him again, her eyes were hurt. "Why didn't you tell me? You shouldn't keep this stuff to yourself, son."

He hadn't told her because she would have just made him feel bad about it. Like she was doing now.

"I didn't want to bother you. You're so happy to be home, and you're still grav-lagged, anyway. The last thing you need is stress. I thought I was doing a good thing. Guess not, though."

"You *were* going to tell me, though."

"Yes, of course," he lied. "It's not even a big deal. They said only one of a thousand who do the advanced testing is confirmed as a mage. The odds are on my side. If you needed to be kept in the loop, I'm sorry."

He hoped she would take the olive branch. She reached her hand across the table, taking his. Maybe things would calm down.

"Lucian, you're my son. You have to let me help you. I know I'm not here all the time, and I know I haven't been the greatest mother. But please, when I'm here to help you, *let* me be a mother."

"I'm not a kid anymore. I know how to take care of myself."

"Don't do that to me. I work hard to provide for you, so you can go to school and get a good job. I try to come home when I can, but it's hard to take off, Lucian. I'm guilty enough already without you making it worse."

"I'm not blaming you," Lucian said. "I appreciate what you do for me. But I'm twenty now. Sure, I'm young, but I'm a man. I can take care of myself. And in another year, I'll be supporting myself."

Working for the League. Not an ideal situation, and not exciting. But he'd have good benefits and get a steady salary with plenty of room for advancement. Assuming he could deal with their bureaucratic bullshit.

There was some emotion behind her watery eyes. Was it guilt? Sadness? It made Lucian want to give up talking to her. No matter what he said, he would only make things worse..

"I know you're twenty now," she said. "I know you're your own man. But this test is a *big deal*. It's okay to lean on me. Just saying . . . I'm here. I always will be."

Lucian didn't bother to call out the lie. When he was younger, he never understood why his mother had to be gone all the time. But as he grew older, he understood the necessity. His father had been dead fifteen years, so she had to support him all on her own. Most of that time, it meant him attending a costly boarding school while his mother was stationed with the Fleet or at the Citadel. And when school wasn't in session, a neighbor watched over him.

But as the years went by, Lucian was more or less on his own, aside from his mother's short furloughs. He almost *never* saw her during the Swarmer War, and that had lasted for five years.

Lucian had mostly repressed the insecurity he felt growing up. He had learned to deal with it quite well. Better than most would have expected him to. Learning to deal with loneliness and insecurity meant learning not to care. It hadn't been easy, of course, but in time Lucian came to prefer solitude.

When the Swarmers finally retreated five years ago, Lucian saw his mother more. But by then, she had missed a lot of his growing up. What would it even be like to have a normal family? Lucian didn't know. And by now, he'd trained himself not to care.

It hadn't been easy, raising himself, but it was his proudest accomplishment. Even if he didn't want to be a bureaucrat, he'd made himself study and work hard for it. That made him a strong person . . . stronger than most, anyway. He rarely drank, never used drugs, and took care of himself. He didn't need *anybody* to make the right decisions.

So of course he hadn't told his mother about the second exam. Like everything else, he'd learned to deal with it on his own. Even if it scared the hell out of him.

One more year and he'd graduate early. There wasn't a doubt he'd pass the grueling exams. After that, he could apply for many government positions and make a comfortable living. It was conceivable that a posting in the League would take him to other planets, too. Lucian had an itch to travel and see the Worlds. He had never even been off Earth, but he was determined not to live his entire life here.

27

As far as he was concerned, he could forget his childhood had ever existed.

He had this stupid fantasy when he was younger, of piloting his own interstellar freighter. A small, barebones crew, or better yet, a crew of only droids. He'd make long runs between the Gates to distant worlds, spending months between the stars. That wouldn't be an easy job for most. But those who could do it were paid very well. They said the loneliness was enough to break most people. He felt he had been training for something like that his entire life.

It was a dumb dream, a fantasy to escape from a lonely childhood. But even Lucian found it strange that his escape from loneliness was an existence even more lonely.

The rest of the dinner passed in silence. Her face was sad as she scraped the last of the food on her spoon. She seemed lost in her own thoughts, so Lucian didn't interrupt her.

She broke the silence with a sigh. "Well, if they find something, I'm coming with you this time. No arguments. You need someone to have your back."

The idea was repulsive to him, but he was too tired to argue. Those dreams during the test had been pretty disturbing – drowning, Luisa killing herself, and that last one especially. What *had* that voice been? It had seemed so real. If he closed his eyes, he could almost hear it whispering in his ear, like a cold wind rustling dry leaves . . .

"You okay, son?"

Lucian shuddered. "Yeah. Fine."

"You know *fine* is never an appropriate answer."

"I'm okay, then."

"No, you're not. I see it in your eyes."

Would it hurt to answer honestly for once? He'd been burned before doing that. But her eyes were so concerned, maybe he could let down his guard this one time.

"All right. I'll admit I'm a little nervous about my results.

That test was . . . something else. They put me in an MMI vat, and then I had these crazy dreams . . ."

Lucian told her about what happened, but left out the more graphic details. Lucian didn't say a thing about the last dream.

"You know, I had to take a follow-up, once," she said. "Nothing came of it, though. Most of those tests are false positives. You'll see."

It was hard to keep his voice calm. "Why didn't you say something before?"

"It was so long ago." There was more to the story. That much Lucian could see. "It was the year after your father's death. That . . . was a bad year." At Lucian's silence, she kept talking. "This might sound crazy, but your grandmother always had these little inklings. She'd walk into a house and *know* things. When she was alive, your father and I were about to buy a house back in Texas. But she said *no* the minute she passed through the door. Said a lot of sad things happened there." She shook her head. "Thank God they didn't test back then. She'd have been one."

The story made his gut churn. Being a mage wasn't *supposed* to be genetic, but many people believed it was.

"It's going to be fine, Mom."

"The odds are small," she admitted. "Tomorrow, we'll go and everything will be okay. You'll see."

Was she trying to convince him, or herself? Lucian had a feeling the odds didn't matter. Either he was a mage, or he wasn't. Either his life was ruined, or it wasn't.

His slate chimed. He picked it up in his right hand, its size adjusting to fit perfectly.

When Lucian read the message, his heart plummeted.

"What does it say?" his mother asked.

He swallowed the lump in his throat. "They want me back at 14:00 tomorrow."

# 5

LUCIAN HARDLY SLEPT THAT NIGHT. Besides his thoughts keeping him awake, the dilapidated A/C unit was fighting a losing battle. The Abrantes' apartment was in Old Little Havana. Many of the tenements were well over a century old. Those who couldn't afford to live in one of the modern arcologies rising from the flooded Florida shoals lived here. The old unit rattled like a dying beast, and seemed to succeed only in blowing warm, humid air.

Nightlife crowds packed the canal below Lucian's window. And they were *loud*, as they were every night. Lucian's neighborhood was where people went to party who didn't want to sell a kidney first. Dozens of clubs and dive bars pulsed with dance music. Coupled with the drunken shouting, the tall buildings lining the canal only served to echo the cacophony below. Usually, Lucian had no trouble ignoring it. But tonight, he couldn't sleep.

He tossed and turned until the noise of the crowds ebbed, if not completely going away. He opened his eyes to the morning sun, and figured he'd only gotten a few hours of sleep.

He faded in and out as the sunlight grew brighter. Morning Levs zoomed over his building, rattling the walls and floors. He didn't wake completely until the smell of lunch drifted into his room, carried by the dying A/C unit. Lucian forced himself up, showered, and brushed his teeth. His face in the mirror looked worn and mournful, his brown eyes listless. When he went out to the kitchen, lunch was ready. Going back to the Health Authority building was the last way he wanted to spend a Saturday. But there was nothing he could do about that.

He and his mother ate in silence, each occupied with their own thoughts. Lucian hardly tasted the food. By the time they finished, it was time to leave.

The light was near-blinding, reflecting off the azure canal below. The hot, muggy air was stifling. The canyons between the shabby buildings were heat traps, especially in the summer. And today promised to be as hot as any other. Lucian thought it was no wonder much of the ice caps had melted long before he'd been born, submerging the majority of the city. There weren't many people out at this hour, which was a good thing. It was only at night that one had to be careful.

Within the hour, the Lev let them off at the revolving doors of the Health Authority. Another few minutes saw them to the fiftieth floor. Besides them, the frigid, gray waiting room was empty.

At the appointed time, two o'clock, the same nurse opened the sliding door to the back offices. "Lucian Abrantes?"

Her tone today wasn't as friendly, but Lucian pretended not to notice as he and his mother followed her. His stomach churned, and there was a lump in his throat that refused to go away.

The nurse showed them into Dr. Ross's office. The beautiful doctor was waiting for them, her features a perfect, neutral mask.

31

"Good afternoon," she said. "Thank you for coming in today."

As if he had a choice. "The results?"

"The test results are in," she confirmed. "I won't mince words. We are . . . detecting clear signs of metaphysical emergence."

The words hung in the air. Metaphysical emergence. That was what the scientists called it to maintain a scientific illusion.

Everyone else just called it what it was: magic.

Lucian felt nothing at the words. Cold. Emotionless. It was as if this were happening to someone else, and not him.

"Do you mean that?" Lucian asked. "Isn't it possible you made some mistake?"

"It must be a mistake," his mother said. "I'm his mother, I've never seen him once act like . . . one of *them*."

"Unfortunately, there is no mistake," Dr. Ross said. "We analyzed three dreams during the lab yesterday, Mrs. Abrantes. The first dream showed no signs of metaphysical manifestation. The second showed some minor signs, but within the realm of error." She paused. "By the third, though . . . it was very clear."

His mother was looking at him for explanation. "You'd only mentioned two dreams."

Lucian remained silent, and kept his eyes on the desk in front of him.

His mother turned back to the doctor. "*How* was it clear?"

"The screen was black," Dr. Ross said. "In every case the screen goes black, it is one hundred percent consistent with metaphysical emergence. Even if – *special abilities* – haven't surfaced yet, it's actually a good thing we've detected it this early. It's the reason we have these tests."

Lucian just wanted her to get to the point.

"With proper training, the ill-effects of metaphysical emergence can be delayed, perhaps even indefinitely. We need to enter your son into a mage academy – as soon as possible."

"Of course," my mother said. "Whatever the cost."

Lucian's skin went cold. How could this be possible? A *mage*. It was unreal. Something that only happened to people in films.

If what he knew about it was true, then he was going to die.

"This can't be real . . ." he said.

Dr. Ross stared at him in silence. Lucian couldn't bring himself to look at her.

"I've shown no real signs of . . . you know. What happens to mages."

"The speed of the degenerative condition, known as *fraying*, varies," Dr. Ross said. "Some experience strong symptoms from the very beginning. Some take years to develop. If there's anything I've learned about dealing with this disease, meta-physical emergence can happen to anyone. All we can do is control the outcome the best way we know how."

Lucian was deaf to it all. He was a *mage*. Destined to go mad as an unknown power burned through him. And it would burn until it took everything from him. His dreams and ambitions, first. Then motor control along with the rot of his skin and organs. And finally, his very sanity, when the sickness reached his brain.

In short, his life was over.

"And there is no cure?" his mother asked. "*Someone* has to have figured something out!"

"The condition can only be managed," Dr. Ross said. "But if Lucian is to get help, it can't be here. Various academies have been set up around the Worlds. Mages run them, and they dedicate their lives to finding a cure to the fraying. From what I understand, they do it through careful control of their . . . abilities. Many, I've been told, can live to old age. We've come a long way in the last fifty years."

"If there are none on Earth, where can my son go?"

"The closest academy is on Volsung. That's where I suggest your son apply."

Volsung. It was one of the First Worlds, and only a Gate jump away. Of course, Lucian realized, even a single Gate jump was a journey of about a month. Interstellar travel was expensive, far beyond the pay grade of he and his mother. Was he doomed to die, then?

"How can we get him in?" his mother asked.

"I don't want to go," Lucian said. "This *has* to be a mistake. You guys told me the odds are one in a thousand with advanced testing. And only one in twenty million people are mages in the first place. How can *anyone* be so . . . unlucky? It's not right. It *can't* be."

Dr. Ross looked at him, her expression filled with pity.

Tears hung in his mother's brown eyes. "Lucian, this is your only chance. As difficult as it is . . . it seems to be the only option."

"Voyages to Volsung set out from Sol Citadel daily," Dr. Ross said. "The government can help you secure a no-interest loan, if you need help. If you work for the League, they sometimes subsidize travel expenses completely. Assuming you can get your son to Volsung, it's a matter of making it to the Academy itself. The leaders of this academy, called the Transcends, must be appealed to personally for training. They . . . do not take on all prospects. As soon as everything is confirmed, I can send a light-message out."

Lucian could only shake his head. "This is my life. Do I not get to decide?"

"Lucian," his mother said. "There isn't any other option."

She was right. Even if he chose not to go for training, most places in the Hundred Worlds banned mages. They were simply too dangerous, especially once the fraying took hold. There were only a few worlds where they *weren't* banned. But even then, mages were quarantined in their own communities. No better than a prison, really.

"So, this academy isn't guaranteed to accept Lucian?" his mother asked. "What happens if he goes there, but they don't want to train him?"

"Well, if not the Volsung Academy, he could travel to another academy. But the other academies are far more distant, and would take many months of interstellar travel."

Lucian noted impatience in Dr. Ross's features. She wanted to wrap this meeting up.

"Thanks for your help," Lucian said. "We can get going now."

"Wait," his mother said. "What if they don't accept him? What then?"

"Well," Dr. Ross said, "assuming that, he could go to a world that hasn't outlawed mages yet. Of course, there are few such places left, and it doesn't guarantee that the planet won't outlaw mages in the future. The closest one is Halia, but—"

"—Wait," his mother interrupted. "You said Halia? My brother lives there."

Lucian's Uncle, Ravis, had emigrated Earth ten years ago to live there. He worked for Caralis Intergalactic, a company that produced droids. There were large-scale mining operations developing on Halia, hence his relocation.

"Yes," Dr. Ross said. "Halia is a rough world, from what I've heard. There, mages have to live in their own communes, and there are no League-sanctioned academies. That is an option, but in my professional opinion, the Volsung Academy would be better. At least that way, there is a chance Lucian can be treated."

"How much does it cost?"

"Assuming you can get there, and he's accepted, nothing," Dr. Ross said. "The Academy is self-sufficient."

Lucian was trying to pay attention, but stress made it difficult to focus. This was too much. Even if he were accepted for training, that was no guarantee. But what could he do?

His life was over.

"I don't want this," he said.

Before either of the doctor or his mother could say anything, Lucian ran out of the office.

# 6

HE DIDN'T KNOW where he was going. He was just running. His mother's shouts cut off as the elevator doors closed. He crouched in the corner, his heart racing and his breath accelerating. When the doors opened again, several people were waiting, looking at him with shocked expressions. He rose and charged forward, one man even shouting as he passed.

Lucian was blind, and deaf, to it all. All that mattered was catching a Lev to *anywhere* but here.

Lucian ran to the Lev station across the canal fronting the League building. He stepped on a timely train, rushing to an empty seat as the doors hissed shut behind him. He was glad the coach was mostly empty as the train shot north, propelled by magnetism. The glittering skyscrapers of downtown Miami blitzed by.

Lucian held his head in his hands, closing his eyes. What now?

Canaveral Spaceport was an hour away. He had some savings, enough to buy a ticket to Sol Citadel, and if not that, one of the L-Cities. He couldn't go anywhere on Earth – he would be tracked. The only thing that mattered was getting *distance.* Maybe he could talk a freighter into taking him on. If he could do that before his government profile was flagged, he might have a shot at escape.

None of that made sense, but Lucian didn't care. All that mattered was getting away. Starting a new life.

The question was, could he go through with it? He knew it was insane. As his emotions ebbed, he hung his head lower. This would *never* work. Even if he somehow made it all happen, the law would catch up to him. And the law out in space was harsh. If he ever found himself on a ship, the captain might decide the most prudent course was a one-way trip through the airlock.

Lucian's slate was chiming. In his distress, he hadn't noticed it. This was the third missed call from his mother. There were also several text messages, each more hysterical than the last.

He was acting like a child, and he knew it. He couldn't run from this, even if it was all he wanted. What would happen when, one day, his powers destroyed him? It likely didn't work like a switch. Day by day, he would only get worse.

There was no escaping. The only thing he could do was accept his fate, and accept to receive training.

Lucian looked at the various passengers, most carrying luggage for the spaceport. He would have traded places with any of them.

Canaveral was only two stops away now. And still, he couldn't decide what to do, even as his slate chimed again.

He picked up the slate and pressed it to his ear. He heard his mother breathing on the other end, but he couldn't bring himself to speak first.

"Lucian, where the hell *are you*?"

Bringing himself to answer was difficult. "The train."

"Oh, Lucian . . ." She sighed. "What are you doing?"

He swallowed a lump in his throat. "I don't know, Mom."

"Please . . . come back. You don't want them to think you're running. You *can't* run from this. You know that, right? It'll follow you wherever you go."

"I know."

"Come back. We have to face this. Together."

Lucian closed his eyes. He couldn't deal with this anymore. He still didn't want to admit the truth, but deep down, he knew his mother was right.

"What am I supposed to do? My life is over."

"No, it's not," she said. "Never give up, Lucian. Never. I didn't raise you like that."

"You didn't raise me at all."

The words were out of his mouth before he could stop them. There was dead silence on the other end. What he said, he knew, had hurt her more than a physical punch. Before he could apologize, she spoke with a thickened voice.

"Just come home."

She hung up.

———

WHEN LUCIAN GOT HOME, his mother was sitting on the couch with her usual cup of strong coffee. Her eyes were puffy and red. All Lucian could do was stand at the threshold. He didn't even know how to start apologizing. An apology felt hollow at this point.

"Sit down, son," she said. Fatigue and defeat strained her voice.

Lucian took up the old, overstuffed armchair across from her place on the couch.

"They've sent me the details of the loan. I can't pay this unless I head back to the Citadel right away."

She let the words hang in the air. There went her furlough.

"How soon is right away?" Lucian asked.

She opened her slate, and a screen projected itself in front of her. "Come here. I'm booking a shuttle now."

Lucian sat next to her, feeling as if he were in a daze. It seemed as if she wasn't angry about him running. Just sad, and tired. In a way, that was worse than anger. Lucian focused on the Pan-Galactic portal that projected from her slate as a holo. It was displaying several voyage options to Volsung. Lucian stared at the projection, unable to believe this was actually happening.

When he saw the price of the ticket, it was more money than he'd ever seen in his life.

"Mom, this'll take years to pay off..."

"I know. I've already sent a message to my C.O. about coming back early. They can help with the payments. There are rumors about the Swarmers coming back. Let's hope not." She shook her head. "Either way, we don't have much time to plan. They're offering a bonus if I'm back within the week. I figured we could catch the same shuttle to the Citadel. From there, you can catch your voyage to Volsung."

"When would all this be happening?"

"Tomorrow."

Tomorrow? Lucian could only stare at her in shock. "So soon?"

"This is the only way," she said. "Mages are outlawed on Earth. The law says we have a month to get you off-world. So we have to move fast." Lucian fumbled for words, but nothing came out. His mother continued to explain. "The Volsung Academy is your best shot. I've been in contact with Dr. Ross, and she's sending a light message ahead so they'll know to expect you. I don't want any argument about this. It's the only way." She sighed. "There, you'll be around people going through the same thing. Maybe one day, a full cure will be found. I hope so."

Lucian was silent as he absorbed this. He couldn't argue with good sense. "What about the money?"

"Don't worry about the money. What's important is keeping you safe. I've been trying to do research on this place with the GalNet, but there's not much information. Maybe it's illegal to publish anything about it, I don't know. I just know it's one of the few legal options for a mage. If you can't get a place here, Lucian, then the only other place for you is a mage commune on a world like Halia. Even Uncle Ravis can't help you, there, even with his connections." She looked at him seriously, as if willing him to accept her point of view. "Volsung is the only way."

Lucian, at last, nodded. There was no use fighting it anymore. Maybe his mother was right. Maybe one day, they'd figure out how to stop the fraying for good.

Just the thought of having his fate in someone else's hands made him queasy. But he had no other option.

"Okay," he said. "I'll do it."

"My stint with the fleet will finish in two years," his mother said. "After that, the loan should be paid off."

"I have some money I've been saving up, too. It's not much, but it'll help."

"I know. Let that be your spending money. Travel isn't cheap. They even charge you for sending messages off ship. You'll need every cred for that."

"All right, then," Lucian said.

"The loan's approved," his mother said. "We can figure out the rest as it comes. Maybe you can do what you can on the journey to find out more about mages and . . . magic." She shook her head. "I can't believe this is actually happening."

"It's happening," Lucian said. "Unfortunately."

His mother confirmed the arrangements. They were booked on the same shuttle from Earth to the Citadel, and from there, they would go their separate ways. They would have a short time to spend together on the massive space station. It wouldn't be enough.

"It's settled," she said. "We leave tomorrow morning."

A silence hung over them. Leaving Earth was something Lucian had always dreamed of doing. But never in a million years had he wanted it like this. But, he would learn to make it, as he always had. After he'd left his mother behind, he'd be on his own. Perhaps he had learned to become so self-reliant for a reason. Maybe everything in his life had been building toward this.

It wouldn't be easy. Life never was. But, as his mother had said earlier, he wasn't going to give up.

Or was he just kidding himself?

The mages at this academy were the only ones who could help him. Stopping the fraying was supposed to be impossible. But at least he might figure out a way to prolong his life, long enough for a full cure to be found.

It was a slim hope, but what else did he have?

He let his mother draw him in for a hug. He couldn't remember the last time she'd hugged him voluntarily. She held him for a long time, squeezing him tight. Lucian only felt numb.

In a few hours, they would both be on a shuttle bound for Sol Citadel.

# 7

IT WAS ALMOST midnight and Lucian still couldn't sleep. He didn't see how it was possible, given the circumstances. When he couldn't stand the hot and stifling air anymore, he got out of bed. He walked to the window, where below, the neon lights of bars and clubs played off the dark surface of the canal. The nightlife was thrumming more than usual, being a Saturday night. He wished he were down there with them, without a care in the world.

He opened the window to let in the muggy, salt-laden air that carried the beat of Latin dance music. He wouldn't see this view for a long time, if not the rest of his life.

He wanted to say he wouldn't miss it. But he knew he was kidding himself. Humanity had colonized over a hundred worlds and moons by now. Even with that, Earth was the crown jewel of the League, and would always be humanity's cradle. Its surface and moon, as well as the habitats orbiting in the cislunar space between, held over a hundred billion souls.

Volsung, from what Lucian understood, was remarkably Earthlike. Its sun was a g-type star, like Sol, while the planet's atmosphere was completely breathable. The main differences were its climate, smaller size, and ocean coverage. It was about the size and mass of Venus, but the main difference was that over ninety percent of its surface was either ocean or covered by its prodigious ice caps.

It would be an adjustment, to say the least.

Laughing and hollering emanated from the canal below. It might be a good idea to see it, one last time. Lucian had never been one for partying, even if Miami was one of the best places in the world to do it. The litany of booze, drugs, and general degeneracy had been a part of the city for centuries. But having lived here for most of his life, there was far more to the city than what appeared on the surface.

Lucian shut the window and sneaked out of his room. He waited a moment in the foyer to make sure his mother was asleep. It felt strange, having to be quiet. But he didn't want her to worry.

Once sure she was asleep, he stepped out the front door and headed for the elevator that would take him down.

———

LUCIAN PARTIED like it was his last night on Earth. It wasn't his usual behavior, but it might be his last chance to act like a normal human being.

The first thing he did was head to the pharmacy. He bought a pill that would mitigate most of the effects of a hangover. He also got a pack of wakers to get him going in the morning, and some sleepers in case he needed them during the voyage. Space travel was notoriously terrible on the circadian rhythm.

Only then did he lose himself in the teeming mass of revelers, drinking copious shots of hard liquor and dancing. He ran into some boarding school friends, with whom he spent a good part of the night. He got drunk enough to forget about where he was going to tomorrow. He smiled. It was the first time he'd felt free in days.

But as his head swam with alcohol, his thoughts took a darker turn. The nightmare was still here, and no amount of alcohol would make that go away. He stumbled out of the club after ditching his friends, walking across the boardwalk toward the canal. He popped his hangover pill. The nightlife partyers were so thick that it was hard to find a table. Dozens of drunk and drugged up people filtered in and out of the bars, the blare of music making his head pound.

At the table, he ordered a sandwich on his slate from a nearby deli, which was delivered in a couple of minutes. If there was one thing Lucian would miss, it would be this deli. He took a big bite, hoping that the thick sandwich and pill would ease most of the effects of his drinking. Boats of partyers with blaring music drifted by on the dark water of the canal.

The peace was disturbed when a group of yammering girls took up a nearby table, yelling, joking, and squealing. One of them hollered at Lucian.

"Lucian! What are you doing out here?"

A chill ran down his spine. He would recognize that voice anywhere. This scene was familiar, and he soon saw why.

This was close to where Luisa had shot him in his dream.

He looked up to see his ex-girlfriend's pale, pretty face framed by shoulder-length black hair. Even if talking to her was the last thing he wanted to do, Lucian couldn't bring himself to walk away.

Luisa was oblivious to his feelings, and seemed drunker than even he was. She stumbled over to his table, a goofy grin on her face, tripping over her heels right before reaching the bench. Instincts kicking in, Lucian caught her before she could faceplant herself. Beneath the alcohol was the scent of her perfume. A rush of memories returned to him, then. It was hard not to be taken back in time, when things were better.

She blinked a few times, then giggled. "My hero."

Without waiting for an invitation, she seated herself and took Lucian's hand. She sat a little too close for comfort. What would she do if he made more space? Would she notice, or care?

Lucian remained in place.

"Oh, that looks good," she said. Before Lucian could stop her, she grabbed his sandwich and took a monstrous bite. "What are *you* doing out? You hate crowds."

"You can have it," Lucian said. The sandwich was a lost cause.

"Hell yeah," she said. "I'm *starving*. I used to hate this place when you wanted to come here. Now, I can't get enough of it."

Lucian let her eat. If she were stuffing her face, she'd be less likely to talk. Or so he thought.

"You seem a bit moody," she said, between bites. "It's not me, is it?"

No, it wasn't her. He had bigger problems in his life now – problems he didn't want to share with her.

Some of Luisa's friends, none of whom Lucian recognized, were making kissing noises.

"He's cute," one of them said.

She turned back to the table, only a fraction of her usual fiery temperament showing on her face. "This is my ex, Lucian. Lucian, my friends."

Her friends got the message from her tone, and backed off.

"Running with a different crowd, I see," Lucian said.

Luisa shrugged. "People suck. Every time I meet new people, I always find out just how fake they are." She searched his eyes. "You're the exception, though. You're the only guy I've met who wasn't *only* trying to get in my pants."

"Joke's on you," Lucian said. "You fell for my ploy."

She smiled. That was dangerous. Why was he flirting with

her? It was probably his drunkenness. That, and the fact he wouldn't even be here tomorrow. There were no consequences.

"What's wrong?" she asked. "Something's got you down. Is the weight of the world too much for your tortured soul?"

The gun. His eyes went to her purse. Could she be carrying it right now?

It had only been a dream. She would never actually *shoot* it . . .

"I'm more concerned about you," he said. "I . . ."

He trailed off, not sure where he was going. He didn't want to tell her about the dream. That would only freak her out, because Luisa believed dreams were prophetic. Lucian, until a couple of days ago, would have thought that ridiculous.

Now, he wasn't sure of anything.

"Anyway," he said, "how are you doing?"

"I'm doing fine, I guess," she said, leaving most of the sandwich uneaten as she picked off the vegetables. "As fine as you might expect."

Lucian felt a tinge of guilt, but what could he do about that? They weren't right for each other. They were great together when Luisa was stable – which was maybe a quarter of the time, and that was being generous. Not that Lucian didn't have his flaws. Not by a long shot.

It was just that their flaws, put together, were explosive. The only thing he could do was step out of the situation, before it was too late. At the time, he told himself it was the only way to help her.

He still wasn't sure whether that was true, or if he had only been running away.

"So, what's new with you?" she asked.

"Nothing, I guess," Lucian said. How easily that lie came to his lips. "Still studying for the civil exam."

It was strange to think that line still *felt* true. He would never get to work in the government. Not ever. The insanity of it all was almost enough to make him laugh.

"I can tell something's weighing on you," Luisa said. "I know we're not together anymore, but I hope you would consider me a friend. And I mean that. It's not just words to me. When I say something, I mean it. Even if I'm a bit crazy."

Lucian couldn't help but smile. "A bit?"

"I'll admit I'm not good at being a friend, especially with guys. They always fall in love with me." She smiled, to show she was joking. But it wasn't a joke. "At some point, guys always seem to want the same thing."

"You won't have to worry about that with me anymore."

For a moment, her shoulders sagged a bit. But only for a moment. She looked at him curiously. "Well? Out with it. I see all these months alone and you still haven't figured out how to open up. Well now, you don't have to worry about getting too close to me. So, you can say whatever you want."

It was a weird sort of logic, but it made sense. He was leaving tomorrow, so no matter what he said, in the end, it wouldn't matter.

When he looked into Luisa's eyes, so filled with concern and pity, a part of him seemed to thaw. Something about her eyes had that effect. They were almost hypnotic. Lucian knew it was a dangerous game – fire always felt nice until you burned yourself. Lucian's mother had accused Luisa of surgery, but as far as Lucian knew, she was completely natural. She was either blessed or cursed with that face. From former conversations, Luisa believed it was more of a curse.

"I'm leaving Earth, Luisa. For good."

Her eyes conveyed a mixture of hurt and betrayal. "Oh. You'd always talked about leaving . . ."

Lucian nodded, but didn't elaborate further.

"Don't want to talk about it, huh?"

"Talking makes things complicated."

"Things are complicated, whether you talk or not. Ignoring what's there doesn't make it go away."

Lucian felt her eyes on him, but he couldn't meet them. "I don't have a choice, Luisa."

"We always have a choice."

"I thought that too, once. Now, I'm not sure of anything."

"What about the civil exam? Did you get a job out there, or something? Did you join the Fleet? Joined a corp?" She paused. "Don't tell me you're going to Triton. The helium-3 mines will be dry by the time you get there."

He sighed and shook his head. What would happen if he just stood up and left? He was never going to see her again. But he wasn't that cold.

"It's better that you don't know the reason," Lucian said, finally. "It would be less painful."

"What the hell does that even mean?" Her voice was rising, a clue that one of her rages could be coming. "You're going to leave without so much as a goodbye?"

Her friends were looking at them, their conversation silenced. If he told the truth, could she handle it? It had gone too far by now for him to make up a lie. Few saw the mages in a favorable light. They had, after all, almost brought the Worlds to their knees fifty years ago.

Admitting that he was one of *them* was the quickest possible road to rejection.

That was what he was afraid of, then. Of course it was. Why did he still care about her so much, when he'd worked so hard to stamp it out? It would be nice if he could just speak his mind, to let her see him as he really was.

"You're running away again," Luisa said, calmer now. "I want to get real, and you run away. It's the same damn thing over and over."

"If I told you why I have to leave," Lucian said, "you'd wish I stayed quiet."

She rolled her eyes. "You're *always* going to be alone, Lucian! All you ever do is hurt people who want to be close to you."

"Well, you should stop trying, then."

The retort seemed to sting her, from the way her eyes watered. Seeing her react that way hurt him, too. Lucian wished he didn't have to go so far, but he didn't want to tell her the truth. Not here in the crowds where anyone might overhear.

"If you want to leave, fine. But I will always wonder the reason why. It's just . . . you're not one to do this, Lucian. Is it about *me*?"

It was just like her to make this about herself. Why had he even come down here tonight? If he had just left, it would have been weeks, even months, before Luisa realized he was gone.

Telling her the truth might be the only thing that would make her leave him alone. The only thing that would poison everything they ever had. It was hard, because deep down, Lucian didn't want that. He had never wanted to leave her. He'd only been afraid of where it was going.

But now it was too late. If the future wasn't even his own, how could it ever be hers?

"I'm a mage," he said, finally. "I found out earlier today."

She looked at him in confusion. She didn't believe him. The admission was so outrageous, so unlikely, that it couldn't possibly be true.

"Seriously?"

"I tested positive just today, so I'm going to Volsung for training. My shuttle leaves tomorrow."

Luisa stared at him. Something disconnected, her manner cold and distant. What he'd said was only now registering.

"Now, you know my secret. Why I'm leaving. In a few years – or even sooner – I might be dead."

"Stop. You're not like them, though," she said. "Mages are evil. Crazy. You're not like that at all."

"Given time, I will be," Lucian said. "It'll start to control me. And then it'll kill me. That's why I have to leave." There was a long silence as she looked away, as she realized he was being serious. "I'm sorry, Luisa."

She turned her face away, but Lucian could see the disappointment. That, and fear. All the tenderness from before, all the calls for openness, had ended up with her being the one to close off.

"You'd better go, Lucian," she whispered.

The words, though quiet, were cutting. A part of Lucian had hoped she would wish him well. There were so many misconceptions about mages, many Lucian himself likely believed. But she had made her choice. There was nothing more to be said or done. It was over, with no chance for redemption.

Lucian left, doing his best to put the conversation out of his head. All he felt was . . . hollow. He truly *was* alone. If a simple statement of truth was enough for Luisa to forsake him, how did he have a chance with the rest of humanity?

He was different now. As if he were branded. Nothing would ever be the same. But Lucian supposed he shouldn't have been surprised. *Everyone* hated the mages for what they'd done, for what they would continue to do. Though the Mage War was fifty years ago, the destruction had been so deep that its scars were still felt today.

These days were different. Mages were controlled by the academies, and those who couldn't be controlled, were imprisoned. This was the only way the Hundred Worlds could ensure the tragedy of the Mage War was never repeated.

Luisa's reaction confirmed everything he already knew. He was alone, and could only help himself.

# 8

WHEN LUCIAN ENTERED THE APARTMENT, his mother was waiting for him on the couch, cup of coffee in hand while leveling him with a fixed stare. He braced himself for the scolding he knew was coming.

But her voice was calm. "You want coffee? Tea? A glass of warm milk?"

Warm milk? What was he, five? At the same time, though, it did sound good. Coffee or tea would just keep him up. "Warm milk."

She went to the kitchen and prepared it for him, while he took a seat in the armchair. When she handed him the cup, he took a drink. She made no mention of the smell of alcohol as she went to sit on the couch.

"A part of me will always think you're eight, or twelve, or even one. At some point, the years all blend together, and ten years ago seems as fresh as yesterday." She took another sip of her coffee. "The shuttle leaves at eleven, so we need to be out of the house by seven. It's a Sunday, so it shouldn't be too busy, but I'd like to leave some room, just in case."

Lucian always trusted his mother with the details when

traveling. She had done it so many times that everything always ran like clockwork. She always arrived with practiced precision, a product of her military training.

Lucian's mind was still reeling from the confrontation with Luisa. It was most likely the last conversation he'd ever have with her. How could she treat him that way? He was really nothing to her, then, now that she knew the truth.

He was better off without her.

"You're an adult now," his mother said. "The sooner I accept that, the better." She regarded him seriously. "Life is harder out there, Lucian. Go beyond cislunar space, and space becomes a wilderness. Even System Worlds and the First Worlds are frontiers compared to Earth. And the Mid-Worlds and Border Worlds?" She gave a harsh laugh. "League planets only in name. I wish this academy were on Chiron rather than Volsung. At least then you'd have some of the amenities you're used to. Volsung is a cold, stormy world. Bleak, except around the equator. I suppose that's why the Academy is there."

Lucian took another drink of his milk, and it went down warm. Why was she telling him all this? The silence dragged on a minute more.

"What a mess," she said. Her hand came to her forehead, as if she were undergoing a massive migraine. "I don't blame you for going to drink. I remember what it's like to be young. To feel like you're not in control ..."

"Mom," Lucian said. "This will change things. Won't it?"

"What kind of question is that? Of course it will."

"I mean ..." He shook his head. "It's nothing."

She looked at him for a moment, her eyes sad. "You'll always be my son. I don't care what happens to the mages, eventually. I don't care about the war fifty years back. You're my son, and I love you. It will change things, yes. But it will not change how much I love you."

He didn't want to admit it, but it felt good to hear that. The alcohol was making him say things he would normally keep to himself. He wasn't sure he liked that, but it felt good to speak his mind and be accepted. He wouldn't have that for much longer, so he had to train himself to get along without it. As he always had.

"There's nothing we can do," he said.

Her expression became distant, her coffee momentarily forgotten. "Being in space for a long time has an effect on you. It's amazingly easy to lose hope. It's as if your soul is bound to Earth, bound to home, and your body and spirit needs it from time to time to go on. It's like going without breath."

"I thought space dementia was a myth."

"So they say," his mother said. "I believe otherwise. When you're out there, you'll know. You'll learn that it's tougher. And when it gets tough, there's only one thing to get you through." She paused, as if to add gravitas to her point. "Hope. You must always hope, Lucian. No matter how dark it gets, the human spirit can push through as long as it finds a silver lining and clings to it with everything. Never forget that – because I can't always be there for you. It's been that way for a while, but it will be even *more* that way in the coming months."

"I'll be fine, Mom. I'll get to Volsung. I'll get the training. Everything will turn out fine."

"You're struggling. I can see it in your eyes. I don't want you to lie about how you're feeling. Hell, *I'm* struggling. I was crying so much in bed. But I just can't cry anymore."

When was the last time he and his mother had talked like this? Perhaps not ever. For the first time, she was treating him as an equal. Was she accepting that he had grown up?

"I just feel . . . numb," he said. "What does it mean? Why *me*? All I know about the mages is from the war – how they almost destroyed everything humanity built. How they were close to destroying Earth itself, before the Tragedy of Isis. I never thought about the mages. They were a bloody chapter in a history book. They weren't a part of my world at all, just an inconvenience I had to go through once a year with my metaphysical." He gave a nervous laugh. "I guess that's how the League *wants* us to think of them."

An uncomfortable thought occurred to him. If the mages were so dangerous, so fallen, why would the League not just *kill* them? Why go through the trouble of sending them to academies? The human race had progressed beyond the point of genocide, but perhaps that genocide might be justified, especially if the mages weren't seen as human. To most, the mages had lost that right when they went to war with the Hundred Worlds. A war that would have seen non-mages as second-class citizens.

Now, those tables had turned. And that was the way it had been for the past five decades.

"It's all so carefully controlled," his mother said. "The Worlds want them out of sight and out of mind. People are scared enough as it is with the Swarmers."

The thought of the Swarmers gave Lucian a chill. The mysterious alien menace had come from unknown regions of space, sacking some science stations a few gates out from the Border Worlds. Within months, they were over the skies of Terminus, glassing humanity's most far-flung colony. Once the Hundred Worlds had stopped arguing long enough to cobble a fleet together, they pushed the Swarmers back. It had taken a good five years, and had cost millions of lives and trillions in world creds.

That war ended five years ago, and the threat that they might return always lurked. Earth's fleet was twice as large now, and better equipped to counter the Swarmers' tiny strike craft. Other worlds had invested in system and planetary defenses, too, but Earth and the rest of Sol System was humanity's main bulwark. If the Swarmers ever *did* return, Lucian's mother would be deployed from Sol Citadel to meet the threat, working from her office on the supercarrier, *LSC Refuge*.

"I just wish *none* of this was happening." Lucian looked at his mother. "Why are there mages in the first place? I know that no one knows. Maybe these Transcends at the Volsung Academy do. If we know how mages emerged in the first place, maybe there's a way to stop it."

"I don't know, son. We can only hope that, someday, they find a cure."

It all felt so unfair. Lucian had barely given the mages a thought. But now, he could not stop thinking about them. As much as he wanted to learn more, there wasn't much information about the mages on the GalNet that could be trusted. He certainly didn't trust what he'd learned in school. All he was sure of was that there *was* a war, and the rebellious mages had lost.

"Up by seven," his mother said, breaking him from his thoughts. "Out the door by 7:30. On the Lev by eight. At the spaceport by nine . . ."

Lucian's thoughts drifted as his mother listed their itinerary. They washed the mugs, and before going to bed, she kissed him on the cheek, as if he were a child again. He wasn't sure what to do with such tenderness.

Later in bed Lucian thrashed in his sheets. He'd never felt so cold and hollow. He'd spent most of his life training himself not to care. But all his carefully constructed walls couldn't stand up to this onslaught.

He wanted everything to go away, to just wake up from this horrible dream. But of course, that would never happen. The memory of his mother leaving ten years ago to fight the Swarmers wouldn't leave him. It was the same day he'd been sent off to boarding school. Every night, he lay awake, haunted by dreams of her dying in some battle, wondering when the next letter would arrive. He would be disappointed when months passed without them. He'd spend those boarding school nights completely alone. His reclusive personality made it difficult to make friends. The pain of not belonging had been overwhelming.

Why was he thinking about all this? He couldn't escape from the past, no matter how hard he tried. The only way out, as he saw it, was not to feel at all. He thought he'd managed to conquer that part of himself, but the events of the last few days made him question that belief.

One thing was sure. He wouldn't get any rest tonight unless he took a sleeper.

After he'd popped the pill, he entered oblivion within a couple of minutes. An oblivion thankfully devoid of dreams.

# 9

WHEN HIS SLATE alarm went off, Lucian was still groggy from the sleeper he'd taken. Well, that could be remedied by taking a waker. Much like caffeine, wakers wouldn't make up for a lack of sleep. But it would make him feel as if he'd gotten a perfect night's rest, at least for the next six hours. And that was all he needed. He could sleep during the voyage to Sol Citadel.

After a quick breakfast, there was little time for sentimentality. They each looked through the condo, revisiting all the rooms. Lucian still couldn't believe this was happening. The home still looked lived-in. How was it possible that they were leaving? What would happen to everything? There were still dirty dishes in the sink. Such things couldn't be considered.

It would be his last time to see this place.

They wheeled their luggage out the door and made the short walk to the Lev station.

Despite the early hour, the city thrummed with life. The last of the clubbers were stumbling home, creatures of the night banished by daylight. The azure water of the canal reflected the tenements looming above. A Lev zoomed overhead, passing over the canyon of buildings. Miami bloomed like a water lily under the yellow sunlight, opening for the day ahead.

Lucian's mother strode with purpose, dressed smartly in her Fleet blues. The uniform would ensure a speedy passage through spaceport security. It was as if she were a different person. Someone Lucian didn't dare to question.

Within minutes, they were at the station, in time for an approaching train. Once on board, the Lev shot north through the sunlight-dappled city. The rising eastern sun shimmered off the facades of skyscrapers, rising above the watery passages between.

Miami's endless sprawl spread in every direction. Toward the western horizon lay a crumbled patchwork of tenements and run-down slums. Crisscrossing electric trains and a grid of blue canals extended as far as the eye could see. Far to the north, he could see the tops of several arcologies, each of which had hundreds of levels. Their surrounding tower farms gleamed emerald green in the morning sunlight. Lucian had always wanted to live in an arcology. It was where most of the rich twerps from his boarding school had lived. Naturally, you couldn't get in without credentials.

The Lev shot north, away from South Miami and through the kilometer-high towers of downtown. Most of the original passengers had exchanged themselves for fresh commuters. Businessmen in designer suits, wealthy wives with extravagant dresses, uniformed kids going to school.

Lucian and his mother got off downtown, taking an escalator to another Lev. This one would see them the rest of the way to Canaveral. His throat clamped as his home passed by. He tried to take it all in, but his mind was so far away he knew he wasn't going to remember it.

They rode in silence above the Florida Shoals, land long lost to the rising ocean. They passed the sprawling cityscape of floating towers, apartments, and condos. The density lessened as they shot farther north. The metropolis didn't end until Port St. Lucie, and the rest of the way to Canaveral was filled with arcologies hundreds of stories tall. How long, Lucian wondered, until the entire surface of the planet was covered with these things? Could Earth bear their weight?

Lucian closed his eyes, but the effects of his waker made sleep impossible. That had been a bad decision, and as with caffeine, his anxiety was through the roof. Or that might just be nerves from the coming shuttle launch.

Lucian watched the blue water blaze by at three hundred kilometers per hour. At times, the track would shoot between the arcologies – Lucian had to crane his neck to see the top of them. Their many terraces were verdant with parks and golf courses. He wondered what life might have been like living in one. Easier, for sure. He might have even been as stuck up as those jerks he'd gone to school with. The thought almost made him laugh.

The Lev slowed as it neared Canaveral Spaceport. Ground cars crammed the streets and highways below. Skycars and larger passenger shuttles streamed above, heading for the landing pads near the cavernous entrance. Lucian could see other shuttles streaking skyward. Most were bound for one of the L-Cities, though some, like theirs, were heading for Sol Citadel. Earth-based launches could reach as far as Mars and the Citadel on one tank of helium-3. The Citadel was the main hub of Sol System, where travelers could get to most major colonies in the solar system, as far as Triton. Interstellar voyages also set out from the Citadel. Most would go to Alpha Centauri, Sirius, Tau Ceti, or Volsung, systems that held the so-called First Worlds. Each could be reached through the four major Gates that orbited Sol, far beyond the orbit of even Pluto.

It was damn far. Physicists theorized the Gates could only work when located far from any major gravity well. The passage took weeks in all but the smallest star systems. Lucian would have to find a way to stay sane during the long journey.

Canaveral was one of the world's oldest spaceports, and one of the biggest. The complex stretched kilometers. Parts of it had even expanded to include artificial islands. Lucian didn't get much time to look at the monstrosity before the Lev floated to a complete stop.

As they got off, his mother reminded him of their itinerary – as if he didn't already know.

"The trip to the Citadel is fourteen hours," she said. "And the Citadel to Volsung is twenty-eight days."

And that was as fast as any civilian could expect to go. Lucian sometimes wondered how sci-fi had gotten it so wrong, where unrealistic engines could bridge the space between stars in days, or even seconds. It was unfathomable. Even by 2364, most interstellar ships couldn't maintain an average speed more than .02 the speed of light. The fastest rigs might get up to .03, and as the years went by, it only got marginally better. It took an incredible amount of energy to get even a modest-sized liner running to .02. And it burned *a lot* of helium-3. The entire outer solar system economy was *geared* toward starship fuel. Still, the outer system was a cold hell Lucian had no interest in visiting, though he would like to see the Forge of Heaven someday – a delving megastructure in the orbit of Uranus, and the greatest helium-3 mine in the Worlds.

Humanity could only reach the stars through the Gates. No one knew *how* they worked, or where they had come from. They had obviously been built by someone, or *something*, though it was hard to imagine the warlike Swarmers, the only living aliens humanity knew of, accomplishing such a feat. One thing most scientists agreed on: the technology the Gates used was so advanced as to be inconceivable to humanity. Some Gates might jump a mere four lightyears, as was the case with the Centauri Gate. Others could jump a *hundred* lightyears or more at a stretch. No one knew how they were powered, and Lucian suspected no one would ever know. Such questions had never really interested him, so he didn't know why he was thinking about it now.

The hypothetical alien race that had constructed the Gates were known as the Builders. They'd had some sort of civilization, as their ruins could be found on many of the Hundred Worlds. It was clear their civilization stretched farther than humanity had so far colonized. Perhaps even to the entire galaxy. Strangely, most of the systems with Builder ruins contained an atmosphere that more or less agreed with Terran biochemistry. For that reason, many surmised the Builders were quite similar to humans, at least in that they preferred a similar gravity and atmospheric composition. Those ruins were thought to be hundreds of thousands of Earth years old, if not more. The only place ruins *hadn't* been found was Earth itself. Lucian wondered why, or if it even mattered.

He'd read a lot about the subject when he was younger, his interest falling off in his later teenage years. But now, those old questions seemed to haunt him. Even if it was pointless to think about them, he still wondered.

"Did you hear what I said, Lucian?" his mother asked.

"Sorry. I was thinking about something."

She sighed in frustration. "*Listen* this time. After you get to Volsung Orbital, you'll have to take a shuttle down to the surface. The Volsung Academy is on an island far to the north, not far from the ice cap. The best way to get there will be from Karendas. It's the closest spaceport. If you don't hear from the Academy by the time you make planetfall, then you'll have to ask around."

"Got it."

They had already passed through the expansive entrance of the spaceport, and were pushing through the roiling crowds. Intermixed with the hurried humans were a few metallic droids. They carried luggage, escorted passengers, and drove trams. It wasn't every day Lucian saw them – they were too expensive to be owned by the people of his neighborhood. He always wondered why they were designed to look vaguely human, with their long metallic legs and arms, and even with a head that contained their central computer. Like FTL travel, full AI sentience had remained out of reach. Advanced metallic droids could still perform basic tasks and communication, and even *sound* human, but there were no deep thoughts happening under the surface. Just highly sophisticated algorithms, that every year got just a bit more complicated. The droids were great for mining, agriculture, and zero-g industry. Not so much for creative work.

"Remember, by the time you pass through Volsung Gate, it'll be harder to keep in touch," his mother reminded him. "It'll get more expensive, too."

Of course, messages could only travel as fast as the speed of light. The only thing that bridged the distance of lightyears were Gates. Interstellar messages had to be beamed through the Gate by data running relays. With luck, any message sent out from Volsung would arrive in Sol in a couple of days or less, depending on backup.

The concept was foreign to Lucian. More people lived on Earth, the Moon, and the cislunar space between than the rest of the Worlds combined.

Space was still a frontier. And it would remain so for centuries yet. It was hard for Lucian not to feel a bit of a thrill that he was going into it, despite his reasons for doing so.

After dropping off their luggage, Lucian followed his mother through the teeming crowds. People parted for her, some even giving respectful nods. Her face was stern, every inch an officer of the Fleet. Even if they sometimes butted heads, Lucian's chest swelled with pride.

They passed through the auto-scanners. After getting the

all clear from the security droid, they walked to the correct terminal.

They waited in the lobby another hour until the gate opened, an hour which seemed to take an eternity.

They lined up and boarded, quickly finding their seats. It was really no different from boarding an orbital skiff. Those technically went into space, too, but only for the purpose of dropping back to Earth. This was different, though. He would be going beyond Earth, into the unknown.

They found their seats. His mother fussed with his safety harness. He let her do it; resistance was futile.

A floating security drone roved up and down the aisle.

"Please harness yourselves," it said in a robotic monotone. "Prepare for liftoff."

Lucian looked out the window, at what might be his last view of Earth from the surface. It would be nice to see the beach, but here there were only runways and towers. In mere minutes, though, all this would be gone, replaced by the cold void of space. Lucian had never felt true weightlessness, not even in a full-body simulation. Those required sim pills, which he had never been able to afford. But now, at least, he'd get to experience the real thing. At least until the artificial gravity kicked in.

His mother reached for his hand. Whether it was for his comfort or hers, Lucian couldn't say. Still, he let her hold it. He hoped she didn't notice his clammy hands.

The shuttle detached from the boarding tunnel and rolled down the runway. After another few minutes, it sped up, and with a roar, took to the air. Lucian grit his teeth as he was pushed back into his seat.

Upon takeoff, it flew at a slight angle, like a plane, before tilting back and burning full thrust. Lucian's teeth rattled at the force, his heart pounding in his chest. His mother's grip tightened over his hand. Over the next few minutes, the blue sky faded into a black expanse of stars. Was that it, then?

Lucian's body floated against his restraints. He was here. Space. He didn't get to experience weightlessness for long. The artificial gravity kicked in, pushing him down with less gravity than Earth's. He'd heard that Martian G, a little over a third of Earth's, was the standard for most ships and habitats. It was enough to offset most of the ill-effects of low gravity, while saving energy. Lucian would have to get used to it for the next few weeks.

The transport sped up, its powerful fusion engine burning them toward Sol Citadel. He was pushed back into his seat before the inertial dampening field compensated.

Lucian looked out his viewport, watching as his homeworld slipped away. Of course, he'd seen pictures and videos of Earth from space. He'd even seen full holographic renderings so real it was a wonder they couldn't be touched. But he'd never seen Earth as he saw it now. That beautiful blue orb, with its streaks of white clouds and green landmasses and vast oceans, rendered him breathless.

The transport was high enough for a space habitat to pass underneath their ship. Earth had hundreds of stations, habitats, and orbitals, though the largest were L4 and L5. Each of the L-cities held tens of thousands, and were major hubs of intersystem commerce. Lucian regretted he couldn't see either. Where he was going, he doubted he would be leaving for a long time. If ever.

Faster than Lucian would have believed, Earth shrunk in the viewport. After an hour, it had become a bright blue dot, one among thousands in an infinite sea of stars.

———

LUCIAN SLEPT most of the way as the effects of the waker wore off. When he awoke, he saw that his mother was sleeping, too. He watched her for a moment, not believing that this was truly happening. It felt like some sort of nightmare. But within a matter of hours, he would be on board a liner to Volsung, and she in her berth on the *LSC Refuge*. The excitement and hope he'd felt earlier were gone now, replaced by an emptiness reflected by the void outside the viewport.

He checked the voyage status on his slate to see there was only two hours left. Somehow, he'd slept for twelve hours straight. He found a small ration in the seat pocket ahead of him, which his mother must have saved. He had one bite of the hardened, tasteless instameal before realizing he wasn't hungry anymore. For such expensive tickets, couldn't they have been provided some half-decent food?

Looking out the porthole, the position of the stars hadn't changed in the least. Of course, the stars' configuration would stay the same as long as they remained in Sol System. He wouldn't see new constellations until he'd passed through the Volsung Gate. How would he feel about seeing that? He thought about what his mother had said, about his soul being bound to Earth. The moment he passed through the Gate, would he feel as if he'd taken a dive into cold water? It wasn't something he wanted to experience. That was how his dreams had felt.

Twenty-eight days. With distances so vast, it was a wonder humanity had managed to spread so far. Though they called it the Hundred Worlds, the moniker was more than fifty years out of date. By now, there were more than that. Worlds Lucian had never heard of. These days, it seemed humanity was spreading faster than the League could incorporate new colonies. One day, it might be that one could make the journey from Earth and never reach the outer worlds in a lifetime. As it stood, it took about half a year to go from Earth to Terminus on the fastest starship. Lucian couldn't imagine going such a distance while keeping his sanity.

Of course, his sanity was already in question, if he didn't learn to handle his condition.

About an hour from Sol Citadel, the captain made an announcement through the speaker.

"Good evening," he said. Lucian wondered what made it "evening" out here. "Time of docking will be 24:22 Olympian. If you think that time sounds weird, remember that a Martian day is thirty minutes longer. Those of you planning on boarding the *Burung* to Volsung, you'll meet a Pan-Galactic attendant at the gate. Thank you, and we hope you've had a pleasant voyage."

The intercom clicked off, Lucian looked at his mother, who had awoken during the message. That was *his* voyage.

"What's going on?" he asked. "He said I need to meet someone at the gate."

She blinked drearily. "I don't know." She unlocked her slate, her eyes widening at a piece of news. "Your ship embarks in two hours! They bumped it up for some reason. Why would they do that?"

The news didn't register at first. "Really?"

"You'll barely have time to make it. The Citadel is huge, and your gate is on the opposite end from where we're docking. That must be why they're having you meet someone."

When she took his hand, Lucian could feel it shaking. Lucian had been expecting to have one last day with his mother, seeing the sights of the Citadel. Now, that would never happen. It was a punch to the gut.

"I'm very proud of you, Lucian," she said, her voice thick. "Never forget that."

"Mom . . ." Several people were looking over at them. Before, he might have been embarrassed, but now, he only felt defeated. What could he say to make it all right? "It'll be fine.

I'll get to Volsung, get the training, and everything will be okay. Once I'm trained up, they'll let me leave." He wasn't sure if that were true, but he wanted it to be. "By then, your stint with the Fleet will be over."

She looked at him, and smiled through her tears. "That's optimistic."

"It'll be fine," Lucian insisted. But beneath those words, he felt things slipping out of his control. He knew he was on a ride he couldn't get off.

Lucian reached into his bag and handed her a tissue. He had to turn his face away, to hide the tears that wanted to come. This stung terribly, all the more so because he had been avoiding her since her furlough started. How stupid and stubborn he had been. What he wouldn't give to go back. Instead of hiding at the university, studying, he might have gone to the beach with her one last time. Or see a museum with her. She'd always wanted to do something like that. It wasn't his thing, but he might have made her happy.

Instead, all he had done was make her sad. But now, it was too late.

"I'm sorry," he managed. "I've been kind of an ass lately."

She looked up, dabbing fresh tears from her eyes. "No, you haven't. I'm too much, I know. Trying to make up for all those years I was gone. I pushed too hard. I would've tried to get away, too."

"Who cares about all that?"

"If you've been an ass, I've been one, too. For a lot longer. I put other things first. You've grown up before my eyes. I've been trying to keep you small. Because of my selfishness. Because I missed almost everything, so I'm trying to live it again. Only, I can't."

This confession was followed by more tears. She had her own regrets, too. And those regrets seemed far heavier than his own.

"It's okay, Mom," Lucian said. "You weren't perfect, but you were doing the best you could. I'm old enough to take care of myself now. When your stint is over, come join me on Volsung. Okay?"

She nodded, wiping the tears from her eyes. "I will. I promise you that. Maybe when all's said and done, we can get a new start on Halia with your uncle. I'll make amends with him."

Lucian closed his eyes, and tried to clear his mind. He tried to remember what his mother had told him. What had she said? To have hope, even when there wasn't anything to hope for. What was the point of that?

Having hope would feel good, though. Damn good. But Lucian didn't know if he had it in him to lie to himself like that. The future was like muddy water – no matter how wide he opened his eyes, he couldn't see far.

Thirty minutes out from the Citadel, the passengers began stirring in their seats. They peered through their viewports for a sign of their destination. While all of them were ready to be off, Lucian wanted the opposite. He wanted to stay here for as long as he needed.

But that would never be.

# 10

MARS HUNG half a million kilometers away, a crimson red drop in the star-studded expanse. It was small enough to be covered by his hand. The Citadel appeared small at first, a silvery star floating in the void easily missed to the naked eye. Lucian knew the Citadel was the largest military installation in the Worlds. Was this it, then?

But as the transport neared, the station only loomed larger. And larger. The first thing Lucian saw was the central spire, the axis around which the fortress rotated. That great spire was filled with viewports and hangars. It seemed more like a skyscraper than the linchpin holding the fortress together, if a skyscraper were ten kilometers long. Around it, the station's gargantuan arms bloomed at intricate angles, a metallic lotus flower. Doors and hangars opened at the ends of those arms. Thousands of viewports gleamed from every surface. Countless bays lay open and ready to receive incoming vessels. Likewise, many small ships zipped silently around the fortress. Lucian's jaw dropped.

Several large battleships and carriers floated a few kilometers from the Citadel itself, far too large to dock there. As the shuttle came closer, Lucian saw that these vessels were mammoths in their own right. The supercarrier *Volga* was over a kilometer long, and half again as wide. Battleships built for brute firepower were in greater number. Lucian counted ten, each armed with plasma cannons, railguns, fusion lasers, and torpedoes. Beside them were even smaller vessels in greater numbers. Tiny fighters by the hundreds swarmed around the capital ships, practicing coordinated maneuvers. Larger destroyers sailed behind, drilling their point defense screening.

War seemed to be looming. These drills seemed to go beyond mere vigilance. Coupled with the rumors his mother had heard, could the Swarmers really be returning?

"Looks like they've started without me," she said, also watching. "Two weeks from now, I guarantee I'll be passing through Centauri Gate. Joy."

"You think you'll rebase at Starbase Centauri?" Lucian asked.

She looked back at him, her eyes hard to read. "A soldier's sense tells me that. If the Swarmers come back through Kasturi, they'll have to go through A.C. to reach Sol."

If that were so, then this would be her last time seeing the Sol for a while, too. It was a dark thought, and one that made Lucian feel numb.

The ship began to slow, pulling toward one of the Citadel's many hangars.

"Time to move," his mother said.

Lucian followed his mother's lead, grabbing his backpack from the overhead bin. He followed her down the empty aisle before other passengers could get the same idea. His heart beat faster. It was a race against the clock. The transport was still pulling in, its deceleration offset by the inertial dampening. With a careful step, it was possible to make it to the airlock.

*"Please remain seated,"* the automated drone commanded. *"Please remain seated!"*

His mother brushed past the drone as if it didn't exist as other passengers grumbled. A male attendant near the airlock was about to address her, when she explained the situation.

"He needs to get to the *Burung*."

The attendant nodded. "That's fine. We should be docking any moment now."

Every action brought them closer to being separated. Hadn't he dreamed of this moment his entire life, being truly on his own? Why, then, did he feel so empty inside?

From outside the airlock door came a resounding click, and the hiss of air. A moment later, of its own avail, the door rolled open. The attendant gestured toward the open tunnel. Lucian entered and his mother followed.

"Mr. Abrantes?" came a female voice, in a Nordic accent.

In his rush to go down the tunnel, Lucian had missed the pretty blonde attendant in a gray Pan-Galactic uniform.

"Yeah, that's me."

"Please, follow me. The *Burung* is almost ready to embark."

Was this happening already? He turned to face his mother, who gave him a firm nod.

"Go, Lucian," she said. "There won't be another voyage. I love you."

"Mr. Abrantes?"

"Go," his mother said. Her voice was firm, but tears ran down her face. "Go!"

The attendant was already walking away, almost jogging, an action she performed easily in the low gravity despite her high heels. It looked comical, but Lucian couldn't embrace the humor of it.

"I love you, Mom," Lucian said, before turning to run after her.

He looked one last time. His mother's face was filled with tears, her posture deflated. Her shoulders shook, as if trying to keep herself from breaking down. It tore at Lucian that he couldn't comfort her. But already, his path had taken him around a corner, hiding her from sight.

Tears stung his eyes, then, but he had to be strong. He was on his own now.

———

"THIS WAY, MR. ABRANTES," the attendant insisted, blind to the emotional parting.

Being addressed so formally was strange – the attendant couldn't have been much older than him. But there was no time to correct her. Now out of the tunnel and in the main concourse, Lucian followed her down several flights of stairs. He didn't even have time to notice his surroundings, other than the fact that the space they were in was *massive*, filled with escalators, stairways, and at least ten decks of stores and restaurants. He felt light on his feet as they raced toward the bottom level of the arm. As with the shuttle transport, Sol Citadel was calibrated to Martian G.

The attendant pushed her way through the crowds to reach an unobtrusive airlock in the station's side. Beyond that airlock was the vacuum of space, but connected to the airlock itself was a small, personal-sized shuttle.

"This isn't the liner, is it?"

She suppressed a laugh. "First time in space? Not to worry. This will get you to your final gate. You'll have to run the rest of the way down X Arm."

She input a key, and the door slid open, revealing the ship's bare interior, which was the size of a small car. There was only a single seat with a safety harness and a viewscreen. Everything must have been automated, because there was nothing to steer with. Lucian realized that the stars outside were spinning slowly. The station was getting some of its own gravity from centrifugal force, which was redirected by the dominating AG field.

As he climbed inside, she leaned inside the door.

"It's self-piloting, so not to worry," she said, beaming a professional smile. "Bon voyage, Mr. Abrantes."

Before Lucian could say anything, the door slid shut and locked itself. It was hard not to feel exposed out here. How many centimeters were there between this metal shell and the cold vacuum of space?

"Please harness yourself," came a placid, female voice from the console.

Lucian followed the directions. Would his main luggage make it in time? How much time did he have left?

Not a moment after he was harnessed, the tiny vessel jolted away, piloting itself under the Citadel. Lucian let out a whoop as he was pushed back into his seat. Once its top speed was established, he began to float against his restraints. The AG field didn't seem to extend far from the station itself.

The ship zoomed out of sight of the arm and boarding tunnel, heading under the Citadel for its opposite side. In the distance, Lucian could see the ships he'd spotted on the way in. Which one did his mother work on? He didn't have time to point his slate at it for confirmation. The vessel was aiming upward now, passing an arm jutting from the station. Another shuttle zipped past soundlessly. He felt a brief moment of vertigo as he gazed into the dark void before him, millions of lightyears of distance encumbered only by multitudes of stars.

The shuttle moved at a low thrum, but other than that, there was deep and profound silence. How tiny he was, compared to the vast cosmos outside this small vessel. How insignificant. He remembered what his mother had said about space dementia, and suppressed a shiver.

The vessel executed a half-flip, drawing underside its target destination. Within the minute, it had docked under an arm on the highest level of the Citadel. The airlock clicked and slid open, revealing a wide terminal crowded with people. This part of the station looked no different from the other one, but Lucian's heart raced when he realized he was close. And the clock was ticking.

*"You have reached your destination,"* the automated female voice said.

Lucian scrambled out of the shuttle, and reached for his slate. Before he could even ask, it displayed direction with a holographic arrow. In the background, an announcement about his ship droned.

*"Attention. The* Burung *is due to depart Gate X76 in ten minutes. This is the final boarding call for Volsung. Once again . . ."*

Lucian ran, his backpack bouncing on his shoulders. He skirted several people on his way up, and ran faster once he'd reached the upper deck. The arrow pointed left, in the direction of the cavernous arm extending for at least a kilometer. Could he run that distance in time?

Lucian sprinted as fast as he could in the Martian G while stars spun outside the massive viewports. It was dizzying, as if he were running along the inside of a translucent drill, spinning and spinning. He passed shops, stores, banks of elevators, and Lev trains running on the arm's periphery. There was little time to wonder at it all. Every fifty meters or so, he passed more gates, in ascending order. He suspected X76 would be at the very end. The crowds thinned as he made his way out from the station's center, until he was only one of a few left. For a moment, he felt a thrill of fear that the gate numbers weren't going high enough. Maybe his slate had led him down the wrong arm . . .

Until at last, he reached the final gate at the terminus of the arm: X76. He heaved a sigh and rushed into the empty waiting area, breathless. He slammed into the reception counter, behind which a young man in a gray uniform blinked at him in surprise.

"I'm here," Lucian said, between breaths. "Am I too late?"

"Mr. Abrantes, no?" the attendant asked. "You have a minute to spare. Walk through the reader."

"What about my luggage?"

The attendant didn't seem to hear him. "The ship will leave in two minutes! Hurry!"

Lucian cursed, then walked through the security arch. There was a moment of hesitation, as if it might reject him.

"You've got to be kidding me ..."

When it beeped agreeably, he charged down the boarding tunnel. He could see the outer hull of the liner through the tunnel viewports. The vessel was many times larger than the one that had taken him here, with multiple decks. The name, *Burung*, was scrawled in all caps on the ship's side. Lucian wondered what that word even meant.

The boarding tunnel doors were closing ...

"No!"

With one last burst of energy, he dove, tripping over the threshold and into the pristinely white ship.

## 11

LUCIAN LOOKED up from his sprawling position on the deck to see he was in some sort of cafeteria or galley. Tables and chairs filled the space, all bolted to the deck. And those tables were filled with people. Some stared at him, others laughed. His cheeks burned as he got up and dusted himself off. Thankfully, everyone went back to their former conversations.

The double doors sealed shut, and Lucian took a few steps forward. Two spiral staircases rose on his either side, leading to an upper deck. Wide viewports lined both sides of the ship. Lucian knew they weren't actual windows, but photorealistic screens serving the same purpose. Lucian knew he was gawking, but he couldn't help it. He never thought he'd get to step on an interstellar liner. And here he was.

Where he stood, the viewports revealed the metallic exterior of the Citadel. The starboard viewports on the opposite side overlooked the star-filled expanse of space beyond. The vista included Mars, the size of his hand and shining a dull monochrome crimson. Mars moved across the viewports, but that was only due to the rotation of the Citadel itself, which the ship was moving in relation to. It was a bit dizzying.

There would be plenty of time to explore later. For now, Lucian was concerned with finding his cabin and making sure his luggage had made it.

A male voice with a German accent rolled out of the speakers, causing conversations at the tables to cease.

"Captain Miller here again. For those of you not in the galley, the boarding door has now closed. That's our cue to embark from Sol Citadel and begin our twenty-eight-day voyage to Volsung."

Lucian checked his slate for his cabin, the holographic arrow pointing the way. He took the stairs to the second deck, heading down a corridor toward the stern. He brushed past a family of four with two young children, the announcement droning on all the while. He tried to pretend he knew what he was doing.

"Now, for some information for those of you who are curious. The *Burung* has a capacity for one hundred passengers. It's one of the largest liners in the Pan-Galactic Fleet. It has two decks, with various amenities. We have a gym, simulation ports in your pods, along with millions of holos and litvids. Our galley serves Worlds-class food. Pan-Galactic's fleet boasts the most comfortable cabins in the Hundred Worlds." Lucian wanted to roll his eyes at the obvious PR. "We are one of the few companies to offer private pods, even to passengers traveling second class. The ship's schedule has been uploaded to your Pan-Galactic app, which you can access on your slate. Later tonight, there'll be a F.N.O. party – that's First Night Out, for all you newbies – timed at our passing of Jupiter at 20:00, which luckily is on our trajectory to Volsung Gate. Trust me, you won't want to miss that. Come meet your fellow passengers, play some games, and I've heard rumors there will be cake."

Meet and greets were the last thing Lucian had expected, but he supposed it made sense. Interstellar voyages could last months. His only experience of star liners came from holos. In those, there was either a mutiny or one of the passengers got space dementia and went on a killing spree. Incidentally, sometimes one of those crazy passengers happened to be a frayed mage. The thought was not a welcome one.

In short, no one could find out who he was. If they did, this trip would get interesting, and not in a good way.

"But for now," the captain continued, "sit back, relax, have a meal, meet your neighbors. You'll be stuck with them for the next four weeks. We'll be departing shortly. Good luck, bon voyage, and Godspeed. And Pan-Galactic thanks you for your patronage."

It was hard to tell, but there might have been a note of sarcasm with that last sentence.

Lucian finally found his cabin, which was almost all the way to the stern. The door opened automatically, somehow recognizing his credentials. The interior revealed two pods, one on each side. Lucian sighed in relief; it would give him some privacy, at least. The cabin didn't have its own lav or showers. He'd have to find that later.

For someone who'd lived alone for most of his life, this would be a long trip, privacy pod or not. Somehow, he'd manage. He had to. Maybe he could pass most of the days in his pod, watching holos. How long could he do that before going crazy?

Lucian's pod was the one on the right. It opened upon his approach, revealing a surprisingly spacious bed that looked clean and comfortable. Lucian sat on the bed, removed his shoes, and placed them in a cubby built into the wall. As soon as he lay on his back, the door closed of its own avail. When it clicked shut, a holographic display lit from the pod's curved interior above him. The interior had a built-in viewscreen, which displayed a menu of options. Among those were movies, games, and holographic simulations. He could book times for the observatory, water pressure massages, or other amenities.

Of course, those things would cost him creds. Creds he regretted not having.

A liner, Lucian knew, was designed to be as entertaining as possible. Its most important priority, besides transport, was preserving the sanity of its passengers.

There was only one option that interested Lucian at the moment: his luggage. It should be stored in one of the compartments connected to his pod. He toggled the command, and a retractable space opened on his left. Upon seeing his main bag, he heaved a sigh of relief.

He lay on his back for a while, recuperating from the stress of his journey. When he felt relaxed enough, he decided to head out and explore the ship.

He opened the pod and put his shoes back on. When he hopped down, it took a little too long to fall to the deck below. This low gravity was going to be hard to get used to. He walked to the cabin's viewport, and was surprised to see Sol Citadel already slipping away. He hadn't felt the ship moving at all, nor had he noticed any deviation in gravity. Clearly, the inertial dampening and AG were top-notch. Lucian knew the larger the vessel, the more efficiently both systems worked. Sol Citadel commanded the entire view. The longer he watched, the more the space fortress shrunk into the darkness, until it wasn't visible at all. How could this be happening so fast?

His new life was starting. It still seemed unreal that he was here, that he was doing this. He couldn't help but feel a sense of adventure, even if the reason for his journey terrified him.

———

IN THE GALLEY, the passengers were busy meeting their neighbors. Of course, Lucian had no one to talk to. He didn't care, but it annoyed him that everyone was already chatting away like they'd been friends for years. People could be so stupid, talking and trusting strangers they didn't even know.

Besides, it didn't look like there was anyone his age to talk to. It was mostly middle-aged and older people, since they were the only ones who could afford the price of a ticket. The only exception seemed to be a table with three young Fleet recruits wearing gray jumpsuits. He instantly didn't like the look of them. Something about their sneering faces and harsh laughter said trouble ahead. One of them even glared at Lucian as he passed. The young recruit had gelled blonde hair and sharp blue eyes set in a pale, hawkish face. A slight smirk played on his lips. If there were a face more punchable than that, Lucian had yet to find it.

It would be best if he didn't interact with anyone. That had been his M.O. for almost as long as he'd been alive. Still, even with all that, he noticed a pretty girl sitting alone on the opposite side of the galley. She had light brown skin, shoulder-length caramel hair, and almond-shaped eyes. No, she wasn't just pretty. She was stunning.

He made himself look away, but that was hard to do. Her brown eyes came up to meet his. Who *was* she? Her face, which had a dusting of light freckles, registered recognition. Had he met her before? He racked his mind, but he was certain he hadn't, because he would have definitely remembered her. And why was she smiling now?

He looked away, but it was too late to hide his embarrassment, evidenced by his burning cheeks.

He shook his head and headed to one of the serving windows, weaving between the crowd. He ordered some coffee. He'd heard spaceships were cold, but he hadn't expected it to be *this* cold. If anything, it was good training for Volsung, which was cooler than Earth. As he waited on his coffee, he glanced around the galley, and found himself looking in the girl's direction again. But this time, it seemed she was ready. Why was she staring at him like that?

Before he could second guess it, he ordered another coffee.

As he approached, she seemed to note the second coffee. His heart was beating faster. God, what was he doing?

He couldn't do this. She was looking down at her slate now, probably pretending not to notice him.

He couldn't do this. It was way too forward. He turned away, looking for another table, but in so doing, stumbled. Hot coffee splashed across his hands. He tried to bite back his pain, but it was *hot*.

"Ow!"

Several people looked at him, some of them laughing at his clumsiness. The girl was on her feet, though, her face filled with concern.

"Are you okay?" she asked. "Here. Let me help you."

She grabbed the two coffees while Lucian dried his hands on his pants. They were stain resistant, so there was no danger of ruining them.

"Thanks," he managed. He shook his hands, and noticed they were red, as if sunburned. At least there would be no blisters. The girl had already set the coffees down on her table.

She gave him a friendly smile. "You didn't have to burn yourself just to talk to me."

At that, his face flushed. "No, it wasn't like that."

"I'm just teasing. I assume this one is for me?"

She held up the half empty coffee. "Yeah. What's left of it, anyway."

She gestured toward an empty seat, and they both sat. He didn't recognize her accent. He couldn't exactly place it. Words lilted and streamed one into the other, in a pleasant-sounding way.

He grabbed his own coffee and took a sip. His mind fought for something to say that wouldn't make him sound like an idiot. How much time had passed, ten seconds? And still, she was just staring at him expectantly.

"So, I'll be honest," Lucian said, not sure where else to start. "I noticed you looking at me and I wanted to know why."

She smiled. "Honest and straightforward. I like it." She took a sip from her cup. "But you were the one looking at me first."

"Yeah, I guess that's true," Lucian said. How much more awkward could this get? It didn't help that she was gorgeous, either. She probably had men hitting on her all the time.

"It just felt like you recognized me, or something," he said.

She arched an eyebrow. "No. I don't think we've met." She smiled. "You seem a little flustered."

Flustered? He had to get it together. "I'm just clumsy, sometimes."

Her eyebrows arched at that. "Well, you're an Earther, that much I can see."

"How do you know I'm from Earth?"

"The tan," she said. "And something about the way you walk. Like you've had gravity pushing you down your whole life. Spacers have a lighter footing. Earthers have a hard time adjusting to lower G's."

"I see. Makes sense."

"My name is Emma, by the way," she said. "You?"

"Lucian. You're from space, then? This is actually my first time here."

Why was he telling her this already? He couldn't think straight.

"Really? I've been told Earthers are pretty insular, but I didn't know it was *that* bad."

"You must have made trips like a dozen times by now."

"More than that," she said, rolling her eyes. "These trips can be very boring. You'll get so sick of holos, sims, and litvids that you'll never want to watch them again. And you run into the same people over and *over*, and some of them can be dreadfully annoying. After a few days, you'll see why they charge so much for a first class cabin."

"Yeah, that's what I was afraid of."

"Is your end port Volsung Orbital?"

"Yeah," he said. She looked at him expectantly. He probably should have thought of a reason for his trip before coming on board. "My . . . uncle works there. I'm going to work for his company. What about you? Volsung, too?"

She gave a knowing smile. "Why are you *really* going to Volsung? Tell me the truth this time."

How had she known he was lying? Lucian cleared his throat, stumbling for an answer. "I *am* telling the truth."

She only laughed. "I guess being careful makes sense, given the circumstances."

Lucian could only watch her. How much did she know?

"You were right," she said. "There *was* a reason I was looking at you. Allies can be hard to find. Especially for people like us."

People like us? Lucian's eyes widened at the implication as the hairs on his arms stood on end. She couldn't be saying what he *thought* she was saying. The odds were too great.

"Yeah," she said, reading his reaction. "I'm like you. I'm a mage."

———

IT WAS PRACTICALLY IMPOSSIBLE. It might be some elaborate prank, but that meant she had to have found out what he was, somehow.

How had she known?

Lucian could only stare in mute shock for what must have been a full ten seconds. It was only then that he found his voice. There was no use denying it.

"How could you possibly know that?"

If Emma knew, *anyone* could know.

"You're not the first one I've met," she said. "And in every case I meet someone . . . like us . . . I just *know*. I don't know how it works, but it does. The instant I saw you, I felt the resonance. That we are the same in some way." She shook her head. "I don't know how else to explain it."

"That's . . . interesting." It was all he could manage to say.

"Interesting? Well, it is that. It's safe to say that we're probably going to the same place for the same reason."

"You're going to the Academy, too?"

Emma nodded. "I am."

Lucian shook his head. "I'm sorry, I don't see how this is possible."

"Well, the only explanation that makes sense to me is that something put us together." What was she *talking* about? He opened his mouth to protest, before she put her hand up. "Not like that. When it comes to people . . . like *us* . . . like can attract like."

"As in . . . fate or something?"

It sounded ridiculous to say that. And a bit . . . forward.

"Something like that," she confirmed. "I don't know why it's happened this way."

Lucian had so many questions, but he had to restrain himself, at least for now. Against all odds, here was someone to compare notes with. But at the same time, he didn't know Emma, and didn't know if he could trust her. Just because they were both mages didn't mean they would be friends.

And yet, what choice did he have but to trust her? She knew his secret, and he knew hers. They could either help each other, or assure each other's destruction.

"It seems impossible," Lucian said.

"It's far from coincidence. The same thing that makes us who we are, also drives the universe in unseen ways."

"Magic, you mean." It sounded so ridiculous to say. But there it was.

"I know it sounds far-fetched," Emma said. "But I know something of magic. Not much, but something."

Now, where had she learned about that? He hoped it was somewhere other than the GalNet, which was an unreliable source, at least pertaining to that.

"Where did you learn?" he asked.

"Someone like us told me. And I believe him."

They lapsed into silence. Through the viewports, Mars was smaller. Sol Citadel by this point would be impossible to see without the aid of the ship's telescope.

"How long have you known what you are?" Emma asked.

"I found out a couple of days ago," he said. "Hopefully, the Academy can teach me to control it."

"I've been told the training is difficult, but worth it. If we help each other, it might be easier."

"It's all so new to me. I haven't fully accepted it, to be honest."

"I know it's not easy to accept," she said. "I've had my suspicions for a while now about what I am. I didn't know for sure until a few weeks ago."

"We should talk about this somewhere else," Lucian said. "Who knows who might be listening?"

No one seemed to be paying attention to them. And they were speaking quietly. However, it was better to be safe.

"That's a good idea," Emma said. "We can talk later."

Before Lucian could respond, she stood up. She was tall and willowy, sometimes a marker of someone who had lived for years in lower gravity. He wanted to talk with her more, about things other than magic. But there would be time for that later.

"Well, Lucian," she said, "it was nice meeting you, but I think I'll have a nap now." She smiled. "Thanks for the coffee."

She stood and left. Lucian finished his coffee while

surveying the other passengers. Looking around, it didn't seem as if anyone had taken notice of their conversation. In fact, most of the tables were empty, and Mars was a red drop in the distance. It was amazing just how fast this ship was going. And a testament to how far away the Volsung Gate was, that it would take two weeks to reach it and then a further two weeks to reach the planet itself.

It was time for Lucian to return to his own cabin. The coffee hadn't done much to wake him up. He climbed the stairs to the second deck and returned to his cabin. It was still empty, and he was grateful he wouldn't have to introduce himself to anyone else yet.

He climbed into his pod and commanded the interior screen to play a holo, which he fell asleep watching.

## 12

LUCIAN WOKE A FEW HOURS LATER, with a slew of missed texts from his mother. He blinked away his sleepiness and picked up his slate. The device expanded to fill both hands. How had he forgotten to let her know he'd arrived?

Hours had passed by now. For all she knew, he was still stuck in Sol Citadel.

*They're stationing me on the LSC* Refuge. *The entire fleet is mobilizing at Starbase Centauri. We're embarking tomorrow. We haven't been told why, but the rumors seem to be true. We'll reach Starbase Centauri in twenty-two standard, and I'll be out of Sol in ten. We have that long to talk without serious delays. I guess you're asleep or something. I'm worried about you. Much love.*

Lucian's stomach dropped as he read. The rumors were truth, then. They had to be. And she was only back with the Fleet because of his need to travel to Volsung.

It wasn't a good feeling.

Lucian began composing his response. By now, the software of his slate knew him so well that he was hardly typing. The words appeared on the screen through eye movements. It wasn't exactly telepathy, but it might as well have been.

*I'm fine. Safe in my pod right now, though I tripped myself pretty bad getting in. It was a close call. I hope the rumors aren't true, but I'm glad you won't be in the thick of it.* Refuge *is supposed to be one of the safest ships in the Fleet.*

Was he trying to comfort her, or himself? He didn't want to think about it. Lucian only had to wait a few minutes for a response.

*Good, I'm glad you made it. Don't worry about me, Lucian. I'll survive, just as I always have. I'll sync some credits to you, because I'm not sure how much transport will be to Volsung. I wouldn't want you stranded. When data's backed up at the Gates, fees can be high. They got me my bonus early. The Fleet is working efficiently for once. I miss you already. They took you away from me too soon. I hope this mobilization will be nothing. Reach out if you ever need anything. Really. Don't hesitate.*

Lucian composed a new message. *I will.* What else to say? *I'll try to do what you said. Not give up. I'll have a lot of time to think about that, I guess. I love you, too. Please stay safe.*

Too many light-messages would get expensive. When no message came back, he slept a bit longer, then watched part of a holo. All he could think about was his conversation with Emma. It almost felt as if it hadn't happened, and part of him felt as if it were a joke. Someone knew his secret. It made him feel a little sick.

Lucian opened his pod to find that the larger cabin was no longer empty. The pod on the opposite side had its door open. There sat a middle-aged woman wearing a nun's habit. Her curly brown hair fell to her shoulders as she looked at her slate, which she held in both hands. She looked up at Lucian and gave a friendly smile that crinkled the corners of her eyes. What was a Believer doing on this ship?

"Hello," she said. "I guess we're neighbors?"

Her accent was hard to place, but it was definitely Latin American.

"I guess so," Lucian said, jumping down from his bunk and landing on his feet. "I'm Lucian, from the States. You?"

"Believer Horatia. Buenos Aires, Argentina."

She *was* a Believer, then. He needed to tread carefully.

He nodded respectfully, and turned to leave, but it seemed the Believer wasn't done, yet.

"Serving the Lord God is my life's calling. I wouldn't be doing anything else." Her gaze was empty, and gave Lucian the creeps. "Is your final destination Volsung, or somewhere else?"

"Volsung." She stared at him harder. She wanted more than that. "I'm going to help my uncle with his business." The lie easily came this time.

Her eyes widened. "That sounds like an excellent opportunity. It's a growing world, and the culture is wonderful."

"You've been before?"

"Several times. Only on the Ostkontinent, though. The Believers are posting me to the new cathedral at Nova Bergen. There, I hope to spread God's message to the people."

"Is that so?" This had nothing to do with him, but he figured it was better to be polite. They would be sharing space for the next few weeks, after all. He didn't want drama, especially with a Believer.

"The Church wants to expand its mission," she went on. "Unfortunately, I'll have to learn Norwegian, and they want me to learn it in a few months." When she smiled, it didn't reach her eyes. Why did all Believers have the same, glazed look? "That's what I'm doing now. At times, I wish the Church were supportive of neural grafting." She laughed, as if this were a joke.

"If only." Neural grafting was expensive, and risky. But it was the fastest way to learn anything.

"Unfortunately, I have my work cut out for me," Believer Horatia said. "And with the mages on the rise, we Believers must increase our vigilance to match."

Her brown eyes intensified, burning with holy fire. This was what Lucian had been afraid of. There was no way she knew what he was, unless of course she were like Emma. But if that were the case, Believer Horatia was in the wrong line of work.

Lucian tried to steer clear of the Believers whenever he could. They had a chapter close to his apartment, and they had no qualms proselytizing to anyone they found. And no one hated the mages more than them. He always walked a bit faster on the corners where they gave their sermons, sometimes to crowds of well over a hundred people. In this new universe with magic, miracles no longer seemed impossible. People had grown impatient with scientists.

It was all bullshit to Lucian. He had always ignored the Believers and their vitriol. But now, he found it terribly relevant, and it made him realize how precarious his existence was. He didn't only have to worry about the fraying slowly killing him. He had to worry about others killing him before that ever happened. On some of the worlds, the Believers had grown bolder. Bold enough to take justice into their own hands.

"I wish you luck in your mission," Lucian said, hoping it was the appropriate response.

He turned to leave, but Believer Horatia didn't seem to think the conversation was over. He had to resist the urge to roll his eyes.

"Most of the Worlds seem to recognize the threat the mages pose. Volsung, unfortunately, is going the opposite direction. The government is even sponsoring that academy. They mean to *train* these mad people in their dark arts! As if the Mage War weren't lesson enough. As if this isn't a cycle that is doomed to repeat itself until their fraying disease has completely purged humanity. Magic is sin manifested, Lucian. Never forget that."

She did not suspect him in the least. In fact, she saw him as an ally. How far had sentiment shifted against mages? Once, mages were seen as victims of fate, unlucky souls ridden with an incurable disease that would one day kill them. Now, it seemed only the scientists and doctors believed that. Much of that had to be due to the Believers' influence.

How long before sentiment had shifted enough to tip the scales of government? How long before mages were no longer allowed to gather in academies in hopes of discovering a cure? How long before all mages were imprisoned or killed on the spot?

Lucian's stomach twisted at the thought. All he wanted was space and room to breathe. Anything but to spend more time with this damnable woman.

But he had to hold out a little while longer. He needed to be above suspicion. Even if it meant his own sanity.

Her features were as sharp as a blade's edge as she continued her sermon. "It may be a war we lose – if we don't turn to God. We must take great care. The Enemy is tainting more every day. The mages are only a symptom of the problem – the problem of sin – but more mages are being born every day. As humanity spreads, its sins multiply. Sin feeds magic, makes it fester and grow." She licked her thin lips, and continued. "Our gravest mistake after the war was suffering them to live. They continued to practice their dark arts, albeit out of the public eye." She shook her head. "If things continue this way, they will regain their former strength. How long before we're in the same situation as fifty years ago?"

Lucian remained quiet. Was there any point in answering?

Horatia continued. "It might be enough to break us for good. The Hundred Worlds can't take another war. When the mages and the Swarmers enter into an alliance, only then will the Worlds realize their error." She sighed. "Forgive me. I can go on and on. I say all this only to warn you, Lucian. You must be careful. Earth is a safe place. There is power there. Power to protect. It's God's chosen world, and as long as humanity holds God in its heart, they can never poison Holy Earth. But you are going away from all that. Volsung is not like Earth. A beautiful world, yes, but a world of darkness. A great evil lies within it, buried deep. One day, that wound will fester. But it will not do so until the time is ripe." Her dark brown eyes were harrowing. "The Believers must always be on their guard. And it is our duty to spread our message to any who have ears to hear." She grabbed his arm, and it was all Lucian could do not to pull it away. "Pray, Lucian. Seek out one of our churches. We are in every major city on Volsung. Only if we come together can we push back the night. There isn't time. And I would sleep easier knowing your soul is safe."

Lucian stood speechless. He didn't dare question her. This woman was far past the point of ever doubting herself. Her beliefs were only a symptom of the problem. The problem being no one knew where magic came from, or why it eventually drove a mage insane. As good as science had been at filling in the gaps of ignorance, it had never been able to explain magic. Even Lucian wasn't sure it would *ever* be explained. It had been over a hundred years since the first mages had emerged, anyway.

By this point, most people didn't want things to be proven. They just wanted it to make sense, so they could sleep in peace – even if the sleep was given by a dose of ignorance.

"I should go," he said.

"Don't be deceived," Horatia said. "God punishes the mages with the fraying. Though they lust for the power the Devil gives them, they will suffer for it." She nodded, as if to confirm that immutable fact. "I will say a prayer for you, Lucian. That God will shelter us both in this fallen universe."

"Thank you," Lucian said. The words took great effort to say. "And I will do the same for you."

"My heart is glad," Believer Horatia said. "Go with God."

This was going to be a long, long trip.

———

ONCE THE DOOR closed behind him, Lucian let out a sigh of relief. How would he survive the next four weeks with that insufferable woman? He walked the *Burung's* empty corridors, brooding. The conversation was a rude awakening that life would never be the same. He could never blend into normal society again.

He saw what Emma had meant about loneliness.

Worse, Lucian understood why people like Believer Horatia held their beliefs. The stories of the mages during the war were incredible and horrifying. Most people on Earth were spared the worst aspects of the war. Some didn't even believe they had happened. But the power-mad mages had leveled entire cities with nothing but their magic. Their magic ensured victories that should have been defeats. Planet surfaces burned with fire, great storms were called from the skies, they poisoned the very air of the worlds they sieged. That *he* might become the same thing someday, without ever wanting or wishing it, made him sick to his stomach.

It was hard to separate truth from fiction. But one thing all accounts agreed on. With their magic, the Free Mages under Xara Mallis wiped out all life from the face of the planet, Isis.

Isis had been a beautiful world, with natural wonders that rivaled Earth. At the end of the war, the League of the Hundred Worlds had finally stopped underestimating the Free Mages. The League had pushed the Mages' Armada to the Border World of Isis, the Mages' capital. Long mad from the corruption of their magic, the mages refused to surrender. They held their planet, and the millions of lives upon it, hostage.

The Hundred Worlds engaged. When victory was near, the mages escaped to the planet surface. There, under a rain of tachyon lances and plasma cannons, they committed their final act, rendering the planet surface a raging inferno of radioactive destruction.

Millions were killed, unable to escape an atmosphere that had turned toxic. The paradise planet had become a post-apocalyptic wasteland. Lucian couldn't imagine the terror of that fight.

Things after the Mage War were never the same . . . and it settled the debate once and for all on how magic-users were to be treated. With the death of Xara Mallis, the last pockets of Free Mages were extinguished. By 2314, the Mage War was over.

In some stories Lucian had heard, the dead spirits of that world forever wandered it. Some said she was still alive, the so-called Queen of the Tomb World. He didn't put much stock in that. The idea was almost too scary to believe.

As the years passed, the cause of magical emergence and the fraying was never discovered. Headway was only made in the detection of mages, through the metaphysical exam. Once identified, mages could no longer fray undetected. At least, in theory. Lucian supposed plenty of mages had escaped the nets, especially on less-developed worlds. They could only exist legally within sanctioned communes, or an approved academy. The Loyalist Mages who fought with the Hundred Worlds now controlled all magekind. Beyond that, Lucian didn't know much else.

But given the way things were going, Lucian could see how even Loyalist Mages might come under fire. Did the Hundred Worlds keep them alive out of necessity? Out of fear?

At that moment, Lucian couldn't say. As it stood, Loyalist Mages hunted the rogues, and those too far gone were sent to Psyche, the so-called Mad Moon in the Cupid system. Which was most mages who couldn't be trained. And any who went to Psyche never left.

Now more than ever, Lucian realized he would never be safe. Without an academy, the fraying would find him and destroy him. Whether it killed him outright, or destroyed his ability to think rationally, his options were few. It was a terrible thing to think about. It felt as if there were a bottomless pit in his stomach, sapping all his energy and life. How could he find hope, when it all seemed so pointless?

His slate chimed, breaking him from his dark thoughts. He pulled it out to see another message from his mother.

*More rumors flying around about the Swarmers. We're expecting an announcement from the top brass later. At this point, though, it's a foregone conclusion. Well, it'll be a few weeks before we reach Starbase Centauri. I'm sure I'll find out more then.*

Lucian's throat clamped. He wanted to scream, but settled instead for punching the wall. That hurt, especially since his hands were still tender from the coffee. But he didn't care.

Things kept on getting worse and worse. What was the point of anything? No matter what he tried, the universe fought back twice as hard. If the Swarmers *were* back, then humanity had more to worry about than a second Mage War. This time, the Swarmers might actually break through, returning in greater numbers. What then?

He stopped in the corridor, having made a circuit around the ship several times. He closed his eyes, seeking refuge from his own thoughts. Where were his walls when he needed them? It seemed nothing could keep out the hopelessness.

Finally, things were happening to break him. His walls wouldn't be enough.

# 13

Lucian ate an early dinner in the galley. He didn't plan on going to the F.N.O. party later. Socializing was the last thing he wanted, especially after his encounter with Believer Horatia. It would be best to eat his first meal on the ship while the crowds were thin.

There wasn't much choice with his cheap meal plan. He could choose Western, Eastern, or Vegetarian. There were premium options, but he didn't want to pay for it.

When he picked Western, a tray spit out from the meal slot ahead of him. Its contents looked sad: a dry slice of turkey breast, half a boiled potato, overcooked green beans, and a dry roll with a slab of frozen butter on top. Worlds-class food his ass.

He took the tray to the same table where he'd sat with Emma. He was the only one in the galley, which he was thankful for. Shipboard time said it was still early afternoon, but his internal clock said it was dinnertime.

When footsteps approached, he didn't turn to look until they were close. A shadow fell over him, making his stomach tense. He looked up to see the pale-faced, blonde Fleet recruit from earlier. His sharp blue eyes held a mocking quality, only accentuated by his superior smirk. He stood too close for comfort. Wherever *he* was from, he clearly had no concept of personal space. On his either side, his two friends flanked him. One was tall and built, with coppery brown skin and close-cropped hair. The other was thin, short, and pale as a ghost, with cloudy gray eyes and matching hair.

"Do you need some money for real food?" the pale young man said mockingly. "You'd like the first class plans. This," he nodded toward the tray, "should be illegal."

Lucian did what he could to control his voice. They wouldn't try anything in such a public space. Not unless they were idiots.

"Can I help you with something?"

"Depends," the young recruit said, taking up a chair and sitting without invitation. His two friends took their own chairs, and all stared at him from across the table. Lucian knew cheaper interstellar liners like this one could attract a rougher crowd. Crime wasn't uncommon, and the ship's crew was usually no help except in the worst cases. Were they trying to shake him down or something? He had no money, and if this piss stain was in the first class cabins, Lucian doubted he needed it.

Which meant they were here for something else. But what could that be?

The ringleader steepled his fingers in a businesslike manner and leaned forward, his smile more predatory than friendly. Lucian's skin crawled. The last thing he wanted was a fight. And it was only day one.

"Earther, aren't you?" the recruit asked.

Lucian nodded, but offered nothing more.

"Traveling alone can be dangerous," the recruit went on. "I admire you for doing it. You never know what kind of freaks you'll be stuck with." He let out a throaty chuckle. "This isn't my first passage. I've been on the wrong end when things get ugly. Believe me, the crew cares about nothing except your money." He held out a hand. "That being the case, I hope we can become friends. My name's Dirk. Dirk Beker. You?"

Lucian hesitated before taking the hand. No reason to stir the pot, even if Dirk's spiel was rubbing him the wrong way. "Lucian Abrantes."

"Nice to meet you, Lucian," he said. "These are my friends." He looked from one side to the other. "Why don't you fellows introduce yourselves?"

The hulking youth with the brown skin cracked his knuckles. "Kasim."

"Paul," the frail one said in a nasally tone. Lucian only now noticed several scars covering his arms. The direction of the wounds suggested they hadn't been self-inflicted.

"Paul, Kasim, and I go way back," Dirk said. "Mars-O is a rough Hab. One of the oldest, too. Filled with mining folks, mostly. It was designed for ten thousand people. Fifty thousand live there now. As you can imagine, things can get dicey. Us three – we're going to Volsung for Fleet training. Me as a fleet officer, these two as pod droppers." Dirk chuckled, and his two "friends" showed no emotion. "I treat my friends well. They're welcome to my meal plan any time. We have each other's backs. It's good to have that, wouldn't you agree?"

"Sure it is," Lucian said.

"I have a friendly question. That girl you were talking to . . . Emma, was it?" Lucian's skin went cold. "Sorry, couldn't help but overhear. Voices carry very well in this ship." He gave a slimy smile. If he had overheard that part of their conversation, what *else* had he heard? "I need some help getting my foot in the door with her, so to speak. I'm a handsome guy, but between gentlemen, I'd rather things not get difficult between us."

Lucian met Dirk's challenging stare. "Is that so?"

"I don't know. To me, it seems you've taken a liking to her. It's easy to see why. She's the finest piece on this blasted ship. Wouldn't you agree?"

There it was. That was all Lucian needed to know about Dirk. It had been obvious before, but now the idiot had tipped his hand. Lucian just stared at him, hard.

"Where are my manners?" Dirk asked. "I grew up in a rough place. It's just how we talk. I've forgotten how . . . *cultured* . . . Earthers can be. You treat us Martians like we're a waste of space. Why mince words, anyway? Wouldn't you agree, Lucian?"

"About what?"

"Emma. Finest piece on this ship, right?"

Paul and Kasim chuckled at that, as if it were the greatest joke in the world.

"She's a looker," he admitted, in a last-ditch effort to avoid conflict. "What's it to you?"

"I'm about to get to that," Dirk said, with a smile. "Why not have a friendly competition? First to bed her gets to keep her the rest of the trip. Sound like a deal?"

"I don't make deals with creeps," Lucian said. "Besides, you're proving everyone's theories about Mars-O true."

"What?"

Lucian's eyes narrowed. "You're a waste of space."

Dirk's eyes became dangerous for a moment, and then he gave a loud, resonating laugh. "He likes her, boys! He might even be . . . in *love*." His two cronies guffawed at that. Dirk leaned forward, until his face was centimeters from Lucian's. They stared each other down like bulls about to charge. "I wouldn't do anything stupid, if I were you. You're alone. What *can* you do?" He smirked. "Nothing."

"You want to test me on that, prick?"

Dirk blinked. He hadn't expected that answer. Lucian knew he was bluffing. He'd been in a few fistfights, sure. But he'd never won anything three on one. And with someone the size of Kasim, the odds were even more against him.

"Lucian, I'm hurt. I was only being friendly."

"Maybe you wasn't being friendly enough," Kasim offered.

"No," Dirk mused, "maybe not."

When Dirk glanced around to see if anyone was in the area, Lucian's instincts kicked into overdrive. He jumped up, knocking over his chair in the process while balling his fists. Paul and Kasim got up to match, while Dirk was gesturing in a placating manner. *Now* he wanted things to calm down? What an idiot.

"Boys, boys!" he said. "No need to fight. We're *friends*, remember?" He smiled at Lucian. He then closed his eyes and inhaled deeply. "Emma. Beautiful, lovely, Emma. Doesn't that name just roll off the tongue? It's an old name. Probably a classy girl. "

"She looks classy," Kasim rumbled.

Dirk shot him a dirty look. "Shut up."

The other one, Paul, gave a slimy smile.

What were his options? He could try to get the jump on them, but any fight here he was guaranteed to lose. Maybe one on one he could beat Dirk bloody, but not with Kasim. He probably weighed fifty kilos, accounting for the lower gravity. And that other one, Paul, had seen things, too, judging by those scars and cold, gray eyes. He could just leave, too, but that wouldn't be a good look.

The only thing he could do was hold his ground, and not let them push him around. If he bided his time, someone else might come into the galley.

So, that was what he would do. Bide his time. Keep them talking.

"I don't want to see you around her," Lucian said, fighting to keep his voice level.

"Or what?" Kasim asked, taking a step forward.

Dirk motioned him back. "I'm not only a good friend, Lucian. I'm a good listener." He smiled dangerously. "Someone with sharp ears like me hears things. That's valuable, you know. My Pa always taught me that. Information is power. Information wins battles, Lucian, not muscle. Of course, muscle is always nice to have."

"What's your point?" Lucian asked.

"You'd better watch yourself. That's all. This is a long trip. And if you keep your nose where it belongs, it'll pass pleasantly enough for the both of us. Me, with a pretty girl warming my bed . . ." He made a rude, jerking motion with his hand. "And you, staying in your pod and familiarizing yourself with the dirty holo catalogue." He chuckled. "If you'd like recommendations, I'm sure Kasim has suggestions." Kasim's expression darkened, but he didn't raise a word against his master.

Lucian looked at him. "You just going to take that, big guy?"

"Kasim and I have an arrangement," Dirk said. "My friends know it's best to stick with me. Isn't that right, boys?"

Apparently, Dirk took their stony silence as assent. It didn't seem as if there was any weak link there.

Dirk leaned back, his features relaxing. "Do we understand each other? Put in a good word for me, Lucian, and I would be in your debt. Maybe mention that you've seen me in the first class cabins? That ought to do. Nothing like a little money to impress a pretty girl, right? With me, she can have all the comforts and sim pills she wants. But it's best if it comes from you. I wouldn't want to sound crass."

So long as Lucian breathed, this creep wouldn't be bothering Emma. Like him, she was traveling alone, and she needed someone to watch her back.

If he didn't do that, who would?

"I won't be doing that," Lucian said. "In fact, I think it's probably best if you left. And left her alone."

Dirk gave a throaty, mocking laugh, his two friends joining him. He nodded toward his two friends.

Lucian raised his fists.

They came forward, fast. Faster than Lucian would have ever believed. Lucian swung, but Paul dodged his blow easily. Next thing he knew, each of Dirk's cronies were grabbing him by the shoulder. They easily shoved him into the wall, pinning him. Against all three of them, Lucian could do nothing.

"Let me go! Get off me, you pricks!"

He yelled as loud as he could, in hopes that someone would hear. Kasim clocked him in the face, making him see stars. The pain rung and throbbed like a bell. Dazed, Lucian could only grunt.

"Enough," Dirk said. "I think he's learned his lesson."

Kasim grunted, as if he disagreed with that. But he obeyed his master's order.

Despite Lucian's shouts, there was no one around to hear. The galley was still empty, and no one would be here until the F.N.O party later.

Dirk stood leisurely, then walked forward. He stood so close that Lucian could smell the foulness of his breath. Lucian struggled, but Paul and Kasim held him in place. Dirk stared, like a snake about to strike. He gave a gleeful little laugh. "I know something that could *ruin* you. Want to hear it? As long as we understand each other, we have nothing to disagree about. Your secret is safe with me." He leaned until his sharp nose was touching Lucian's, who fought harder to escape the pin he was under. Paul and Kasim redoubled their efforts to hold him against the wall. "Some advice. *Don't* cross me. It's not fun to be on the wrong side of public opinion. All I have to do is say a few words, and the witch hunt begins."

Lucian did his best to meet Dirk's gloating stare. He knew the truth. Somehow, someway, he had overheard his and Emma's conversation.

"So, what'll it be?" Dirk asked.

Finally, the moment Lucian had been waiting for arrived. He heard voices coming from down the corridor.

"Hey, get off me you assholes!"

"Let him go," Dirk commanded.

The loyal dogs let go and backed up, giving Lucian space.

"Don't forget what I said," Dirk said.

He nodded toward his friends, and they walked out of the galley toward the bow of the ship. Several others filtered in – an old man with snowy white hair and an eye patch, a red-headed woman. None looked his way, and none seemed to know what had happened. Even if he told them, why should they care?

Lucian shook his head. He could try to catch Dirk alone, but he had the feeling he didn't go anywhere without his guard dogs.

But he couldn't ignore his threat. He *knew* what he and Emma were. Had all but said it. In Dirk's mind, Lucian's silence was guaranteed. What mage would dare out himself, especially with the likes of Believer Horatia on board?

It wasn't only him at risk. Dirk could use the information to blackmail Emma into a compromising situation. Just the thought of that set his blood boiling.

He slammed his fist on the table, ignoring the looks he got from the others, sitting down to their coffees or meals. Of course, it could all be a bluff, but Lucian couldn't assume that. If he went to the crew, then Dirk would out him. Could he live with that?

Lucian couldn't even count on the crew to intervene. There were always stories of fights, crime, and worse on interstellar liners. The liner's job was to get its passengers from one point to another. Maintaining anything more than the minimum of security cut into margins. There was the brig for bad cases, but a little bullying would likely not get anything more than a slap on the wrist.

Well, at least that meant they wouldn't kill him. Probably.

The one thing he could do was find Emma and tell her what to expect. He couldn't stand idly by, no matter the consequences. Lucian had no idea how to do that without tipping his hand. He didn't even know where her cabin was.

Whether he wanted to or not, it looked like he was going to the F.N.O. party tonight. That was due to start in a couple of hours. That being the case, Emma was probably in her cabin now.

Maybe the best thing was to have a look around the ship. She might be in one of the ship's public spaces.

He got up and bussed his tray. He headed back in the direction of his cabin.

Once he'd reached the door, he looked back over his shoulder, finding the corridor empty. He rounded the corner, past his cabin, toward the starboard side of the ship.

Around the corner, just ten meters from his cabin, was where they jumped him.

There was no time to react. A fist landed squarely in Lucian's jaw. He stumbled back, his back slamming into the wall. Kasim and Paul shoved him in tandem. They kept him pinned while Dirk landed punch after punch, his eyes smoldering like blue fire. Lucian tried to call out, but all he could manage was a belabored hacking. He curled his fists to defend himself, but his arms were immobile.

They were going to kill him.

Even as he screamed, the beating continued. Paul caught his right wrist and twisted. The pain was sharp, and Lucian howled. The three boys slammed him into the corner. He fought to escape. Panic clutched his throat, panic drowned by a sea of pain.

For the next half minute, he endured that hell. All three used their weight to keep him grounded, clobbering him in his stomach and face. Lucian held up his arms in a feeble attempt to defend himself. Where *was* everybody? He couldn't even shout for help.

Dirk's face above him was twisted and monstrous. He gave Lucian one final punch in the jaw, hard enough for Lucian to see stars. His vision was hazy. He just wanted it to end . . .

And when it did, his breathing was labored and raspy. Any more, and they'd kill him.

Dirk's pale face swam in Lucian's vision. Somehow, Paul and Kasim had forced him into the kneeling position. When Lucian tried to stand, he was forced back down.

Dirk's icy eyes glinted murderously. "Don't say I didn't warn you. We know what you are. A *psycho*. If we killed you, trust me, no one would shed a tear." He leaned forward. "Now *apologize*."

Lucian didn't care if his next words killed him. He spit in Dirk's face, blood mixed with phlegm.

"Fuck you."

Dirk punched him once again in the gut, knocking the wind out of him.

"Dirk, you've done him good enough," Kasim said, nervously.

"Yeah," Paul agreed. "People are gonna ask questions."

"Will they, Paul? *Will* they?" Dirk spat with disgust. "Get yourself to the med bay, mage. Get yourself fixed up good. Or I tell everyone."

Where were people when you needed them? The ship, Lucian realized, was larger than he had ever thought. Or people had heard the commotion and decided to keep out of the way. That was just like people.

"Let's go," Dirk said.

They ran, leaving Lucian sprawled against the wall, fighting for breath. The pain was excruciating, like nothing he had ever felt. He needed to get to the med bay. The thought of being found in this state was humiliating. But the pain was too great.

The med bay was on the other side of the ship. In this state, he might have to crawl to get there, leaving a bloody trail.

Somehow, though, he forced himself to stand. His eyes were so swollen that he could barely see. But he had to keep moving. Get himself fixed up.

And he had to warn Emma.

# 14

Lucian hobbled down the empty corridor to his cabin. It wasn't far, but the door wouldn't open for him. He banged on it, breathing a curse.

"Open, damn you ..."

His voice seemed to trigger it, because the door slid open soon after. His face must be so messed up that the reader no longer recognized it. He stumbled inside, finding Believer Horatia's pod closed.

He needed a med bay appointment, so what was he even doing here? He couldn't think straight. His ears were ringing, his head swimming. With a shaky hand, he raised his slate to his mouth.

"Med bay appointments."

The holo display immediately showed him time slots for a treatment pod. He had his pick of appointments. A quick nano-treatment should get rid of most of the bruising and swelling before anyone could notice. Maybe he could tell others how bad he'd been messed up, but Dirk would let out his secret, and maybe Emma's, too. And Lucian couldn't abide the shame.

He made an immediate appointment and headed for the

door. But before he could step out, Believer Horatia's pod whirred open, revealing the zealot within. She gasped, her eyes wide. He must have looked worse than he felt.

"My God," she said. "What happened?"

All he wanted was to get out of here.

"Ran into some trouble. Nothing to worry about." He stepped toward the cabin door.

"Lucian, we must get you to the medical bay at once!"

"That's where I'm headed. I'd appreciate it if we kept this between us."

"Allow me to help you."

Why wouldn't this woman leave him alone? "I'm fine. Just get back in your pod."

His head swam, and he leaned on the door for support. Damn. *Could* he make it on his own? If she knew what he was, she might finish the job.

Without a word, she stepped next to him to support his weight. The small, wiry Believer was much stronger than he would have guessed. Then again, the gravity was less – which spoke to his weakness that he couldn't get there on his own. Short of fighting her off, he wasn't going to get rid of her.

"Fine," he conceded. "Let's move."

Out in the corridor, Lucian's slate pointed the way. The corridor seemed to be clear all the way toward the bow. The Believer and Lucian walked down an empty corridor that would pass above the galley. Would a crowd already be gathering for the party? There was nothing to be done about that, though. There was only one way to the med bay.

"What happened? Who attacked you?"

"I fell," Lucian said.

She tsked. "In this gravity? You wouldn't have gotten a scratch." She clicked her tongue. "I think I know who did it. Those Fleet ruffians I saw earlier. Those types think they own every vessel they step on." She shook her head. "The crew will do nothing to stop them, because the military will protect them. It's not worth their trouble."

Lucian remained silent. Maybe she would let the matter drop.

"Even if reporting it won't do anything, we should consider it."

"I'm fine," Lucian said. When would she get the message? "It's my problem to deal with."

"Don't be foolish," she said. "Men and their pride!"

At this point, they were passing the galley from the second deck. By now, it was busier, with people filtering in early for the F.N.O. party. Lucian moved to the side, trying to let the Believer shield him from view. Still, he couldn't help himself. He had to look down and see who was there.

Sure enough, Emma stood by the high viewports on the starboard side. Those viewports looked out on a majestic vista of Jupiter. The orange and white-streaked orb, along with its gargantuan, baleful eye, dominated the ports. The planet couldn't have been more than a million kilometers away. Despite everything, the beauty of the solar system's largest planet gave him vertigo. He could feel the world's power reaching out to him, as if its gravity were pulling him.

Only after he managed to pull his gaze away from Jupiter did he notice Emma wasn't alone. Standing beside her, Dirk was all smiles and suave. Kasim and Paul lingered a few steps away.

Seeing that was a punch in the gut. He should go down there right now, call him out in front of everyone, bloody face and everything. He was about to do just that . . . until something stopped him. No. He could win this. He could find a way to get them back, while keeping his and Emma's secret safe. Besides, who was to say what would happen once Dirk told them all what he was?

For all he knew, he might be the victim of mob justice right there. Believer Horatia's presence right next to him only edified that feeling.

The only way he could protect her was not allowing anyone else to see him like this. There would be time for revenge. Later. For now, all Lucian could do was ball his fists, and get himself fixed up.

"Thank you, Believer Horatia," he managed. "I can make it from here."

Before she could protest, he increased his pace, his pain rising to match. Almost there.

Lucian found the med bay easily enough, the slate's arrow pointing him toward the rightmost of two medical pods. They didn't look much different from his own bunk. As he approached, it opened to accept him. He lay flat on his back, and closed his eyes. He'd never been in a med pod before.

He just hoped it didn't hurt.

———

WITHIN SECONDS, Lucian's head swam in a sea of painless bliss. Muscles relaxed as his mind drifted, completely at peace. It was almost worth getting beat up just for the feeling. The poking, prodding, and application of nano-healing gels became something far away.

He lay dreaming in that state for what seemed like hours. A curious itching had set into his knees and swollen eyes. That itch was powerful enough to cut through the drugs, but he couldn't move. But neither did he care. Whatever pain and fears he had were washed away by the meds. When the dose increased, he nodded off.

Lucian woke what must have been hours later. There was still a dull throbbing in his knee, but otherwise, his pain was gone. He reached up to touch his face, and his hand came away clean, finding no blood or tenderness.

How much would this set him back?

The pod hissed open, and Lucian crawled out. He stood, favoring his left leg. After walking on it a bit, he realized the leg was just stiff, which should go away after a few hours.

He checked his slate to see it was now two hours past midnight. Which meant he had been in the pod for what, eight hours? Whatever the case, his stomach growled as if he hadn't eaten in a week. One of the main side effects of nano-treatment was increased hunger. When the body healed faster than it was supposed to, it demanded energy to compensate.

When he reached the deck above the galley, his eyes widened upon seeing Emma sitting alone at her usual table with a mug of coffee. His movement above must have caught her eye, because she waved at him. It looked as if she didn't know what had happened.

"There you are! Get down here."

How would he go about this? He went down the spiral staircase, wondering what it was she and Dirk had been talking about.

"You all right?" she asked. "You're limping."

"Let me eat, first. I'll tell you everything."

"All right," she said, worriedly. "Is everything fine?"

"Yeah," he said.

Lucian went to the serving window, this time not skimping. He ordered a premium meal, steak and potatoes with a side salad. He also got a cup of soma tea that would work wonders for his nerves, while giving him some pain relief. He couldn't have too much, though. He needed to stay sharp.

He went back to the table and ate quickly. He was so hungry he didn't care what Emma thought of his lack of manners.

"Okay," she said. "*What* happened?"

Lucian swallowed, took a sip of his tea. "How are you doing?"

"I'm fine," she said. "I asked about you, though."

"I came by the party earlier," Lucian said. "Saw you talking to Dirk."

"You were at the party? I didn't see you."

"What were you guys talking about?"

Her eyes widened. "Nothing. He was just introducing himself. Why?"

"That's it? Nothing else?"

"No," Emma said. "What, are you accusing me of something? Why does it matter who I talk to, or . . ."

"No, it's not that," Lucian said. "I wanted to warn you about Dirk."

"What about him?"

"They know, Emma. Or at least, strongly suspect."

Lucian didn't have to explain further. Her mouth opened in surprise, and she was at a loss for words.

"I swear, I didn't say a word," she said.

"Me, neither," Lucian said.

"Then how . . ."

"I don't know. They overheard, or something." Emma watched him for explanation. It was hard to tell the truth. He'd just end up embarrassing himself. Even if it was three on one, it didn't look good.

"Whatever's on your mind, just tell me," she said.

"They were waiting for me by my cabin," Lucian explained. "Three against one, there wasn't much I could do."

Emma watched him, incredulous, as Lucian told her everything. Her expression soured the more he talked.

"Anyway, that's where I just came from. The med pods. I've been set back almost half the price of my ticket."

"I . . . just can't believe it," Emma said. "That asshole. Are you going to report him?"

"That's the thing," Lucian said. "I can't. If I say anything, he'll just let our secret out."

Her face twisted with disgust. "What a creep. From the

minute he started talking to me, something felt off. He seemed to know things about me already. He never said so up front, but just his questions. It's like he knew what to ask me. How did he find all that out?"

"I didn't say anything, and you didn't say anything. And they were too far to hear us. That means that *someone* heard us, somewhere."

"He might have an ocular implant," Emma guessed. "I've heard of those. It would let him listen at a distance while filtering out competing noise. Worse, they also record conversations. So if we denied the truth, he'd have the evidence."

"I thought those implants were illegal."

"They're supposed to be in most places. When has legality ever stopped a rich person from getting what they wanted?"

Lucian didn't have an answer for that. "So we're screwed."

"There's only one thing we can do. Go to the captain, and ask for his protection."

"Out of the question."

"Why not?"

"Because, we don't know what *his* stance on mages is. We need to think of something else."

"We could just ignore him."

"So, hiding."

"Do you have a better idea?"

"I don't know. All I know is you should feel safe and not have to worry about the likes of him."

"I *do* know," Emma said. "Unfortunately. This isn't the first time I've dealt with unwanted attention, and it won't be the last. Space has a way of making bad people even worse."

"My cabinmate is a Believer."

"The old nun?" Emma asked. "I saw her at the party. She kept to herself, except when she tried to proselytize." She rolled her eyes. "Don't worry about Dirk. He was bragging about how he was going for officer training in Nova Bergen."

"You shouldn't underestimate him," Lucian said. "He was saying some . . . pretty vile things."

"*Great*," Emma said. "If I'm right about that implant, then we'll have to be careful what we say and where we say it. I'm sure the cameras caught something, and you have your medical bill to prove what happened. I understand liners don't exactly *guarantee* their passengers' safety. But stuff like this should *never* happen. I think you have a case if you want to bring it to the captain."

"Wouldn't it be worse if Dirk outs us?"

Emma frowned. She looked beautiful even doing that. "That's hard to say. Do you choose the devil you know, or the devil you don't?"

"The one I know, for sure. I just need another option."

"Like what? Kicking his ass?"

"I would, but seems his dogs follow him wherever he goes. Still, might be worth a try."

"Are you daft?" Emma asked. "You just spent money you can't afford to lose on a med pod. You're going to deal with three Fleet recruits with a penchant for violence, all on your own?"

"Maybe."

She shook her head. "Are you *always* this stubborn, Lucian Abrantes?"

"I've been called stubborn a few times in my life," Lucian admitted. "I don't want you getting involved. These guys are dangerous, and I don't want you to be a target, too."

"I already *am* a target, and I don't need a White Knight," Emma said. "We were meant to help each other. But to do that, you actually have to let me *help you*."

The mere thought made him queasy. He didn't need *anyone* to help him. He set to finishing his meal, and Emma just stared at him, seemingly unwilling to let the point go.

"Well," she finally said, "thanks for telling me about him. We don't have to figure it all out tonight, I guess."

"Stay away from Dirk in the meantime."

She sighed and shook her head. "I'm tired, so we should exchange slate ID's. That gives us a way to talk without anyone overhearing us."

Her ID? Now he was getting somewhere. "Yeah, that's a good idea."

She smiled. "Well, you can message me anytime. Far as I figure it, we're friends now. You didn't have to tell me about Dirk. And . . . I appreciate you standing up for me."

"Of course," he said. "If he bothers you any more, let me know, okay?"

She nodded, then stood to leave. "Sure. I will."

"Can I walk you to your cabin?"

"What, so you'll know where I'm staying?"

Lucian's cheeks burned at the suggestion. "No. It can be dangerous, and . . ."

She smiled. "I'm just messing with you. Don't worry about me. I can handle myself."

She surprised him then by kissing him gently on the cheek before leaving. All he could do was stare after her in shock, touching the place where her lips met his skin, still warm.

# 15

WHEN LUCIAN AWOKE the next morning, his stomach twisted with hunger. He got up, used the lav, and showered. Once back in his cabin pod, he grabbed his slate, which held a message from Emma.

*Meet me in the galley.*

Believer Horatia was gone, thankfully. He headed toward the galley, wondering what this could be about.

Once there, he found Emma eating breakfast. Whatever she had looked half-decent – an omelet with fruit and seasoned potatoes. He got his basic option, a bowl of rice porridge flavored with mashed onion and garlic, and likely fortified with a nutrient paste. It wasn't much, but it was something. After his treatment, he'd have to be careful with his wallet.

He took a seat. "What's up?"

She looked at his breakfast. "I won't even ask what that is."

"Breakfast," he said, taking a large bite.

"Poor thing," she said. "Let me get you a steak or something."

He waved her away. "I'm fine, Emma." Looking out the

viewports, he could see a bright spot in the distance. Saturn, maybe? They were getting farther from home every day. It was testament to how far the Volsung Gate was that on the second day, they were well into the outer solar system and not even ten percent of the way there. It was the first time in Lucian's life he'd experienced the vastness of space firsthand.

"So, have you given any thought to . . . the situation?"

Lucian tried to slow down his eating. He didn't want Emma to pity him anymore. "I still need to come up with something."

She laughed. "*You* need to come up with something? We're in this together, remember? I have the same problem you do."

He couldn't argue with her there. "I don't know. Haven't had much time to think about it."

"Well, I have an idea which might be useful."

"What's that?"

She smiled, hesitating a moment. For effect, Lucian supposed. "Every pod has the ability to connect to the ship's sim network. I could share some of my pills with you, and we'd have a place to hang out without anyone disturbing us."

Lucian almost spit out his food. She'd share her pills, with *him*? "I wouldn't want you to waste that on me."

"Don't insult me," she said. "I've got plenty to share." She frowned. "Or is it you just don't want to sim with me?"

Where had she gotten that idea? "Of course I would. It's just . . . they're expensive."

She shrugged. "It's just money. Aren't some things more important?"

In theory, sure. But that was something well-off people often said. When you had a lot of money, you took it for granted. The attitude had sickened him in boarding school, when he had to turn down invitations to practically everything since he couldn't afford it.

The short of it was, accepting something so expensive from her would put him in her debt.

"You were watching out for me," Emma continued. "Least I can do is share my stash." She took out a large pill bottle from her handbag, filled with gray sim pills.

Lucian's eyes popped. There were well over a hundred. It could pay for this voyage several times over. "What are you doing?"

Her cheeks colored as she hid them away. "Sorry. I buy in bulk."

Hopefully, no one else had seen. That was another thing rich people did. Not knowing the value of something because they took it for granted. Who exactly *was* Emma? Where did she come from? He found himself wondering, but he didn't want to ask right now. He'd hazard a guess at one of the L-Cities. She didn't have their posh accent, but only an Eller would offer sim pills like candy.

"Take one," she said. "I insist."

"That's the thing. I've never simmed before."

"You're kidding. That settles it." She opened up the bottle and handed him a small, gray pill, which he stared at dumbly. "Just go to your pod, pop the pill, and close your eyes. You'll be in the lobby in under a minute. I can show you the ropes."

"That easy?"

"We already have each other's ID's, so our slates will put us together. I can manage everything."

Lucian blinked and stared at the pill. "I don't know . . ."

"What, you got something better to do?"

"No. Guess not."

She rolled her eyes. "You have a real way with the ladies, you know that?"

"Of course I'll go," Lucian said. "Who wouldn't want to sim with a beautiful woman like you?"

She smiled. "Okay, too much." She was already getting up. "Finish your breakfast. And make sure to use the bathroom first, if you haven't for a while. You might regret it."

"I feel like there's a story there."

Her cheeks colored. It was satisfying to see her embarrassed for once. "Just saying. You won't feel anything in the real world once you're in. Accidents can happen. I'll meet you in the sim lobby."

Before she went back to her cabin, though, she came by the table again, getting him a plate of eggs.

"Emma, you really don't need to . . ."

"Just say thank you like a normal person."

He smiled. "Sure. Thank you."

"See you in the lobby."

She left, and he ate the eggs. He couldn't remember when something had tasted so good, but it was probably just the hunger. There was even some salsa on the side he could spread on it.

He took her advice and used the restroom, not even taking the pill out until he was safely back in his pod. There, he examined the little gray pill in his hand. Was this really happening? Within minutes, he'd be in an alternate reality. The thought made his stomach flutter. A lot of simmers were completely addicted, preferring to live in false game worlds. The fantasy was more preferable to their own lives, but only the richest could afford to do that.

Emma definitely didn't fit the profile of a typical simulation gamer. She was healthy-looking, for one. Simmers could spend hours perfecting their online avatar while not running a comb through their hair for months. Then again, like hard drugs, there were people who were experts at managing their addictions. Emma was hard to pin down, and Lucian would only learn more by spending time with her.

The prospect made him a bit queasy. The last thing he needed was a pretty girl to complicate things. Things were already complicated enough.

He couldn't keep her waiting. He thumbed a new message on his slate.

*This won't kill me, right?*

Her response was near-immediate. *As long as you didn't hack the safety conditioning.*

*Hack the what?*

*It's the program that detects when you're too hungry or thirsty to continue. Some people hack into that to get longer sessions, but it's illegal. Some have died. But don't worry about that. A session can only last six hours, max. My pills are legal and come straight from Event Horizon.*

Event Horizon. It was the biggest gaming company in the Worlds.

*All right, then. What now?*

*Simple. You swallow the pill, and in a minute, you'll enter the game lobby. It's a bit jarring the first few times you do it, but you'll get used to the sensation. Most things can be done with directed thought commands. Just will yourself to leave, for example, and you can jump out. But no matter what you do, the program will kick you out after six hours.*

That ensured people kept having to buy pills.

*The sim will also bring you out if it notices anything unusual,* she went on. *It's monitoring your biosignatures at all times. It's safe. And it's the perfect place to talk.*

Lucian decided to take her word for it. Besides, he didn't see another option. If they were to talk about magic without anyone overhearing, it was the only real option. Unless they happened to crawl into the same pod together. That thought made his cheeks burn.

*Okay. I think I've got it.*

*See you on the other side.*

Lucian looked again at his pill. Had Emma already taken hers? Before he could second-guess things, he popped it in his mouth and swallowed.

He closed his eyes and waited.

Nothing happened for a few seconds. Was the pill a dud? That was when a channel flipped inside his mind.

In an eyeblink, he was somewhere else.

# 16

LUCIAN STOOD IN A GRAY, featureless room with no doors or windows. There needed to be more light.

At the very thought, windows popped into existence on the walls, letting in a flood of sunlight. A door materialized ahead of him. Over the next few seconds, the simulation produced a rustic country cottage.

Lucian blinked at the sudden change. Had *he* done that, or had the simulation read his thoughts, giving him an approximation of what he wanted?

There was a knock at the door and he went to answer it. There Emma stood, wearing a shimmering silver dress that shone like diamonds. He couldn't help but gape.

"Too much?"

He cleared his throat. "No. It's perfect."

"Just wanted to show what you could do in these things," she said, stepping inside. "You can wear whatever you want, and it takes no time at all!"

Lucian looked down at his own clothing, which was exactly what he had been wearing on the outside – gray pants, a white T-shirt, covered by a dark denim jacket.

She walked in and took a look around. "It's so quaint. Is this your home back on Earth?"

Lucian shook his head. "No. It's not half as big as this one. Not sure how this popped into existence."

"Sometimes, if you don't have specific instructions but an idea of what you want, the sim fills in the blanks."

He watched her as she went to stand by the window. She had been beautiful before, but in the sunlight, she was radiant. None of this was *real*. He had to keep that in mind, but to his brain, it might as well have been reality.

Lucian looked out the nearby window to see a countryside filled with green, rolling hills. When he turned back to look at Emma, she had changed into her normal street clothes. But even her clothing was far better quality than what most people could afford on the outside, perfectly tailored and of fine material. Lucian was sure she came from money.

"What happened to the fancy get-up?"

She shrugged. "Well, we're here for business, right?"

"That's a funny way of putting it."

"I don't know. Maybe we should learn about each other a bit, first. Have you ever been to New York?"

"Sure," he said. "I was a kid, though."

"Have you ever been to New York in the year 2120, though?"

What was she getting at? "Can't say that I have."

"I thought we might go somewhere familiar, but still a little different. New York was the first full-scale sim they rendered. And that was back in 2120. It's sort of . . . a *historic* place to go."

"I'm game if you are."

"Okay, then. Follow me."

How did that work? He didn't have time to ask. Emma disappeared, leaving him alone in the cottage. How was he supposed to follow her?

Maybe it was as simple as a command or a thought.

*Follow her.*

In the next instant, the cottage was gone, and Lucian appeared on the streets of New York. The air was cold, tingling his skin. A slate gray sky expanded above him, mostly blocked by tall skyscrapers. Huge crowds bustled around him, while blaring holo-billboards and neon lights glowed in the late afternoon gloom. Those ads displayed companies and products obsolete for over two centuries. The smell of hot dogs and sauerkraut wafted by as an old man rolled his food cart past on squeaking wheels. He was in New York, 2120, or at least its closest approximation.

He looked at the food vendor again, who had been dead for over two hundred years. He turned around, a sense of vertigo almost sending him stumbling. The sights, the whirring electric engines, the cold air, were exactly as they should have been. If there were one difference, everything had a barely perceptible washed out appearance. Other than that, he might as well have been there.

A high-lev blazed overhead, wrapping around a building. Others were taking pictures and selfies with their slates, though this far back in time, they were still called phones. The nanotech that let slates change size and shape wouldn't be invented for over a century.

Emma only watched Lucian as he gawked. He'd done VR before, but this was on a whole other level. He was *here*.

People were even looking at them as they walked by. It wasn't only an environmental rendering, then. The same environment was programmed to react to them.

As time passed, there were more differences. The cold didn't make him feel uncomfortable. He could smell the various food carts around him, but the aroma was not as strong as he expected, as if he had a slight cold. No matter how far technology progressed, reality would still be reality.

Emma walked toward a building of twenty or so floors that tapered toward the top. *The Paramount Building*. Somehow,

Lucian knew that without having to be told. The sim was feeding him information in real time.

"Well, what do you think?" she asked.

"Amazing," he said, watching the crowds. A group of girls in 22$^{nd}$ century retro garb with long capes walked by. No, not retro. It was the real thing. No one had worn clothing like that in over two centuries.

"So, we can talk about anything here," Lucian said. "And no one can hear us?"

"That's right," she said. "The server is private. Maybe we can start off by walking around Broadway. Maybe grab a bite?"

To Lucian's surprise, his stomach twisted with hunger. "I could eat."

Emma led Lucian down a street, until they reached a restaurant jampacked with people. Despite the fact that it was full, the host seated them immediately at the best table.

They ordered whatever they wanted, with no regard to cost. And there they talked for a long time.

When they were served dessert and coffee, the conversation turned more personal.

"What's your story, Lucian?" she asked.

"Not much to it," he said.

Her eyes narrowed. "Seriously? You've got to give me something. How'd you find out you were a mage?"

Lucian then told her about the test, and even the dreams he'd had. He found himself hesitating about the last dream, with the dark voice that had told him to find the Aspects. It felt wrong to talk about it, for whatever reason. As if he would be betraying someone. Lucian pushed down the confusion.

"Next thing I knew," he said, "I was on this ship, heading to Volsung. With no future."

"Don't say no future," Emma said.

"Well, I don't even know if the Academy will accept me."

"No one does. That's part of it, unfortunately."

"Doesn't that freak you out?"

"Yeah," she said. "A little."

It got quiet after that. What would he do if he wasn't accepted? He didn't want to even think about it.

"Have you emerged yet?" she asked.

"That means . . . actually *using* magic, right?"

Emma inclined her head. "So, have you?"

"No," he said. "Why, am I supposed to have?"

"No," she said. "I haven't, either. In fact, that's my main problem."

"That you haven't used magic?"

"That's the paradox," Emma said. "Using too much magic will get you killed. Not enough, and it builds up inside you, sort of. At least, that was how it was explained to me."

"By whom?"

She seemed to hesitate. Was there a story there? "By a friend, a long time ago."

When she didn't elaborate, Lucian didn't push it.

"Anyway, I've got this . . . condition, I guess you would call it. I should've been enrolled in an academy a long time ago. Without training, it won't be long before . . ." She hesitated, and her voice came out thick. "Well, before I fray."

Lucian couldn't say anything. He tried to, but his throat clamped up. She was dying, then? How much time did she have?

"Don't worry," he said. "We'll get you to Volsung in time."

Her smile was sad. "I hope so. My parents have been in contact with the academy. I should be accepted, but it's possible that I won't be."

When she said that, her voice was emotionless. As if she'd trained herself not to care by now. Lucian knew how that was.

"It'll be all right," he said. "How long have you known about it?"

"Almost two years," she said. "That's a whole other story,

though. Suffice it to say, time's running out. You're lucky, Lucian."

"How's that?"

"Because you have time. Me? I might not make it."

"What do you mean?"

Her eyes became distant. "It's nothing. I would rather enjoy my time here. Not think about sad things."

"Sure," Lucian said. "Head back to Times Square?"

She nodded, and forced a smile. "It's almost time."

"Time for what?"

"You'll see."

They left the table without so much as paying the bill. When they reached Times Square, it was near midnight, and mostly empty. They stood in the center, and almost had the whole place to themselves.

"What are we waiting for?" Lucian asked.

"Wait for it."

The cold touched him, but didn't make him uncomfortable. In that moment, he felt warmth from her presence. He tried to put what she'd said out of his mind, but how could he? He was afraid to ask what was bothering her. Maybe it was too soon for all that.

Still, he surprised himself when he reached for her hand. And was more surprised when she took it, warm.

The snow started to fall. Lucian had never seen that in person. It fell gently at first, and then in droves, landing cold on his face and melting rivers down his cheeks.

"You've been here a lot, haven't you?" Lucian asked. "To this very day. This very moment."

She nodded. She was so beautiful standing there with the snow. She was looking up at the sky. Then, she turned to face him, letting go of his hand.

"Thanks for humoring me," she said. "Some things are hard to talk about, you know? I don't know what will happen with either of us. One thing I'm sure of, though, is I want to enjoy life before the inevitable. When they invited me to the Academy, they mentioned I'd have to give up most of the things I was used to. And that includes this."

"I guess there are no sims on Volsung."

"Not for mages. The Academy made that clear in their messages to me."

"What do you mean?"

"They live an ascetic lifestyle. No sims, no electricity, no GalNet. And not even personal items. It's why I packed so light."

"Wow. Seriously?"

"I'm afraid so."

Lucian realized he knew next to nothing about this academy. Before he could ask Emma anything more, she spoke again.

"Our six hours are almost up. This was . . . nice. If you're worried about the Academy, don't be."

Lucian nodded. "Of course."

At that moment, he couldn't help but look into her eyes. She looked back, seeming expectant. He longed to hold her in that moment. Something in him wanted to keep her safe. Why was that?

He wanted to turn away, afraid of that longing. But he found he couldn't. They were standing closer to each other now, and she was smiling.

That was when footsteps ran up to them. Lucian turned to see a most unwelcome sight.

What was Dirk doing here?

## 17

DIRK STOOD SEVERAL METERS AWAY, the expression on his stupid face incredulous. Was he real, or part of the simulation?

When Emma gasped in surprise, Lucian knew that wasn't the case.

Before Lucian could say anything, the scene disappeared. In the next moment, they were in the room they'd started in. Lucian looked around, but it was only he and Emma.

"Shit," she said. "I'm so stupid . . ."

"What happened?" Lucian asked. "Why was he there?"

"It's my fault. I must've forgotten to lock the server."

"What? Seriously?"

She nodded. "Yeah. I just looked it up. Seems to be the case. Usually people have the courtesy to stay out of where they haven't been invited."

"Not everybody," Lucian said.

She shook her head. "Guess not. He's already blocked. I'm just so stupid . . ."

"Hey," Lucian said, taking her hand. "Don't feel bad about it. He's the creep, right?"

"I'm sorry," she repeated. "He won't be able to follow us anymore."

That left another problem. Dirk now knew the both of them were talking. And they might have to deal with his reprisal.

"Well, now he knows for sure we've teamed up," Lucian said. "That means trouble."

Would Dirk make good on his threat? Or would he use the information as leverage? Lucian couldn't begin to guess.

"Maybe the time has come to not hide what we are," Emma said. "If we get ahead of it, we can control the narrative. I mean, it's not *illegal* for mages to travel as long as they're going to an academy. Which both of us are. The crew knows who we are, anyway."

"They do?"

"We're already being watched," Emma said. "But our identities are confidential."

"Not anymore. I have a Believer for a roommate, remember? All it takes is one crazy person to ruin us. In fact, that's probably why he followed us in there. To see if we were talking."

"I'm almost positive he has an ocular implant," she said. "Probably hiding around corners and stalking our every move."

The only question was, what to do about it? There was no telling how long he might've been tailing them.

"I don't want you to feel too bad about it," Lucian said.

"Easier said than done." After a moment's pause, she forced a smile. "It's time we left anyway, before the sim jolts us out."

"Okay," Lucian said. "We can talk soon."

"Of course. See you."

With that, Emma disappeared. Lucian focused his own thoughts on leaving.

He blinked, and was back in his pod. He got up to use the lav and brush his teeth. He was tired, and though it was only early afternoon by now, he could hardly keep his eyes open.

Lucian went to grab lunch. Emma wasn't there, though Paul and Kasim were. They ignored him. It seemed they needed an order from their master before they messed with him. Lucian ordered a quick meal, finishing it in a few minutes before going back to his pod.

He had to decide what to do. Only thing was, he wasn't sure what that would be. Was it too much to hope that Dirk might behave himself? Was the answer to just hide until the trip was over?

Once back in his pod, Lucian drifted off, thinking of how Dirk might exact his revenge.

———

THE WORRYING SEEMED to be over nothing. Things remained quiet as the *Burung* traveled deeper into the outer solar system, beyond the orbits of Uranus and Neptune. Lucian took his meals in the galley, sometimes with Emma. When Dirk and his cronies were there at the same time, they barely paid him any attention. And anytime they were in the public areas, they only talked about safe subjects.

But any time he tried to learn more about her, she had a way of redirecting questions back to him. He wrote it off the first few times. Maybe she just wasn't ready to talk about anything deeper.

He did his best to keep himself busy. He spent time in the ship's gym. It was nice to lift three times what he was used to in the lower gravity. Of course, there were endless media entertainment options in his pod. When that failed, he could go to the galley or the viewing deck.

He often crossed paths with Dirk or his friends, but when he did, he avoided eye contact. Either Dirk wasn't making good on his threat, or he was still planning his revenge.

But judging from the other passengers' behavior, Dirk

hadn't breathed a word. That didn't mean he *wouldn't* tell someone at some point. Believer Horatia was still friendly enough. The day she turned cold, he'd know.

Unlike his first day, Lucian never made the mistake of being alone. He ate at normal times, and never stayed out too late. Being restricted grated at him, but he couldn't afford another trip to the med bay. So far, in his short texts to his mother, she hadn't mentioned anything about an extra bill. He wondered when he'd be hearing from her about that.

He tried to get to know other passengers, too, as fake as it was to force social interaction. It would help to be remembered favorably if Dirk ever tried anything. It might be the difference between staying safe and becoming a target.

He couldn't help but lock eyes with Dirk a few times in the early days of the voyage. And Dirk would always stare back in challenge, his face pale and jaw clenched, with blue eyes burning fiercely. He was definitely plotting some form of revenge, of that Lucian was sure.

# 18

ON THE FOURTH NIGHT OUT, Emma shared another sim pill with Lucian.

This time, she took him to Kasturi, one of the more developed Border Worlds. Kasturi was a balmy planet, known for its beaches, pink coral seas, and long chains of archipelagos. Lucian remembered it was in the Kasturi system that the Swarmers had been pushed back during the last war. Looking around at the pink-tinged landscape, however, there were no signs of that past conflict.

They sat on a beach under a pink-clouded sky. That water was still as glass, save for in the distance, where several long, dragon-like creatures plied the tranquil waters. Their forms were long, their heads angular, designed for deep diving in the Infinite Ocean. Their coos resonated over the water. Kasturi was too sparsely settled, too far out from Earth and the First Worlds to have been spoiled. Give humanity a century or so and it would happen.

The atmosphere was also filled with a strange form of microscopic life that was as hallucinogenic as it was deadly, from where the sky got its pinkish cast. Colonists living on Kasturi couldn't go outside without a rebreather that filtered it out. But in a sim, of course, that wouldn't matter. The sim could even replicate the positive effects of its unique atmosphere, though he and Emma had it dialed down. There was just enough to have a pleasant buzz for a more open mind and looser tongues. Maybe here, Lucian could learn more about her past.

But it wouldn't be safe to steer the conversation that way first.

"Dirk is planning something," he said. "I *know* it."

"*Him* again?" Emma asked. "Forget him. I already have."

Lucian remained quiet. Maybe she was right, but it was hard to let a grievance go.

"Dirk is all talk, anyway," Emma said. "They won't try anything."

Had she forgotten what they'd done to him? They might do it again.

But there was nothing he could do, not three versus one. So, Lucian put Dirk out of his mind. Or at least, he tried to. He instead focused on gentle waters, pockmarked with slow-falling drops of rain. Through the haze, a couple of rainbows arced in the distance.

"I've always wanted to come here in reality," she said. "It's on the complete opposite side of the Worlds that I'm from, though."

"It makes sense a person from L5 would be into simming," Lucian said. "There isn't much room to breathe up there."

"It's more spacious than you would think," Emma said. "I'd love to show you around."

"The time's almost up," Lucian said. "Maybe next time." Now was the time to ask her about the past. "So, are you from L5 originally, or somewhere else?"

"I hesitate to say I'm from anywhere." She paused for a

moment. "If I had to name one planet, though, it would be Aurora."

"Aurora. It must be outside the League."

There weren't many non-League worlds. They weren't incorporated for some reason or another. Perhaps they somehow violated the League Constitution, as in the case of a world ruled by pirates or one of the crime syndicates. Perhaps they extended beyond the originally sanctioned Border Worlds, thereby not falling under the League's purview. Or maybe they bucked certain laws all League Worlds had to adhere to, such as harboring mages.

Non-sanctioned worlds usually didn't last long, prey to pirates, crime, or even the Swarmers. Their safety was not guaranteed by the League, but it was the only way an entire world, or the factions that existed on such a world, could exist outside the League's purview.

In short, it made Emma even more interesting.

"What was that like?"

"It's a long story," Emma said. "Not one I want to go into right now."

There it was again. Lucian tried to hold back his frustration. Something must have happened back there, something that was hard to talk about.

"Okay," he said. "Sorry about that."

"It's fine. Maybe one day. I think I'm done. I'll see you around."

"Okay."

Soon after that, Emma exited the sim. Why was she so touchy about the subject? He felt a fool for even bringing it up. He usually wasn't this nosy, but he was curious about her. But the last thing he wanted was to lose trust by pushing it.

ONCE OUT OF THE SIM, his head was pounding. He'd read that could be a side effect of simming. Usually it meant dehydration. He was thirsty, and his bladder was about to explode.

He headed to the lav, and then took a shower. It was rather late by now, so it was a bit of a risk to be out and about. But the corridors were empty, and Lucian was ravenous.

He ate in the galley, with no one interrupting him. His mind was still buzzing, and he walked around the ship to settle his nerves. Just a few days in space, and he was already feeling his strength atrophy. The white, empty corridors were eerie and silent, the only sound his footfalls as he walked. He looked out at the starry expanse out the large viewports on the ship's periphery. An emptiness pulsated within him, an emptiness echoed by lightyears of space around him.

When he rounded the corner again, he was no longer alone.

Someone he'd never seen on the ship before stood by the furthest viewport sternward. It was an elderly woman, wearing a travel-worn robe of dark gray, almost black. Her hair fell in silver waves over narrow, bony shoulders, and the profile of her face revealed a sharp, hooked nose set in a face that was a maze of deep-set wrinkles. At his approach, she turned her head toward him. When her dark eyes met Lucian's, his skin crawled.

He didn't know *how* he knew, but he sensed the woman was dangerous, far more to be feared than the likes of Dirk. It was too late to pick another direction, and he didn't want her to know how unsettled he was. So, he kept walking, deciding this would be his last round before returning to his cabin.

As he approached, her gaze did not turn away, as he expected. It only intensified. Those dark eyes seemed to see to the marrow of his bones. There was something . . . *strange* about this lady, to say the least. Why was she giving him that impression? If there was one thing he learned growing up in Old Little Havana, it was to trust your gut. If you didn't, it could be your life.

Finally, she turned her face away, to look out the viewports. For some reason Lucian couldn't explain, he went to stand a few meters away from her. What was he doing? And yet, the action felt right for some reason he couldn't fathom.

As time and silence dragged on, he tried to pull away, but his feet remained rooted in place. *What* was he doing? Why was he even standing here?

He couldn't answer that. He stood there for one minute, two, the silence stretching on and on.

At last, the elderly woman broke the silence with a quiet, scratchy voice. Though restrained, the voice carried great authority.

"The stars," she said. "Like us, they are born, they live, and they die – and their remains give birth to new stars again. All life, all *existence*, is a cycle. Birth, life, and death, in an endless sea of stars."

Not much for small talk, this one. But the proclamation was fitting, given what they were both looking at.

"I guess that's true," Lucian said.

"Has this trip been satisfactory for you?" she asked.

The voice commanded Lucian's attention, but more than that, it compelled an honest answer. The voice seemed to drill inside his mind, unearthing the secrets within.

"No," he said. Why had he just told her the truth? "It's been . . . difficult."

He had to get it together and walk away, now.

But he couldn't. He wanted to answer whatever she asked. No matter her appearance, she could be trusted. It somehow felt right – even as it felt wrong.

"Why has it been difficult?"

He shook his head. "I don't know. It's a long story."

The woman seemed to consider. "Adversity should be welcomed, not denied. Hardship is an old friend. For what doesn't kill you, makes you stronger."

For some reason, the expression didn't sound trite and overused when she said it. She had spoken those words as if she'd *lived* them her whole life. As if she *owned* them.

"Maybe," he said. "There are some things that don't have a clear answer, though."

Like Dirk.

"There's nothing you cannot overcome, if only you have the will," the woman said. She sounded so certain. How could she be that certain about *anything*? "What is this problem you're talking about? Perhaps I can help."

Now, why would she want to do that? And yet, she had asked, and someone of her experience might be able to help. For some reason he couldn't explain, he *wanted* to tell her.

"I've been having problems with someone on board," Lucian said. "Normally I'd fight back. But if I do . . ." He was saying too much, but the woman was listening intently. He didn't want to stop. "Let's say he has an ace up his sleeve. He could use it to destroy me."

"You've said enough. I have the gist of things."

"I don't see a way I can deal with him." This next part would be hard to admit, but he couldn't stop himself. It felt as if she were pulling the words out of him, though she was doing nothing more than watching him. "He and his friends attacked me a few nights ago. I had to go to the med bay."

"And you didn't report him, because of this so-called ace up his sleeve. Am I correct?"

"He still has it out for me. Because . . ."

No. He couldn't go there. Not even if he was tempted to say the reason.

"There is no fate worse than being a slave," the woman said. "Some wear the collar, metaphorical or not, easily enough. It is often that a person will exchange their freedom for a guarantee of security. The ability to have *will* that affects your world and others should be one's highest aspiration." She turned to face

139

him in full. Her dark eyes seemed thunderous, full of hidden meaning. The effect was mesmerizing. "You must impose your will on this problem. It is a sign of strength and resiliency. The problem is merely one of your will, nothing more."

Lucian shook his head. "My will. Are you serious?"

"Yes," the elderly woman said. Her voice took on a sternness that was surprising. "A slave trivializes conflict, and would rather wear chains than fight. *That* is weakness."

"I'm not weak," Lucian said.

The woman gave a dark chuckle, then turned her face away. Her eyes shone curiously, the dark orbs glowing with reflected starlight.

"The most important war to win is the one within yourself. The universe is vast, and the only space we can truly call our own is the one between our ears. *That* is the only thing guaranteed. As long as you have that, nothing of consequence can be taken from you. To allow anything into that sacred space, to bend your self-appointed reality, is a sacrilege to your soul. Consciousness, mindfulness, awareness – all gifts to be nurtured carefully, to be guarded jealously. As a flame in a winter storm. Abandon the flame but a moment, and the darkness sets in. And with the darkness, come the wolves."

What was she getting at? How had he failed to notice this woman so far?

"Who are you?" he finally asked.

The woman hesitated, as if considering her answer. "You are not ready to learn that. Your test will come soon, Lucian. Meet it head on. Stop running."

With a swirl of her cloak, she stole away, leaving Lucian to stand before the viewports. He was reeling – he hadn't once said his name, but somehow, she had known it. Unless she had heard it from somewhere, or had the same trick as Dirk, how could she have known?

There was something about her that sparked recognition

and familiarity. And then, it came to him. She had been in his third dream during the metaphysical. He couldn't believe it at first, but there had been an elderly woman there, with long white hair, dark eyes, and a dark cloak. It had been nothing more than a passing image, but he was almost certain it was her. With that startling image, he realized *Emma* had been in there, too. A flash, nothing more.

What did it all mean, if anything at all?

The answer came to him, though he knew not how. It made a chill pass through his entire body.

He and Emma were not the only mages on this ship.

# 19

ON HIS WAY back to his cabin, he turned the corner and found Dirk and his dogs waiting for him. How had they *known* he would walk by at that particular moment? Lucian didn't have time to question it.

Lucian's heart raced as he balled his fists. Kasim cracked his knuckles while Paul stalked forward with a predatory smile.

In between them, Dirk's eyes glinted murderously.

"Get him in the cabin," he instructed.

He knew he should have run, but he remained rooted. Kasim was on him first, practically throwing him into the wall. The shock of it rattled him to the core.

Kasim and Paul pulled him through the open doorway of the cabin. Dirk watched as he passed inside, rolling up his sleeves with narrowed eyes.

Paul and Kasim slammed Lucian against the wall, keeping him immobile. Dirk entered the cabin, the door sliding shut behind.

Now, he was dead.

"You shouldn't be walking alone at night," Dirk said, with an easy drawl. "It can be . . . dangerous."

Well, if he were going to die here, he'd make it a fight to remember.

With strength he knew not where, he pushed free of both Paul and Kasim. He circled around and threw a wild right punch at Dirk. But the ringleader only grabbed his wrist and twisted it in his firm grip. Lucian yowled, turning his body to relieve the pain. Lucian ripped his hand from Dirk's grip, turning to throw himself at Paul, who now blocked the door. If only he could get through, he could run the rest of the way to his cabin – what he should have done in the first place. Paul braced himself to eat the tackle, and despite the force of Lucian's attack, there wasn't enough momentum behind it to clear a path.

His only gambit to escape had failed. Paul pushed back with surprising strength despite his scrawny form. The boys guffawed as Kasim caught him and threw him against the wall. Lucian tumbled to the deck, scrambling up as quickly as he could. All three ringed around him to prevent escape.

Paul came forward and threw a hard punch, which Lucian dodged. But Kasim hit him square in the jaw, causing him to stagger back. Dirk and Paul set upon him again, landing more punches. Lucian tried shielding himself, but it was impossible. Paul and Kasim were holding him in the corner, making escape impossible. Once secured, Dirk approached, cracking his knuckles.

"You didn't listen," he said.

"Something's *wrong* with you," Lucian said.

Dirk chuckled. "No. Something's wrong with *you*, mage. Someone ought to kill you. A hero." He laughed. Lucian struggled against his assailants, but couldn't break free. "One day, mage-hunting will be legal, and we'll cleanse the galaxy of your filth. It seems you need a bloodier lesson than last time for my point to sink in."

The last thing Lucian needed was another trip to the med

bay. And of course, there was always the danger that they would go too far this time. He might only have a few minutes left to live, if that. His heart raced at the mere notion, as paralysis coursed through him. No. It couldn't end like this . . .

He had to defend himself, but how? There was magic, but he didn't know how to use it.

But maybe *they* didn't know that. It was a desperate ploy, but it was all he had.

"I'm warning you," Lucian said, fighting to make his voice sound confident. "Don't make me use my magic on you. I held back last time. But I'm allowed to do so if it's in self-defense."

Lucian had no idea whether that was true. And to his surprise, Paul and Kasim's grips loosened, almost allowing him to break free. But Dirk added his own weight with snarl.

"He's bluffing! He's going to that damn academy on Volsung, and until he gets training, he can't do jack shit to us." He smirked. "Now, take your beating like a man!"

Paul and Kasim exchanged worried glances, and Lucian prepared to go after the weak links. He had only one shot. He had to make them more afraid of his vaunted powers than they were of their leader.

Lucian closed his eyes and concentrated, doing his best to make a real show of it.

"What are you doing?" Kasim asked, fear creeping into his voice.

Paul's response was the exact opposite of Kasim's. He pummeled Lucian in the stomach, knocking the breath out of him.

Lucian had made them scared, which was exactly what he'd wanted. Unfortunately, that fear was causing them to lash out more. Even in this moment, even with this pain, there had to be a way to take control. Maybe it was a matter of will, as the old woman had said.

He still had his mind, and that could never be taken from him.

His voice escaped with a rasp. "I . . . *won't let you win!*"

He was rewarded with another punch to the gut, courtesy of Dirk.

A voice seemed to come from outside himself. *Control your mind. In the midst of chaos, stillness is the key . . .*

That voice sounded like the old woman's. How could that be possible, though?

Lucian didn't question it. He was sinking lower and lower from the weight of their attacks. His body was bruised, and several stray hits to his face caused blood to fall.

That was when they started to kick. Each impact was like a hammer, pummeling him again and again. A few minutes of this, he would be lying dead in a pool of blood.

They wanted him to beg for mercy, but Lucian couldn't give them that satisfaction. Not after all this pain.

Stillness was the key. He went into himself. The pain seemed to fade, through either a loss of consciousness or something else. There was something . . . *there*, in the distance. Was it a light? Or was it death? Whatever it was, his consciousness latched upon it. As soon as it did, a sort of mad power seized upon him. He let out an insane laugh, a laugh that seemed to give his attackers pause, if only for a moment. A fire seemed to be spreading through every fiber of his body, threatening to boil over.

What *was* this? It was like a build-up of static electricity, only it refused to be let go. The hairs on his arms stood on end. This power, whatever it was, needed an outlet.

It could only be *them*.

"Stop." His voice came out commanding and strong, so much so that for a moment, it seemed to give them pause.

That was the only opening he needed. Lucian scrambled

up, but Dirk wasn't having it. With a roar, Dirk charged, his face twisted with rage.

The fire burned hotter, enough to make Lucian cry out. His *hands* were glowing now. What was this? A purplish aura radiated outward, illumining the interior of the cabin with an ethereal glow. Now, the three Fleet recruits *did* back away, their eyes wide and faces pallid.

But it was too late for Lucian to stop it. If he didn't let go, and soon, the fire within would burn him alive.

He gave a shout, and the pressure released from his hands in a single burst. The fire dissipated at once, along with the glow around his hands.

Dirk screamed. His hands grasped his face, where blood coursed through his fingers. It poured through in rivers of red, dripping onto the deck in big, fat drops. Lucian felt a cold stab of fear. Had *he* done that? How could that even be possible? His rival wailed in pain, his words escaping in an incoherent babble as Kasim and Paul looked on in horror.

There would be no better opportunity. Bruised and bloody, but still in control, Lucian pushed past Paul and hit the button to open the door, staggering into the corridor.

Dirk's screams were cut off by the closing cabin door, and Lucian ran.

# 20

When Lucian jumped in his pod and closed the door, his heart was pounding madly. Whatever he'd done to Dirk, it was magic. He didn't know *how* he'd done it, but he'd felt that fire. He saw the way his hands had glowed. He saw the looks on their faces when they realized the truth, too.

He was a mage. Before, there had still been room for deniability, but he no longer had any such luxury.

He grit his teeth, and let out a yell as he punched the interior screen of the pod. The force of his blow did nothing to break the inner viewscreen, though it made his hand throb something fierce.

The pain of his beatdown felt like something distant. Though his muscles and bones ached, and there would surely be bruising, it hadn't been as bad as last time. They had held back this time, even if it hadn't felt like it at the time. Even so, Lucian didn't regret what he'd done in the least. He just didn't know what this meant for the future.

His mouth tasted of metal. He drank from a nearby bottle of water, but the taste didn't completely go away. An aftereffect of the magic, maybe, or just blood.

The only question was, what did he do now?

Even if using magic hadn't been his intent, no one else would see it that way. If Lucian were lucky, Dirk would get healing in the med bay and be completely fine and not breathe a word of it. If he were unlucky, he would report it to the captain. And there would be terrible consequences.

Of course there was the worst option, the one that made Lucian sick to his stomach. Dirk might have bled out and died.

If that were the case, Lucian's life was all but over.

He tried to slow his breathing, and think. What were his options? How might he defend his actions? He didn't feel one iota of guilt about what had happened. Dirk had it coming, though he wished he could have handled him in a non-violent manner. No one would see it that way, though. Maybe not even Emma.

Would *she* know what to do? He wanted to keep it to himself, but unless Dirk kept quiet, she would find out, anyway. Within hours, the entire ship would know.

He had no choice, then. He had to tell her, and hope she might know a way to salvage the situation.

He took out his slate and made a voice call to Emma, before he could second guess his decision.

When she answered, her voice was sleepy.

"Hello?"

"Emma . . . " he started.

There was a tense pause. "Yeah?"

There was nothing but to tell the truth. "I messed up pretty bad."

"What do you mean, *messed up*?"

"I might need some help."

He then told her the story, and she listened. He tried not to think about what was running through her head, though that was impossible. It took all of two minutes before he went quiet again, waiting for her reaction. What was she thinking? Had she lost all respect for him? Did she even believe him about it being an accident? He had meant to hurt Dirk, but he hadn't meant to do it to that extent.

"Are you there?"

Finally, she cleared her throat. "Yeah, sorry. Just thinking."

"What do I do? I didn't mean to hurt him like that. Not that bad, anyway."

"You were trying to defend yourself," Emma said. "I mean, *they* pulled you from the corridor into their cabin. That had to have been caught by cameras. From your perspective, they might have been killing you. Magic, though?" Emma paused. "*That* will be seen as more severe, even if it was self-defense."

"I know," Lucian said. "So, what do I do?"

"I'd tell you to run, but that's impossible, isn't it?"

"That bad, then."

She left that question unanswered. "Is this the first time you've used magic?"

"Yeah . . ."

"Well, now you know for sure. You're a mage. Somehow, you streamed magic without any sort of training. That's rare, except when a mage starts to fray. But from what you've told me, you should be nowhere near that point."

Those weren't things Lucian wanted to hear. And what was streaming? "You're saying I might be fraying already?"

"No, that's not likely. I've been told that in times of stress, even an untrained mage might be able to control magic, if only for a brief moment. That's what it sounds like. You had a short, uncontrolled stream directed right at Dirk. And the stream somehow injured Dirk's eyes."

"I see."

"Forget about that for now. Let's worry about what *you're* going to say. You have to remember that *you* were the one who was attacked. Any time they ask, repeat that over and over. Even if using magic without belonging to an academy is against

League Law, there may be exceptions for self-defense. It's the difference from getting leniency to a one-way ticket to Psyche."

The mention of the prison moon was enough to send a chill down Lucian's spine. "Trust me, I'll be telling them the truth about it being self-defense."

"They're *going* to question you," Emma went on, "and it's *not* going to be fair. Even if they have a recording of what happened, they may choose to ignore it. It sort of depends on how sympathetic the captain is. His word is law in space."

"Not doing much for my confidence."

"I'm sorry," she said. "I'm trying to plan ahead, no matter how bad. I believe everything you've told me. The problem is getting others to believe it, too."

There was silence for a long moment. Lucian didn't want to feel defeated, but what Emma had said was sobering. His future hung on by a thread, and the smallest breeze could send him over the edge.

"Lucian? Let's meet in the galley. We should speak in person about this."

"I've already involved you enough. I wouldn't want people to think you're helping me."

"I won't take *no* for an answer. Get to the galley, now."

There was no convincing her otherwise. "Okay. See you soon."

———

BY 5:00, it was early enough for a few people to be in the galley. Emma was already waiting for Lucian, her pallor paler than usual.

"Heard anything yet?" she asked.

"Nothing," Lucian said, taking up a seat.

He couldn't figure out what to do with his hands. And he couldn't help but glance in the direction of the med bay. No doubt, that was where Dirk was right now. Had they told the captain anything yet? If they had, Lucian could be expecting a visit soon. Maybe it would be best to go to the captain himself. To get ahead of it, as it were.

Minutes passed as he and Emma outlined a strategy – a strategy that stuck to the truth, in case he were questioned. If there were cameras and med bay logs, then they could see it was self-defense. If Dirk and the others lied about that part, then the cameras would tell a different story. That was, assuming there *were* cameras, but it was inconceivable that there weren't. Even given that, though, there would be consequences. The sick wrenching in his gut became unbearable.

"It'll be all right," Emma said.

The words didn't help. He knew she was only trying to make him feel better, and those words had no bearing on reality.

The reckoning came sooner than he thought when footsteps approached from the direction of the bow. Lucian turned to see who must have been Captain Miller. He was a tall, middle-aged man, with salt and pepper hair and sharp blue eyes. He was dressed in a white Pan-Galactic captain's uniform, complete with captain's cap bearing the company's retro rocket logo. Two male crewman flanked him on either side, both in plainer gray uniforms. One was tan-skinned, bald, and glowering, and the other tall, with graying hair and solemn features.

One thing was clear: they considered him dangerous, and were taking no chances.

"Lucian Abrantes," the captain said, "follow me to the bridge."

There was no getting out of this. "Okay."

"He was just defending himself," Emma said, as he stood.

Captain Miller nodded, as if he were aware of that much. His blue eyes watched her for a moment. "Rest assured, we're doing what we can to get to the bottom of it."

Emma watched him, her expression pale, while Lucian straightened his back to appear more confident than he felt.

"I'll be fine," he said to her.

Just words, too. Words that didn't seem to have any effect.

"Let's move," the bald crewman said. "We don't have all morning."

He followed the captain and his two crewmen back to the ship's bridge with a leaden weight in his stomach. They couldn't kill him for this, could they? He had a vision of himself being blasted out of the airlock, a form of justice only reserved for the worst offenders. It was hard to get that thought out of his mind as they went upstairs to the second deck.

When they passed the door to the med bay, Lucian looked at it, but couldn't tell if there was anyone inside. If there had been any blood trail leading to it, it'd been cleaned up by now.

They passed the first-class cabins, all the way to the sliding doors marking the bridge's entrance at the corridor's end. Those were doors usually inaccessible to passengers, and Lucian wondered why he was being led directly to it.

Those doors opened at the captain's approach. The bridge beyond was smaller than Lucian anticipated. And it was crowded. Captain Miller's navigator, a brown-haired woman of middle age and chubby red cheeks, stood to the side. She watched Lucian with wide, green eyes, as if he were a snake that might bite her. A couple of younger female attendants he'd seen around the ship were also present. One had red hair and a pale face, and the other had dark skin and high, regal cheekbones. The ship's entire human crew had been gathered here, likely out of concern for the captain's safety. Each carried a shock baton at his or her belt. Used in tandem, those weapons would have enough kick to knock Lucian out for hours, if not stop his heart cold. The bald crewman that had led him here was already touching his baton, as if itching to use it.

Captain Miller faced Lucian, standing before a wide

panorama of stars. Lucian felt small under the weight of that gaze. What could the captain be thinking behind his icy blue eyes?

"Clear the bridge," he said. "Everyone but Lucian."

The five crewmen looked at their captain as if he were crazy. But an order was an order. They left, if a bit hesitatingly.

The bald crewman hung by the door. "Captain. Permission to speak?"

Miller gave a terse nod. "Granted."

"I advise against staying alone here with this . . . mage. He might've already frayed."

"I'm aware of the risk," Miller said. "Thank you, Emerson."

The crewman nodded before casting a glare in Lucian's direction. The doors closed behind him, sealing the captain and Lucian inside.

Captain Miller regarded Lucian a moment before speaking. "I analyzed the med bay's log. The . . . diagnostic was not a pleasant way to wake up. Corneas ruptured with kinetic force. It's as if he took a particle impactor shot to the eyes." Captain Miller stared Lucian down. "Dirk Beker would have bled out had his friends not gotten him to a med pod in time. Count yourself lucky they did."

"He's alive, then?"

"He's alive. But without organ-growth surgery, he'll never see again. Maybe there are artificial options, I don't know. I'm no doctor. He'll be in the pod a while longer, that's for sure."

It was worse than he thought. Well, Dirk could have died. Lucian didn't see how he could talk his way out of this.

"I've heard their side," Captain Miller said. "Now, I'd like to hear yours."

Lucian took a moment to get his thoughts in order. His fate on this ship hung in the balance depending on his next words.

"I'm going to Volsung to train at the Academy. First of all, I'm *not* a frayed mage, as your crewman suggested. It's legal for me to be on this ship, since it's taking me to Volsung. With all that said, it's only fair to point out they've had it out for me from day one. They eavesdropped on a conversation I was having with another passenger–"

"—Emma Almaty, I presume," Captain Miller said, with a nod. "Continue."

"Well, after Dirk learned about that, he and his friends have had it out for me. The first night out, they cornered me in the galley. A few minutes later, they jumped me in the corridor by the starboard viewports. Believer Horatia can verify this."

"Your cabinmate."

Lucian nodded. "That's right. I had to spend money on the med pod. It didn't end there, though. Just now, they pulled me into a cabin – Dirk's cabin, I guess." Lucian looked the captain in the eye. "I could tell just by looking at Dirk he meant to murder me. I didn't want to get involved, but it was three on one. How else would you expect me to defend myself? I'd be dead otherwise. He hates me for what I am. I have no control over being a mage, Captain. I'd choose another life any day."

Captain Miller watched him, his eyes not seeming to miss a single detail.

Lucian continued. "My mother took out a loan to afford this ticket. I'm determined to make it to Volsung, or die trying. I never expected it to be easy."

"It's true, that your . . . kind have great difficulties," Captain Miller admitted.

"I can't afford half the stuff on this ship. But somehow, I'm expected to make it. I can't control my magic, Captain. Not unless I get training. They pushed me to the breaking point. Whatever I did was self-defense. Maybe it would have been less complicated if I'd died. Then again, you'd have to explain to the Volsung Academy why their newest mage didn't arrive."

That last bit was a lie. As far as Lucian knew, the Transcends there didn't know to expect him, but Captain Miller would have no way of knowing that. Then again, it would end up meaning nothing if the captain hated mages as much as Dirk or Believer Horatia.

Captain Miller was watching him, and from what Lucian guessed, without much sympathy. He at last came out of his silence.

"You've put me in a difficult position."

"I'm sorry," Lucian said. "I handled the situation as best as I could. I was never taught to take a beating without fighting back. What I told you is the absolute truth. Check security footage."

"The funny thing about the truth is that it can be irrelevant, at least in matters of public opinion."

"What are you talking about? There's got to be footage. Either from a few hours ago, or even day one. You'll see I'm telling the truth."

"We did get footage of the second incident, at least from the corridor as they're pulling you into the cabin. Of course, there's no telling what actually happened *in* that cabin. We can only see that you were pulled inside in a rough and abrupt manner. What happened inside the cabin is speculative, at least from a legal viewpoint. Whatever you did to Mr. Beker's eyes could not have been done by hand."

He forced down his anger. It would do him no good here. Instead, Lucian lifted his shirt to show the captain the nasty bruises that covered a good half of his torso. "These are fresh, Captain. The med bay from the first night would have taken care of it, so these bruises would have to be from tonight."

Captain Miller noted the injuries mechanically. "Be that as it may—"

"—And what about a few days ago, when they ambushed me in the corridor? Nothing was done. I'm sure you have footage of that, too."

"Nothing was reported," the captain said in a neutral tone.

"Disciplinary actions against passengers are not taken unless a report is filed. Reviewing today's case, however, I will go back and have a look at that."

What kind of captain couldn't keep peace aboard his ship? Not a particularly good one. Captain Miller would rather avoid problems than deal with them. Lucian couldn't expect such a person to treat him fairly. True, Lucian could've reported the first incident, but nothing would have happened. It was just a convenient excuse for the captain to not take responsibility.

The captain continued. "I know that Mr. Beker's intentions were not good, but we have no evidence he and his associates actually hurt you. Those bruises could have come from anywhere, at least as far as the lawyers will be concerned. I'd rather not involve them at all. All we have is the evidence of the ruptured corneas."

"That's bullshit, Captain."

It was just his luck to be placed on board the same ship with the likes of Dirk. Why couldn't he have just stayed in his cabin and watch holos? That had been his original plan.

"As I said earlier," Captain Miller continued, "all this is pointless. I quite sympathize with your predicament. At the same time, I must make a difficult decision. In space, a ship is its own world. The captain is the unquestioned ruler of that world. Your fate rests with me. I also have to write a report that will be interpreted as a factual account of the events." Captain Miller's expression was icy. "Until the *Burung* docks at Volsung Orbital, your life is mine."

Lucian bit his tongue. Panic warred within him, threatening to take over. If all that were true, then Captain Miller could destroy him.

Stillness was the key. Nothing good would come from emotion.

"Mr. Beker could sue Pan-Galactic for thousands," Captain Miller said. "Personally speaking, I believe you. But to satisfy everyone, I have to come up with a punishment that fits the crime. Something that will placate Mr. Beker and any passengers who might be sympathetic to him. People talk, and the version they hear in the coming days will be far from the truth."

Logically, that made sense. Emotionally, Lucian fumed at the injustice.

The captain turned his back on Lucian, facing the stars filling the viewscreen. That action alone proved the captain didn't fear him. Why else face away? "Another ten days will see us to the Volsung Gate. I think that's a suitable length of time in the brig to satisfy most people. And it's the best you're going to get."

Lucian could hardly believe what he'd heard. Ten *days*?

"I understand what the mages have is an affliction," Captain Miller continued. "An affliction that can't be controlled without training. I also know that training won't help everyone. We knew what you were, of course. Contrary to what most people think, Pan-Galactic is happy to transport mages to Academy Worlds. The subsidies we earn are more than worth it." He frowned. "In most cases."

He had no choice, then. Fair or not, it would be his life for the next ten days. It could have been death, had Captain Miller been a different person.

It was best to accept the verdict peacefully.

"I understand," Lucian said. "What about after?"

Captain Miller shook his head. "I don't know. If I had my way, that would be the end of it. It's too soon to say."

"But can't you decide what you want, Captain? You just said you made the rules."

Miller chuckled at that. Perhaps the question had been naïve. "That's true for as long as this ship is in deep space. However, when we get to Volsung Orbital, Pan-Galactic and perhaps even the Orbital police will look into the matter. I'll do whatever I can to prevent that, and make sure your side of the case is heard. I can't guarantee anything. If all goes well, then yes. You'll be out in ten days, and that will be the end of that."

It was the best he could hope for. "All right, then. Will people be able to visit me?"

"Unfortunately, no. Your food will be delivered by one of my crew. If I let you go without at least something of a punishment, I might be out of a job by the time we get to Volsung."

"I understand," Lucian said.

Summoned by an unseen signal, the two male crewmen entered the bridge once again.

"They'll escort you to the holding cell," the captain said. He was already focusing his attention back on the ship's controls. "Good day."

Nothing more was said as the crewmen led Lucian away.

## 21

THE CELL below the main deck, set among pipes, machinery, and cargo, was small. Terribly small.

It was five paces wide and five deep. There were only a few centimeters of space above Lucian's head. If he stood on his tiptoes, he could press his head into the ceiling quite firmly. There was a toilet, a sink with soap, and on the opposite corner, a metal bunk with no mattress or blanket.

He wouldn't need the fraying to go mad in such a place.

In the end, he lay down and closed his eyes. There was nothing else to do. They'd even taken his slate, so the only break from the monotony would be mealtime, whenever that happened to be.

The ship would be approaching the Volsung Gate in ten days. Ten days of confinement. Ten days with nothing but his thoughts. How long could he exist in such a state?

As the hours ticked by, all Lucian could do was think. How had he used magic? He didn't know how it worked. All he knew was that he'd been desperate, and he'd felt that fire. And with that fire, came the violet aura emanating from his hands.

Lucian went to the small window in the door and peered

out. He studied everything in that room, seeking out new details to keep his mind occupied.

But he couldn't do that forever. He went back to his bunk, lying on his back and trying to make his mind blank. If he could manage that, he might lose track of time, and these ten days would pass all the faster.

Rumors had certainly spread by now. Lucian wondered how other passengers were taking the news. Lucian got the feeling more people would sympathize with Dirk's plight than his.

So, here he was, waiting and hoping that his sentence would only be ten days.

"I have control of my mind."

His voice, though quiet, filled the small cell. The words felt hollow and empty. A desperate ploy to give himself hope.

It couldn't have been more than four hours by this point. Back home in Miami, he could go days without speaking to anybody without it bothering him.

Now, human contact was all he could think about. At this point, he wouldn't have even complained about a conversation with Believer Horatia.

How was *she* taking the news?

He kept thinking of Emma. What was she doing? He imagined entire conversations with her, for so long that they almost felt real.

Almost.

At some point, Lucian ran out of things to say. Emptiness pulsated within him, each peal rippling hollow pain through his body.

Lucian sat up on his bunk and gave a sudden shout of frustration, punching the wall. The pain throbbed in his knuckles, but at least pain was a feeling.

Ten days.

WHEN LUCIAN OPENED HIS EYES, he wasn't sure how long he'd slept.

He soon saw the reason for his waking up. A clicking was coming from the door. A face appeared in the window. It was the sorrowful, long-faced crewman.

The door slid open, and the crewman quickly left a tray of food on the floor, before closing the door behind him.

Lucian scrambled up and put his face on the window. "Hey! Can I get my slate?"

The crewman either couldn't hear him, or was ignoring him. A moment later, he was out of the cargo hold and out of sight completely.

Lucian cursed, then took the tray to his bunk.

Lucian peeled off the aluminum seal. A scentless steam curled from a meal of dried turkey, overcooked rice, and soggy broccoli. It was all the nutrition he needed in the most flavor-less package possible.

He finished the meal in less than five minutes, washing it down with some water from the tap. He didn't even have a cup to drink with.

He picked every stray bit of rice, every crumb of broccoli, even licking the bottom of the tray for traces of turkey juice. If he was going to be in here for the next ten days, he needed every calorie. It didn't look like they'd be feeding him as much as he needed.

The hollow feeling of loneliness pulsated within him. It was hard to tell whether this meal was lunch or dinner, since he wasn't sure how much time had passed.

If that was dinner, then it meant he could expect at least one meal a day. Perhaps two, if there was breakfast tomorrow.

All Lucian wanted was to sleep again, but his head was already swimming with oversleep. His mind demanded stimu-lation, but there was nothing to keep him occupied.

Why were they doing this to him? What gave Captain

Miller the right? Lucian remembered his words clearly enough, and his explanations.

It was all horseshit, regardless.

"Could be worse," Lucian said, just to hear a voice. He laughed. A ridiculous joke.

Lucian could talk out loud if he wanted to, or even sing. No one was around to hear, and any sound was better than the pervading silence. If he listened closely, he could hear the thrum of the fusion engine, and even feel its vibration through the deck. These were details he would have missed only yesterday.

He paced back and forth, did some push-ups, jumping jacks, and mountain climbers. He pushed himself off one wall and into the other, to see how fast he could do it. No one was there to stop him, and if they tried, well, at least that would give him someone to talk to. He pushed himself until it felt like his heart was going to pound out of his chest. Gasping for breath, he sprawled on the bunk.

After using the toilet, Lucian thought about flushing, over and over, as an act of rebellion. Until he realized that would only earn him more time in here.

One day. It had only been one day. Right?

He wondered if his mother had been informed of the news. He hadn't even thought to ask Captain Miller. The longer he went without speaking to her, the more worried she would get.

Lucian closed his eyes, the physical activity at least making him somewhat tired. He went into a light doze.

———

LUCIAN WOKE on what might have been day two, though of course it was impossible to say. The lights remained steady, despite the hour. He would have thought they'd have the decency to dim them at least, but he guessed not.

He sat up and began what would no doubt become his daily ritual: staring at the wall.

That was when a voice entered his mind.

*You're awake.*

That voice wasn't his. He couldn't say why, but it brought to mind the old woman he'd spoken with two nights ago.

Even if it was himself making things up, it was conversation. At this point, he didn't care whether it was real or not.

*Is this real?*

*Yes,* the voice responded.

*I'm not imagining this?*

*You are,* she said. *Psionic links, like this one, always take imagination. But that doesn't mean it's not real. Belief, especially when it comes to the Manifold, makes reality.*

*The Manifold?*

*You will learn soon enough.*

He waited for more of an explanation, but nothing came.

*I don't even know your name,* Lucian said. *But somehow, you already know mine.*

A moment's hesitation. Was she gone?

*You may call me Vera,* she said.

*And you're a mage. Right?*

*What do you think?*

*You'd have to be, to be speaking to me like this.*

*Yes,* she said. *I'm a mage, if you need me to spell it out.*

*How is this even* possible? *Forgive me for saying, but at your age, wouldn't you have frayed by now?*

When there was silence on the other side of the link, Lucian knew he had blundered. She could have manifested her powers recently, even if she were elderly. But for some reason, Lucian didn't believe that to be the case.

*Lucian,* she said, *there is so much you have to learn. Nothing is as you think. You know little enough of mages, magic, and the Mani-*

*fold. But what little you do know, you would do well to forget. This very instant.*

Lucian figured that would be easy enough. As she had said, he didn't know much to begin with.

*I've read your thoughts,* she continued. *Yes, I'm old. Contrary to popular belief, magic doesn't doom all mages to the fraying. That disease only touches those who use their magic with insufficient care. Some would say to never risk yourself, to limit your magic to near-uselessness.* There was a pause. *But there is a better way. And I can teach you.*

*You can do that?*

*Yes,* Vera said. *Streaming magic is not the main object of the mage. It is to do so from an unassailable foundation. That foundation doesn't matter, as long as they come from a place of soul's truth. That is the base upon which a mage must begin constructing their power. Nothing more, nothing less.*

Lucian was silent as he absorbed this information. Could he trust this Vera? From their one, short conversation, she had given him the creeps. But if she knew about magic, what was the harm in getting a leg up? It might help in his admittance to the Academy.

*I don't even know what the Manifold is. Is it magic?*

*Magic is only a useful word to explain a phenomenon that is beyond explanation. And the word serves well enough. The Manifold itself is* not *magic – it is the higher reality that supersedes our own. The perfect version of our world, the solid foundation, whereas reality as we see it is the shadow. You can think of the Manifold as an engine, or a computer program, that manifests all we see in our day to day. These are imperfect analogies. The Manifold is much more than that.*

Lucian's mind was still not grasping it. He let Vera continue.

*Reality – what you and I see every day – is not reality at all, but a shadow cast by the Manifold. When a mage uses his or her powers, they are influencing the Manifold itself. Adjust a parameter there,* and the corresponding parameter will adjust in the universe before us.

*So reality – what we see and sense – is a lie?*

*No,* Vera said. *What we can see is no more a lie than your own shadow. The shadow you cast isn't false, but rather an unclear version of what is actually true. We see but a drop of a vast, dark ocean. Beyond the bounds of our perception lie wonders and horrors beyond conception. The Manifold is that ocean, and mages are islands, able to inhabit both worlds. Our fate is to exist in both planes; we stream our thoughts and intents from one into the other. Mages are bridges, touched by this deeper reality.*

Lucian wondered why she was telling him all this. *I don't think I get it.*

*In a word,* Vera continued, *the physical world is not immutable. We can shift it with our beliefs. Reality, the shadow, can be manipulated by the Manifold, true reality. Our magic is a gift, and it is our responsibility to use that gift with great care. We must use it to transcend human weakness, the source of the fraying. For the human mind and body cannot handle the truth of the Manifold, and will become destroyed by it with repeated exposure. But, by bringing our thoughts in line with the Manifold's will, the conflict is resolved. Learning to do so is a lifelong journey. Suffice it to say, we are not material beings, as the scientists say. A new era has arrived. One day, when you are ready, you will see things as they are. And on that day, the real world will seem like the shadow. When that day comes, you will drink of the Manifold's gifts. That which is poison for most will become power to you. And power is that which affects change.*

Already, Lucian's mind was objecting. This was not what he had learned. The mages were doomed to fray, and not even training was a guarantee. Only the lucky ones survived to an old age, while the rest died horrible deaths from the fraying. Not even their minds were safe from the rot of magic.

But Vera seemed to think the opposite. That with proper training, one could be kept safe from the fraying. Indefinitely.

*You must believe it is possible, Lucian. Or it never will be.*

*It's a lot,* he said.

*I can teach you,* Vera said. *If you are willing.*

He held off on his questions for why she might want to do that. He had a feeling he wouldn't like the answer. Something told him not to trust her. He couldn't explain why. Then again, what was the harm of learning more?

*Learning is hard to do in a cell,* he said. *Is there anything you can do to get me out of here?*

And for that matter, how had she known his predicament? Word must have already spread upside.

*If I helped you escape, you would learn nothing. And that would benefit neither of us. And pray tell, what would you do if I actually did help you to escape? What comes after that?*

Lucian knew she had a point there. *You got me there.*

*You are blind,* Vera said. *And still unready. I'll leave you with this. A final thought to ponder. You must accept your physical reality. Your mind, not your physical circumstances, is the key to freedom. Meditate on the Manifold, Lucian. Recognize that it is the only reality that matters . . . not the Shadow World we inhabit.*

*I still don't understand, Vera.*

*If I gave you all the answers, then you would never learn. A lesson given is a tenth of a lesson earned.*

*But it's easier to learn when someone teaches you.*

*Wrong,* Vera said. *Meditate on what I've said.*

Lucian felt her departing his mind, though he couldn't have said *how* he knew that. He felt a sense of numbness as her words bounced around in his head, the only thing he had to latch onto in this cold cell.

Acceptance of physical reality. Reality was only a shadow of the Manifold. Mages are islands, and the Manifold is the ocean...

All mysteries, or more likely to Lucian's reckoning, all nonsense. But the Psionic link connecting them had been real enough. Assuming it wasn't his mind being addled by the fraying already. She knew something of magic and the Manifold, that much was clear. If she were taken by the fraying, he would have no way of knowing it.

Who was Lucian to question anything? For once, he could try taking someone else's advice.

So, he meditated. He thought about her ideas, as foreign as they were to him.

And somewhere along the way, Lucian fell asleep.

# 22

Vera's voice didn't enter his mind again. Lucian remained immobile, almost catatonic, for untold hours. When not sleeping, he lay with his eyes closed, trying to master his thoughts. He tried to detect that awesome source of power that Vera said was the engine behind reality: the Manifold. But Lucian sensed nothing except his own increasing frustration. If he could not detect the Manifold, then streaming magic was impossible. He saw now that the magic he'd used against Dirk was a fluke.

He meditated, going deep within himself. His meals went uneaten, and were taken away by the crewman without a word spoken. He sought that inner stillness Vera had talked about. He had nothing else to latch onto.

The idea he might avoid the fraying was tantalizing. But he still didn't know whether it would make a difference.

Hours bled into days. The anger at being thrown in here became distant as his silence deepened. There were times where Lucian *might* have felt something like a fire. But the flame would never kindle. He was still missing something. Something he couldn't control.

He realized Vera was right. He needed instruction. And he needed to be ready for it. But how?

He got the feeling Vera had lived decades as a mage. She could have the secret, the key, which had eluded humanity for over a century since the mages first arose.

Was it too good to be true? What were *her* motives for sharing such a secret with him?

It was impossible to know. All Lucian could do was move forward and hope for the best.

Lucian tried to recreate the anger that had caused him to stream magic against Dirk. Of course, he wasn't successful. He had wanted to hurt Dirk bad, then. That had been his soul's truth, at least in that moment.

Hours ticked by as if they were minutes. Every time the long-faced crewman came, he left a new meal for Lucian that went untouched. And every time he returned, he took his unopened tray and replaced it with a fresh one. That was the only outside interruption to Lucian's succession of days.

But one day, Captain Miller interrupted that succession. The cell door opened, and Lucian opened his eyes.

His ten days had passed.

————

"DAWSON SAYS YOU AREN'T EATING."

Lucian stared at the captain. He didn't feel the need to say anything. It was as if he had turned into a statue.

"We are approaching the Gate," the Captain continued. "The general sentiment on board is that most think it was an accident." Miller watched Lucian for a response. "You have your friend to thank for that."

Lucian forced himself to come out of his long silence. "What do you mean?"

"Miss Almaty has been your best advocate, or so my crew

has told me. Otherwise, people's opinions would be quite different."

"That's good."

"Be that as it may," Captain Miller went on, "you still have your opponents who want you to remain in here." He shook his head. "The lawyers have told me your hunger strike could be a liability issue."

"So, I'm free to go?"

"Yes," Captain Miller said, with a stern note in his voice. "Of course, if there's any more trouble, I'll put you back in here as fast as I got you out."

"I understand," Lucian said. "I won't cause more trouble."

The fact that the captain was here himself was proof he didn't believe so, either. Miller nodded, as if that settled it. He stood aside, allowing Lucian to see the cargo hold beyond for the first time in days.

He exited the cell.

# 23

MILLER POINTED Lucian down a service corridor running beneath the main deck. Lucian emerged out close to the stern by his cabin. There was no one out here, for which Lucian was thankful. With the Gate so near, everyone was likely in the galley or the viewing deck. He was sure Emma would be there, too.

Lucian was reluctant to be around people, so he decided to watch the passing on his own. He walked to the sternward viewports, as far from the galley as he could get. There, he stared out at the thick inner band of the galaxy. It shone with a white-hot brilliance in front of the distant galactic center. He marveled at the amount of color. Had the stars ever looked so beautiful? Having the space to move and breathe seemed a rare treasure.

Despite the lack of food, Lucian wasn't hungry. It'd been at least six or seven days since his last meal. He was lightheaded, but he felt new purpose. There might be hope he could learn to control his condition.

He wanted to learn magic, now. And he wanted to avoid the

fraying. He knew both of those journeys would require a lifetime of dedication. But that no longer fazed him.

He was ready.

He knew what Vera had been trying to teach him. They could imprison him on the outside, but they couldn't change his mind or his beliefs. Only *he* could.

Lucian stood there, enjoying rare serenity. When footsteps approached from behind, he hardly even noticed them. He knew who it was without even needing to turn. Vera was wearing the same gray cloak as over a week ago. From the side of his vision, he could see her long white hair and beak of a nose. She inclined her head toward him, and he felt the weight of that gaze.

At some point, she faced ahead, to look out into space.

"What have you learned?" she asked.

If there was any doubt about their Psionic conversation, it was gone now.

Her forthright manner was not as disconcerting anymore. "I don't feel like I've learned much. Except for the fact that I'm ready to learn more."

She nodded, as if satisfied with that answer. "Ten days you've spent alone. It seems you've weathered it well enough. Has it affected you for ill, or has it made you stronger?" After a moment's pause, she continued. "You needn't hide your insights."

Lucian felt a twinge of annoyance. "What's the point? Can't you go inside my head?"

She gave a throaty chuckle. "No. Only if you allow it. Or if my will overpowered yours. There are certain . . . methods to achieve that, but rest assured, I'm not going to use them." She gave a long sigh. "Long ago, I was a formal teacher in the arts of the Manifold. In that busy life, I would have given anything for one day to myself, free from outside interruption. To get ten full days of uninterrupted thought . . . *that* is a luxury indeed." She watched him with great intent. "I would ask you to dig deeper. Did you learn anything?"

The woman was very persistent.

"I suppose I learned to accept my condition. Sort of like you said. It was easier once I did that."

"Good," Vera said. "You seem calmer. More in control. Control is the first lesson a mage must learn. Stillness is the key. Only from stillness, can you find your Focus. And from Focus, streams magic itself."

"Who are you, exactly?" he asked. "What are you doing on this ship? How do you know so much about the Manifold? Were you a teacher at the Academy?"

She had a laugh at that. It was the last reaction Lucian had expected.

"The Transcends mean well. Unfortunately, meaning well does not translate into doing well. In fact, it can be dangerous."

"Dangerous, how?"

"We've diverged from our main point," she said. "I sense your skepticism that power grows from stillness. That stubborn set of mind will keep you from learning."

"What if I'm right, and *you're* the stubborn one?"

"Who here is the teacher, and who the student?"

Lucian opened his mouth to protest, until he remembered he had accepted to learn from her. At least, for now.

"Not to say I have nothing to learn myself," Vera said. "The path to knowledge comes from recognizing we are all ignorant fools."

"Well, that's another thing you know more than me."

"Don't be snide. Say what you mean, if you have anything to say at all." When Lucian remained silent, she continued. "I hoped to teach you the power of perspective. With perspective, even a prisoner can be free."

Lucian was getting annoyed with her cryptic sayings.

"Knowing something and living it are two different things entirely."

"Good," Vera said. "That is an important distinction to recognize. You have two choices. Accept. Or reject. Accepting is far less painful."

All his former commitments to change seemed forgotten in the face of her questions.

"What do I accept, then?" Lucian asked. "That I'll never live a normal life? That I'll go mad and die after the fraying rots my mind and body?"

Vera considered that for a moment. Her dark eyes were hard to read.

"I've been a mage for decades, and I haven't frayed yet. I've learned to control my gift, and to control it from a place of conviction. I've *accepted*. And if you don't accept, the fraying will be inevitable. As it is for most mages."

Lucian was quiet for a long time. This Manifold, whatever it was, had chosen him. As it had chosen Vera, as it had chosen Emma, as it had chosen one in twenty million human beings in the Worlds.

The worst part was, deep down, Lucian knew Vera was right. He had to accept this part of himself.

It wasn't easy, though. Not by a long shot.

"Why me?" he asked. "Why *anyone*?"

"That's the best question you've asked so far," Vera said. "No one knows. Some are chosen, some are not. There are theories, of course, though most are doubtful."

"What are the theories?"

Vera shrugged, as if those theories were of no consequence. "The most popular one is genetics. Nonsense, of course. They have been testing for that for over a century." Vera pursed her lips. "Nor are mages more prevalent in one part of the Worlds over another. So, it can't be environmental. There can be clusters, but still, the spread is quite even." She paused, as if considering. "We can only conclude that whoever the Manifold touches is arbitrary."

Lucian didn't like thinking of the Manifold as an entity, choosing who to touch. Was it a force of nature, or something more, like a god?

"I will admit most mages will fray," Vera said. "Could most mages learn to save themselves, if only government invested the resources?" She shook her head. "Instead, they corral and control us. Rather than give us an equal place in society, they would use us to keep them in power, while they send those of us who can't fulfill that role to the Mad Moon. It makes one think, no?"

"Think what? That they'd rather us be dead?"

She arched an eyebrow. "Don't they?"

Her words chilled him, but as usual, they had the ring of truth.

"It's convenient, isn't it?" she asked. "What better way for the mages to never rise again? Turn them against each other. People can't stomach an open purge . . . not yet, anyway. The next best thing is to let the mages fight amongst themselves, silent and forgotten. And those mages that *can* be used, are quarantined to the academies. There, they can be controlled."

It was sobering how much that made sense. The mages only existed by the grace of the League of Worlds. Millions, if not billions, would welcome mages being killed on the spot. Dirk was just one example of that, and Believer Horatia another. How many others on board were of a similar opinion? Mages weren't even allowed to set foot on most worlds. And the worlds that *did* allow them had strict regulations.

And of course, there was the uncomfortable truth Vera had mentioned. Any mage not under the purview of an academy had only one recourse. The prison moon of Psyche. Any mage sent there, never came back.

If Vera wasn't associated with an academy, then it meant

only one thing. She was a rogue mage. If she were ever discovered, then the League would do everything in its power to hunt her down. That she had survived this long was a testament to her skill and wile.

"You said you could teach me," Lucian said. "You also said the Volsung Academy has it wrong. But I'm sure if I went there, they'd tell me the same thing about you."

Vera smiled, as if Lucian had told a funny joke. "No doubt they would. My ways and theirs have a key difference in philosophy. Their teachings instruct their pupils to limit their powers. They train them to bury their inborn abilities, and if they *do* use them, it's with great limitations. All with the purpose of preventing the fraying. Of course, that only slows the fraying. Any mage must stream some of their power sometimes. That is unavoidable. Otherwise, Manifoldic poisoning results."

"Manifoldic poisoning?"

"Every mage draws power from the Manifold, a stream that builds up over time. And it must be dispelled. The longer they go without streaming their magic, the worse the effects. Seizures, mental instability, and burning pain are the main symptoms."

"It sounds like the fraying."

"It will develop into the fraying, given time," Vera said. "That's why it is important to learn to stream consistently and effectively. I hope to teach you."

"Okay," Lucian said. "Then where does magic come from? It all started sometime in the late 2200's, right?"

"More or less," Vera said. "For decades, I've been seeking an answer as to the ultimate why. My theory is that magic is connected to the Builders. I could be wrong on that. It may be a heretofore undiscovered force of nature. But it is my quest to seek an answer all the same."

"And if there *is* no answer? Then you'd be wasting your life."

If that fazed Vera, she didn't show it. "It's not a waste, for I find value and truth in my journey. That truth is the bedrock upon which I build my life and power. One could not ask for a stronger foundation. My entire existence has become unshakeable."

Lucian grew bolder in his questioning. "So, if you die without ever finding that answer, it wouldn't bother you?"

She waved a hand in dismissal. "If I'm dead, nothing can disappoint me then, can it? Life isn't about attaining a goal. The universe goes on, year after year, century after century, eon after eon. To what end does it go on?" Vera watched him for an answer. When he didn't give one, she continued. "It goes on toward nothing, for nothing, by nothing. The only higher truth we know – the Manifold – is itself wrapped in mystery. It's the reality that drives the Shadow World. If there is any ultimate truth, it's *that*. Our lives are what we make of them. Our beliefs shape our reality. And the universe is the canvas upon which we paint our will." She looked at Lucian, and at his further silence, she stepped back from the viewport. "Think on what I've said. Later, you can share any new insights you have."

"I'm not sure I'll have any."

"All the same, there is great value in introspection and seeking the truth. It's important to know *why* you believe the things you do, and in the case of a mage, it's paramount. The Manifold will destroy those who can't stomach it. A paradox. For truth is what we make of it. Like an optical illusion, truth changes depending on one's vantage point. The journey to truth is a long, winding path that bears fruit in and of itself." She withdrew her hands into her sleeves. "We'll be approaching Volsung Gate, soon. That is something you can think about, too."

"What do you mean? We're going to pass through, right? In one side, out the other."

She shook her head, as if in disbelief he'd said that. "These ancient Gates, crafted by a long-dead race we know little to nothing about. Do you think it's as simple as passing in one side and out the other?" She chuckled. "Mark my words. These Builders, as we call them, understood well the secrets of the Manifold. It would not surprise me in the least if these structures streamed the Manifold's magic."

"Whenever people can't explain something, they turn to magic and religion," Lucian said. He thought of Believer Horatia.

"Call it magic, or not. It is reality. It is power." Vera looked back out the viewport. "These Gates. I've often wondered if they're somehow connected. Is it coincidence that the rise of magic happened within a century of humanity's first discovery of them?"

Lucian thought back to his history lessons. The explorer Erik Nielsen and his crew had been the first to pass through a Gate. That was back in 2186, decades after humanity had colonized a good chunk of the solar system. The first recorded mages appeared in the middle of the 23rd century, a little over a century ago.

Vera might be onto something, there. Could it be as simple as that? It seemed doubtful. There were still too many missing pieces . . .

Lucian's mouth worked for an answer, but as had been the case so many times, he came up with nothing. At his silence, she took her leave.

## 24

LUCIAN REMAINED by the viewport long after Vera had left. This corner of the ship was empty, and that was good enough for him. He stood there for a long time, waiting for the inevitable passing.

When footsteps approached, Lucian turned to see Emma walking toward him.

"There you are." She surprised Lucian with a hug. The warm human contact was a shock after his isolation. His body tensed, before relaxing. "I heard you got out. Have you been standing here the whole time?"

"Yeah," he said, parting from her. "Just can't be around people right now."

"Oh," she said, her face falling. "If you need some space . . ."

Lucian shook his head. "No. You're an exception." He cleared his throat. "Captain Miller told me you turned a lot of people around. Thanks."

"Of course," she said. "You doing okay? You look kind of . . . rough."

"I feel kind of rough."

"Well, the passage will be soon."

She was standing close enough to his side to feel her warmth. After so long in that cold cell, the feeling was welcome. It made his throat clamp up, and tears almost came to his eyes. His hand brushed hers, and of its own volition, held onto it. Her grip in his was firm, yet soft. It felt so good to touch her, but he had to let go. He might lose it otherwise. He turned his face slightly away, so that she couldn't read his expression.

"You've lost weight," she said. "Did they not feed you?"

At the mention of food, Lucian's stomach rumbled. He chose to not tell her it was his choice. "Not much."

"After the passing, we can head to the galley. Or, I can bring you something to your cabin. You'll have to tell me where it is, though."

"We'll figure it out." Despite his hunger, food was far from his thoughts. In the viewport, he could see his reflection staring back. Emma was right. He *had* changed. His form was thin and haggard. His eyes looked tired, the light in them having departed. Dark circles underlined his eyes, and his complexion was pale. It was as if he hadn't seen the sun in months.

"Almost halfway there," she said. "After the Gate, it's on to Volsung."

"I'm still not sure how I'm going to get down there, yet," Lucian said.

Or even if it was *worth* going down there. Vera had sown seeds of doubt. Maybe the Academy was no longer the best choice. It was all too much to think about, and all Lucian wanted to do was lie down.

"The shuttle from Volsung Orbital goes to Karendas, a city on the surface," Emma said. "One of their Talents is supposed to meet me at the spaceport. I can tell them that you're coming, too. You said the doctor sent a message ahead, right?"

"They said they would."

"Then it should be no issue."

"There's no guarantee the Transcends will accept me, though."

"I don't know if they'll accept me, either," Emma responded. "We have to try, right? What other choice do we have?"

Well, there was Vera. He wasn't ready to tell her about that, yet. He needed to learn more.

"So, once we're accepted, then what?" Lucian asked.

She shrugged. "I guess we learn whatever it is they have to teach us."

"And if we get rejected?"

From Emma's troubled expression, Lucian could tell that the question bothered her. "Let's think positive, okay? It'll be better if we go together." Emma looked out the viewport again. "I don't think I can do this alone."

"You're not alone. You've got me, right?"

She nodded. "I know. It's . . . painful. My magic will kill me if I can't learn to control it."

"Kill you? It'll kill any of us."

"What did it feel like?"

"Magic?" He frowned as he thought. "It felt as if every part of me was infused with fire. It . . . *hurt*, almost, but not quite. But it definitely felt good, too. It made me feel powerful. Like nothing could stop me."

She nodded. "I haven't streamed, yet. But sometimes, I feel that same fire . . . and nothing happens. But it has to go some-where." She heaved a sigh, as if what she was going to say was weighing on her heavily. "So, it directs inward. The pain is unbearable. It's like a dam bursting, and the pain doesn't go away until the stream is over. Eventually, it'll kill me."

Now, she was the one hiding her face. He wanted to reach out for her, comfort her. As useless as that might be.

"Emma . . . I had no idea. I'm sorry."

"It's not your fault," she said. "It's why failure isn't an option. My parents have tried everything else, whether it's medication or physical therapy. The longer I go between seizures, the worse it gets. It's been two weeks since my last one, so the next one should be pretty bad."

"That's horrible."

"It's because I wasn't detected early enough. Eventually, this happens to everyone if they don't learn to stream in time. Some figure it out on their own, others don't. I'm one of the ones who hasn't." She shrugged. "So, here I am."

"I don't know what I'm doing, either," Lucian said. "Whatever I did to Dirk was from a lack of control." Lucian looked over at Emma, who was staring out the viewport. "I want you to know that I'm here for you. Whatever you need . . . let me know."

She gave a slow nod. "I appreciate that."

There was a silence after that, the two of them just staring quietly at the stars.

"What's the word with Dirk the Jerk?"

Emma smiled at that. "He wears a bandage across his eyes now. The med pod couldn't completely fix him. He needs more advanced surgery. He's been brought low, that's for sure. And his two friends . . . Paul and Kasim, was it? They keep to themselves now, too."

"You think I should feel bad about that?"

"No. People do it to themselves, you know? It's not our problem."

"It felt . . . good," Lucian said. "I mean, at the time. I felt powerful, like I could take anyone on."

"You should be careful about that," Emma warned. "That's why magic is addicting. Some say it's the power that makes you go mad. You open yourself up to it, wanting to feel more and more. But that power has a price."

"So, the more you use magic, the worse it becomes?"

Emma nodded. "That's the gist of it. The fraying happens when a mage finally gives in. They completely abandon their ego, instead live only for the feeling, no matter how much it destroys them. The Manifold – the place mages say magic comes from – pushes the mind past its breaking point. Some can deny that temptation long enough, but in the end, it becomes overwhelming. Like a siren calling you to your death."

Her words were interrupted by the chime of the ship's intercom. Captain Miller's cheery voice emanated through the speakers. The tone sounded strange to Lucian, after hearing his sterner side.

"Greetings, passengers of the *Burung*. We're five minutes away from Volsung Gate. If you haven't already, there's still time to get to the nearest viewport to watch the passage. No need to go to the bow; all the viewports will give the vantage from the bridge. Don't blink, or you might miss it."

The comm clicked off.

"What did he mean by *don't blink*?" Lucian asked.

"We're going .02C," Emma explained. "Every second, six thousand kilometers go by. The passing will happen in less than a second. The moment the Gate becomes visible, we're through it."

"Sounds dangerous. What would happen if we crashed into it?"

"That's a little morbid."

"Those Gates are supposed to be indestructible, right?"

"So they say. It would be a quick death, at least."

The math of computing a safe course was routine for navigation computers. The central plane of every Gate was more than a kilometer wide. More than enough space for any ship to pass through, even the largest supercarrier in the League fleet, *Volga*. The only thing that had to be arranged was passage order. It wouldn't do for two ships from opposite ends of the Gate to collide into each other. That had happened only once, as far as he knew. And when the force of the collision cleared, the Gate remained behind without so much as a scratch. Such a thing was beyond Lucian's comprehension.

Lucian wasn't nervous about the passing. He was thinking about what Vera had said. *Were* those Gates powered by Manifold, or by the theoretical vacuum energy proposed by physicists? That was the reason they said the Gates had to be located far away from any major gravitational well. Now, though, he wasn't sure. Nothing made sense anymore.

The image on the viewport changed, as Captain Miller had said. A new vista of stars appeared, this one pointed toward the darker, less dense outer band of the Milky Way. It was only moments now. Lucian held his breath, focusing intensely on the viewport.

Then, a new star appeared in the center of the port. It grew brighter and brighter, a purplish aura of light blue-shifting as the ship hurtled forward.

As Emma's grip tightened on Lucian's, the burst of light dissipated. There was no jolting and no thunderclap. A momentary flash of brilliance, then nothing more. The stars had shifted once again. But this time, it was from distance, not the display itself.

"That's it?" Lucian asked.

"That's it," Emma said.

It felt so . . . anticlimactic. And all Lucian could think about was how far he was from everyone and everything he ever knew. He thought of his mother then. Now in a new system, their messages would take much longer to reach each other. They had to pass through the mail relays set up outside the Gate.

She had to be panicking. She'd probably sent a million messages by now.

"I have to go," he said. "I have to get my slate."

"Yeah, you better check on that. Dinner later? I'll give you a premium meal, on me."

Lucian nodded, then ran back to his cabin.

———

WHEN LUCIAN RETURNED to his cabin, Believer Horatia was sitting on her bunk with the pod door open. As soon as her eyes met Lucian's, she glared with hostility.

He expected a fight then, but he only felt her cold gaze as he climbed into his pod, closing the door before she had the chance to say anything. A holo he'd been watching from before his incarceration started to auto play. That film seemed to be from another life.

His slate was waiting for him in the compartment. He unlocked it, and saw thirty-six missed texts from his mother. He was surprised it was so few.

They started off concerned. Then angry. And finally, panicking.

And none of them mentioned Lucian being in the holding cell. Captain Miller hadn't shared that minor detail with her.

Her messages stopped two days ago. That likely coincided with her passing into Alpha Centauri.

Lucian swiped out a response, knowing it would not be adequate in explaining things.

*Sorry for not responding, Mom. I lost my slate. I know, I'm an idiot. Lucky for me, someone returned it to one of the crew. That's why I haven't been able to message for a while.*

Lucian doubted she would accept that lie, but it was better than telling her the truth. That would only worry her sick.

*We're two weeks out from Volsung. We passed through the Gate. I'm fine. I'm just ready to get there. I don't know what else to write. I've been watching a lot of movies to pass the time. There's not much else to do, so I'm going stir crazy. Love, Lucian.*

Lucian pressed send, only for the server to give him the following message: *Not enough credit.*

Lucian blinked. Did his ticket not allow for interstellar messages? Or had the med pod been more expensive than he remembered? Lucian found his virtual wallet. His balance from Earth hadn't synced with the new star system. Data must be getting throttled at the Gate relay.

Whatever the case, if Lucian didn't get some money from somewhere, he was as good as stranded.

## 25

Lucian went to dinner with Emma. Believer Horatia had closed her pod, thankfully. He didn't want to deal with her, but it was a tall order to avoid her the rest of the trip.

The galley was full when he arrived. Everyone went quiet upon his entrance. He did his best to avoid the stares, not even checking Dirk's old table to see if they were there. He half-expected someone to challenge him, but none did. It was clear he'd been the main subject for the past week.

It was fear. They *feared* him, many shying away or leaving by the other exit.

Lucian went straight to Emma at their usual table. As promised, she already had a tray waiting for him.

"I hope you like seafood," she said. "They were out of steak."

"Seafood's perfect." Despite everything, his chest swelled with happiness to sit down to his first meal as a free man. The smell of the salmon, over garlic potatoes and glazed carrots, was tantalizing compared to what he was used to. And the lack of food for the past few days made the smell all the more enticing.

As he wolfed it down, what few people were left in the galley cast surreptitious glances his way. Let them. Nothing could ruin this moment.

"That good, huh?" she asked, smiling with amusement.

He took a swig of soda and nodded. "Never tasted anything better in my life."

"Now I *know* you were starving," she said. She picked at her own food, but didn't seem to have an appetite for it.

"Now, I just have to survive the rest of this trip."

"We're over halfway there. After what you did to Dirk, no one's going to mess with you."

"Except the lawyers. Let's hope the captain is putting them off." Lucian leaned closer. There were still things they had to catch up on. "Should we sim later? There are things I want to talk about."

"We can tonight, if you want."

"That'll work. Right after dinner?"

After Emma gave him some of her sim pills, they returned to their cabins.

———

They met each other in the default game room.

"Where should we go?" Emma asked.

"Doesn't matter."

"Okay. I think it's time you learned a bit more about me. Only a small part of Aurora was mapped out, but that includes my old village. You can show me your home on Earth, too. If you want."

"Sure," Lucian said. "Lead the way."

Within the minute, they had left the game lobby and were loaded into a new reality.

Sharp, cold air pressed in around him, touching him but not causing discomfort. They stood in the middle of a snow-field, wearing thick winter clothes. They found themselves in a forested valley, white snow-clad mountains surrounding them. A dark, violet sky stretched above, laced with bright streams of stars. Aurora borealis shimmered from horizon to horizon, multicolored, luminous, and breathtaking. A cracked moon, molten red, floated in the sky above. It was smaller than Earth's, but far brighter, glowing with a hellish red light.

"This way," Emma said. "We're close."

They walked until they stood on a precipice high above a valley filled with tall, spindly trees. In that valley shone several lights of a small village in the distance.

"That's home," Emma said, her breath coming out in clouds. "That's Vale."

"How come I've never heard of this world before?"

"Rogue mages settled it twenty years ago. They were drawn by the Builder ruins. Open-minded people followed them, my parents among them. They lived separate from us, of course, but the world's main draw is the ruins. The artifacts my dad found made him a rich man."

"Artifacts?"

Emma nodded. "You can get to Aurora through Sani's Border Gate. Even then, you won't find it for another three Gates."

"Tier Three, then."

A planet's tier was calculated by how many Gate passings it took to reach it from a League world. Assuming a month of travel per tier, the standard, Aurora was probably about three months from the Border World of Sani.

Emma continued talking as they plodded through the snow. "Needless to say, Aurora doesn't even have an orbital. At least, as far as I know. Things might have changed."

"And you said mages found it?"

Emma nodded. "Rogues try to get as far from the League as they can. I . . . wasn't supposed to talk to them, but I did anyway. That's how I learned things. No one knew the ruins like the mages did."

"Was it always cold, like this?"

"Whoever uploaded this to the GalNet must have taken readings in winter. That said, Aurora is cooler than Earth, especially here in the mountains. The Builders seemed to prefer to build their cities in mountains."

"Seems like an interesting childhood."

Emma laughed. "Well, I hated it. All I wanted was to live on Earth or a First World. I was born on Sani, which is remote enough. When we moved to Aurora, I was not a happy child." Her smile was tinged with sadness. "Now, I recognize that even if those times were hard, they were happy. I cried when we left Aurora, four years ago. My mother wanted to be closer to family, but it's possible she was beginning to sense something wrong with me."

"You think she knew?"

"Suspected," Emma said. "To this day, they believe that's how I 'caught' my magic. From one of the many artifacts they handled."

"Could it have happened like that?"

Emma smiled. "You ask a lot of questions." She shook her head. "No. It didn't. Mathias – the mage I talked to – told me that it's not something you catch. So, I trust him."

Emma gazed down at the valley. Her sad expression was easy to see by the light of the stars, which were twice as numerous as in an Earth sky. Aurora must have been located in a dense starfield.

"I didn't start showing symptoms until I was fifteen, when we left," she said. "All the usual stuff, like weird premonitions and dreams. The convulsions didn't even start until I was eighteen. By then, we were living on a station orbiting Hephaestus.

The doctors tested me, but I came up negative. That's when we moved to L5, where the best doctors are." She paused in recollection as the lights of the town drew closer. "For a whole year, we lived on starships. We crawled across the Hundred Worlds toward Earth, Gate to Gate, orbital to orbital, station to station. Things kept getting worse. Sometimes, the seizures were bad. Sometimes, they'd stop. When we finally arrived, the doctors could find nothing wrong with me. Almost as a last-ditch effort, they tested again, not expecting anything." She went quiet. "That's when I learned. After that, life was never the same."

The silence of the world pressed in on them, completely foreign to what Lucian had grown up with. There was no sound of animals from the surrounding woods. Aurora might be a purely arboreal world.

"That was when it occurred to me," Emma went on. "I thought about Mathias, and some of the other mages I'd met. They looked *different* to me, as if they had some aura surrounding their faces." There was a silence as she thought about it. "I always thought everyone could see it. It was more, though. So much more." She looked at Lucian. "That's how when I saw you, I knew."

Lucian was chilled by those words. "And now you're here."

"More or less," she said. "I turned nineteen a few months ago, by the standard calendar. That's when my parents reached out to the Transcends on Volsung. It only took a couple of weeks for them to respond. They told me to come in person, and that my case seemed promising." She gave Lucian a sidelong look. "Only me, though. My parents still have to work on L5. Not like they could see me, anyway, with the Transcends' rules. They made it clear enough that only I was allowed to come."

She was quiet for a while. Talking about this couldn't have been easy, and he could see why she had been hesitant to say anything before.

Lucian thought about her story as they wove through a forest of billowing trees laden with snow. They picked up a trail until the trees came to a sudden end. They stood on the periphery of the village now. Most of the buildings were one story, constructed of wood. Smoke emitted from chimneys, lending a sweet aroma to the cold air. Lucian felt as if he had stepped back centuries in time. On the frontier, pioneers had to reconstruct civilization from scratch. Lucian had a feeling it would take centuries to civilize this wilderness. But if it were as rich with Builder ruins as Emma said, it might take less time.

They walked through the village of Vale, until they stood at a central tree. The tree was the largest he had ever seen in his life. It was about as tall as the Redwoods of Earth, but its canopy even wider, filled with slender bows that billowed above.

"I've always felt like there was something special about this tree," Emma said. "It has nothing to do with the size. The feeling is absent in a simulation, but if you were to go there, you would see what I mean."

"Special, how?"

Emma was quiet as she looked up at it. "I don't know. Its effect is calming, for some reason. Like it has a spirit of its own, similar to how I can tell when someone's a mage." She smiled nervously. "I know it sounds silly, but that's what I think." She looked back at him. "The main mage enclave isn't far, up the path to those mountains there." She pointed. "You can see the smoke of their fires hidden by that ridge."

She led Lucian to her old home on the periphery of town, one of the rare two story cabins. It was empty, but only because the sim's camera drones hadn't mapped it out. It was up to Emma to populate it with her memories. Within another moment, there was furniture – nothing fancy, but comfortable, made from local wood and padded with cushions and blankets. A warm flame burned in the fireplace. There were bookshelves, a couch, two chairs, along with a basic kitchen and dining table of carved wood. A set of stairs led to a loft up above.

She looked at Lucian. "Well, this is home. *Was* home. Thanks for humoring me. After all, we didn't come here to talk about my life."

"It's fine," Lucian said. "I'm glad you shared that with me."

"You'll get your turn, soon. I've never been to Miami before."

They took up seats on the couch in front of the blazing fire.

"So, what did you want to talk about?" she asked. "You didn't come here to just hear me talk."

There was nothing but to get right into it. "There's another mage on board."

Emma's eyes widened, but she recovered quickly. "I think I know who you're talking about. The old woman, right?"

How had she known? "Yeah. Could you tell?"

"I suspected. There was no aura around her, but I still had a feeling something was off about her. I saw her one night when I couldn't sleep. Seems she only comes out when everyone else has gone to bed."

"She's definitely a mage," Lucian said. "I've spoken to her twice. Once right before the second time Dirk attacked me. And again, right before you found me during the Gate passing." He paused. For some reason, it felt strange to talk about Vera to Emma, almost like a betrayal of confidence. That was silly, though, because Vera had never told him to keep their conversations private. "Her name is Vera. She had some interesting things to say. I'm not sure what to make of them, but somehow, she knew what I was."

"What did she say?"

"Everything and nothing. She keeps talking about reality being a shadow of the Manifold. That the Manifold is the true reality that casts the shadow. How a mage should use the Manifold to make themselves stronger." Lucian gave a nervous laugh. "Stuff like that."

"You should be careful around her," Emma said. "Even if she was up front with you, she was hiding her true nature from me."

"Well, wouldn't she *want* to do that?" Lucian asked. "She's a rogue."

"Whatever the reason, something's off about her." Her cheeks colored, as if from embarrassment. "I'm sorry. I don't know how else to describe it."

"When I mentioned the Volsung Academy, she didn't have good things to say."

"You told her you were going there?"

"Why shouldn't I have?"

"I don't know," she said. "I just don't trust her."

"That was my initial reaction, too. She knows things, though. She's been a mage longer than both of us have been alive. Maybe twice as long."

Lucian summarized most of his and Vera's conversations. How Vera thought the Transcends had it wrong about magic, that her way was better. She said it was important to use the Manifold with care, to nurture it as a gift and not lock it away like a curse. At least, that was how Lucian figured it. He probably didn't explain things well enough.

For now, he omitted the part about Vera speaking to him in his cell. At the time, it hadn't seemed strange, but he realized how much it might seem like a violation of his privacy.

Emma stewed on what Lucian said for at least two minutes, her light brown eyes looking into the flames. At last, she responded.

"Mages have been trying to use the Manifold in a safe way for over a century. Ever since there *were* mages. I may not know much, but I do know that no one has been successful at it. Not completely. That kind of thinking was what led to the

Mage War. When the fraying was connected to magic use, academies changed their training to focus more on safety. But that didn't sit well with many mages. They followed Xara Mallis and other influential mages into exile, forming the Free Mages. From what Mathias told me, the Free Mages taught their followers to not restrict themselves. Of course, we know where that led."

Lucian didn't have to ask. The fraying. "I guess they weren't successful."

"No," Emma said. "At the Free Mages' height, Xara had as many mages following her as the Academies. In fact, the mages were fighting each other before their war spread to the League."

"So you're saying Vera's way of thinking lines up with the Free Mages?"

"The Free Mages died in the Siege of Isis," she said. "Those who weren't were hunted down by Loyalists and sent to Psyche. I wonder, though. It's not hard to imagine a few escaping the net..."

"No way Vera is one of them," Lucian said. The old woman was a bit creepy, sometimes, but to be one of the mages who had almost caused the destruction of the League? How was that even possible?

"She probably isn't," Emma said. "It was fifty years ago, after all. Then again, from what you've told me, it sounds like her philosophy isn't far off. Seeking a final answer to the fraying seems noble on the surface. But it has led to nothing but the death of millions. There may not even *be* a final answer to the fraying. *That's* the danger of that kind of thinking, Lucian. It made mages think they would find a final answer, and they never did. Half of the League burned."

She had a point, but Lucian also thought he wasn't doing justice to Vera's arguments. "She's old, Emma. I don't know *how* old, but it wouldn't surprise me if she's pushing a hundred. For her to live that long without fraying is incredible. She must know *something* about keeping the fraying away."

Emma's expression darkened. Something Lucian had said bothered her.

"What?" he asked.

"I don't know. If she's been a mage that long, she's definitely old enough to have participated in the war. And some of her beliefs line up with the Free Mages, especially the part about using the Manifold as a means to strengthen oneself."

Lucian wasn't sure what to think. Vera was a little strange, sure, with her cryptic sayings and cold manner. But those things, coupled with her beliefs, didn't mean anything in themselves. She was a rogue mage – if she were ever discovered, they would send her to Psyche.

Then again, she'd managed on her own for this long, eluding capture. Didn't it stand to reason that a rogue mage's thinking might not be in line with the norm? Did that necessarily make her wrong? Lucian was old enough to not trust authority blindly, but Emma seemed to see things in terms of good and bad.

It sounded a bit naïve.

"What if she *was* a part of the Free Mages?" Lucian asked. "She would never admit that, would she?"

"Probably not. But if there is even a chance, you should avoid her at all costs. The Free Mages were magic maximalists. They believed magic would be humanity's salvation. So, they didn't hold back. It made them powerful, for sure. Because they trusted the Manifold would produce a cure, if only they worked hard enough." She shook her head. "Of course, that didn't happen."

"You know a lot," Lucian said.

"I've asked a lot of questions with Mathias. I won't forget those talks for the rest of my life. I found them fascinating, and Mathias was open. For a mage, I mean." Emma looked at

Lucian worriedly. "The Manifold is dangerous. Mages should follow the consensus of the Transcends. A mage should use magic only when necessary. The more we stream it, the greater the risk of fraying. The Volsung Academy opposes Free Mage ideology. It's been proven not to work. And in the end, the promise of unhindered magic is empty, especially when the Academy has had promising results in recent years."

"Promising results like what?"

"Well, most of the Transcends themselves are quite old, from what I understand. Most untrained mages make it five or ten years before fraying. Sometimes less than that. But if my research is right, the Academy's teachings have more than doubled the time it takes for mages to show signs of fraying. And many live *much* longer than that symptom free. The symptoms can even be reversed. Given enough time to figure it out, they might even find a complete cure."

It sounded too good to be true, but it also meant limiting one's use of magic. It meant becoming a Minimalist, as Emma had put it. Lucian didn't see how it was possible. As Emma herself admitted, magic built up over time. A mage *had* to use it, at some point. Unless they found a way to stop *that*, then how could anyone hope to stop the fraying?

"With enough time," Emma continued, "we could be free of this one day."

Lucian tried to imagine that future, even if it seemed distant. He couldn't picture it, though. "I hope so."

"Just be careful, Lucian. Promise me, okay?"

Lucian nodded. "I promise. I won't ignore her, but I won't accept everything she says without thinking about it first."

That answer seemed to satisfy her. "Let's get out of here. We still have a couple of hours left before we're kicked out."

"Sure," Lucian said. "You still want to see my house?"

She nodded. "Of course!"

Lucian wasn't quite sure how to get there. So, all he did was imagine his home city – its sunny blue sky, sultry air, blue canals, and gleaming skyscrapers. And he willed them to go there.

The ease of it all surprised him, for in the next moment, Miami's humid heat was baking his skin.

## 26

LUCIAN TOOK Emma to South Shoal on the Lev. She watched the approaching nova-deco hotels rising from the canals in awe. Restaurants and bars spilled over the multitiered board-walks. Several artificial islands spread in the distance, filled with sunbathers and swimmers. The sky was blue, the sun was bright, and the tall silvery skyscrapers were blinding in their brilliance.

It was surreal to be back, if only in a simulation.

Her eyes were glued to the window in childlike wonder. "You grew up here?"

"Not this part. This is where the rich people live." Lucian pointed at an island they were passing, filled with mansions and high rises. They rose in strange proportions, possible only with anti-grav masonry. "The weirder the house, the richer the jerk who owns it."

"I'm sure my parents could afford one of those houses. One of the smaller ones, anyway."

Was she *that* rich? "Seriously?"

"I don't know, probably. Where do *you* live, then?"

"Well, I don't live there anymore," Lucian said. "It's definitely not like those houses."

"I don't care," she said. "You saw my house on Aurora. It's nothing crazy."

It was still nicer than most of the other buildings in the village. If she saw where he lived, she would be in for a rude shock.

"You'd rather see my dingy, sad apartment than the city? We only have an hour left."

"Yep," she said, without hesitation. "Let's go!"

It was hard to say no to her enthusiasm. Rather than shift there in an instant, Lucian and Emma boarded another train. He said it was to show her more of the city, but the truth was, he was afraid of how she might react. His neighborhood was pretty rough, and he wasn't sure how accurately the sim would portray that.

They got off at the station in Lucian's neighborhood. He wouldn't have called the area a slum, but it was somewhere between that and middle class. The buildings crowded together, seeming to lean over the canals beneath. Most needed a new paint job. Homeless people in shabby clothing clustered in the dark corners. Emma made no comment as they strolled along a walkway strewn with litter, though she stood closer to him. He'd been jumped before, once when he was fifteen.

Soon, they stood before the familiar door, its outside coated in faded yellow paint. Though his home wasn't much, he felt a strange sense of longing for it. He'd likely never see it again in real life.

"This is it."

He opened the door, and they went inside. Its interior was as Lucian remembered, from the ratty old sofa and arm chair to the faded wooden dining table. The cluttered kitchen needed a good organizing, and the air was hot and stuffy. And it was *loud*. The shouts of neighbors outside, as well as the din of motorboats below, passed through the thin walls as if they weren't even there. Even if he'd only been gone for a little over two weeks, it felt smaller. Was that the simulation, or had his conception of it changed?

Emma walked past him into the living room. It was strange having her here. She wore nice, well-tailored clothing that complemented her slender figure well. Expensive clothing like that would only make her a target in his neighborhood. It only took a moment for her to take in her surroundings.

"It's homey," she said. A table filled with framed pictures caught her interest. She picked up the largest one, with Lucian as a young teenager posing with his mother. She wore her League fleet blues, giving a stoic smile, while Lucian wasn't smiling at all.

"You don't look too happy here," Emma said, with a smile.

"My mom was deploying," he said. "I don't know why she kept that picture."

It brought back memories, most unpleasant. Lucian hadn't understood why his mom always had to deploy. Back then, he was lucky to see her twice in a year. Not having a father around made it harder, too. After the skirmish with pirates that had killed his father, Lucian had always worried the same thing would happen to his mother.

Lucian pushed the thought from his head as he gave Emma a tour. It didn't take long. When she was in his bedroom, she looked around and took everything in. He just hoped she wouldn't start snooping.

They returned to the living room.

"That's the grand tour," Lucian said. "Now you know how the other side lives."

"I'm sure this area has a lot of history."

Lucian knew that was code for, "your house is old as sin," but he decided to take it as a compliment. "Ready to head out?"

"Not yet," Emma said. "Maybe we can talk a bit more?"

What did she want to talk about? "Sure."

Emma sat down on the couch as if it were her own home. Lucian did the same.

"Lucian," she said. "You're acting weird. If it's about your house, I don't care. I still like you as a person."

"I don't know what you're talking about."

She rolled her eyes. "Yeah, you do. Why is money such a big deal to you?"

Lucian almost defended himself, but stopped himself in time. "I know it's not fair." He paused to collect his thoughts. "I went to boarding school, right? Well, my mom couldn't really afford it, but I went anyway. The public school systems here are . . . well, awful. You need a private education to have a shot at a good government job."

"That was smart of her," Emma said.

"Yeah, it was," Lucian said. "But I also didn't fit in there. Compared to everyone else, I was dirt poor. I begged to go somewhere else. But with Mom on active duty, it wasn't possible. When it got out where I lived, the kids made fun of me. They were merciless. It's safe to say my dating life was nonexistent when I got a little older." He forced a laugh. "Guess I had to learn to get along without others."

"I'm sorry about that," Emma said. "I guess your reaction makes sense."

Had she really understood him so easily? Luisa would have somehow used his past to make him feel guilty. She had a knack for doing that.

"I appreciate that. I know it's not fair to you. I have no reason to think you're like that. Old habits die hard, I guess."

"I'm not like that. Yeah, my parents are rich, but how do you think it makes me feel when people think I'm too good for them? Some people are snotty, but I never grew up rich. I lived most of my life in a log cabin on a frontier world. I *knew* we were rich, but not *how* rich until we moved to L5. And even then, I was sick half the time."

"I'm sorry. I guess I rushed to judgment, there."

"It's fine," Emma said. "We understand each other, so let's move on." Her gaze went back to the picture. "Was your mom really away from home a lot?"

Lucian nodded. "Most of the time. I've had to take care of myself since age ten, basically. If not earlier."

She smiled, as if something had clicked into place. "So *that's* where you get it from. You've had to do it all yourself, huh?"

"Yeah." He didn't want to talk about it anymore.

"I can't imagine that," Emma said. "My parents have always been there for me. *Too there,* if you know what I mean."

No, he didn't know.

"This trip has been hard," she went on. "I'm missing them a lot. But what choice do I have? If I don't do this . . ."

"You're not used to being alone, are you?"

She shook her head, and tears came to her eyes. "No. I'm not. I wish I could be more like you, but it's just not me."

That explained why she had been so trusting of him from the beginning. That could have worked out badly for her. Anytime she had fallen, a net was always ready to catch her. On this ship, she saw *him* as her net.

The question was, could he accept that burden? He had so much to worry about. Then again, he couldn't deny how he felt when he was around her. As if he could forget himself for a moment, forget the pain of his past and just feel . . . warm. And hopeful. That was a dangerous feeling.

She was watching him now. How long had he been looking at her? But her smile was expectant, unjudging.

That scared him. Already, he could feel himself closing off. As good as that might feel to let her in, the mere thought of it set his heart racing.

Emma shifted in her seat. "Can I ask you something, Lucian?"

He cleared his throat, not trusting it to come out without cracking. "Sure."

She gave an embarrassed smile. "This will sound silly, but . . . if there's ever a time I need you, will you be there for me? No matter what?"

They were binding words. Lucian thought about them, and knew he couldn't answer this lightly.

"Absolutely."

"Would you think less of me for it?"

"No."

"What about the other way around?" she asked. "If you ever needed me for something, would you ask for help?"

The question was like a punch in the gut. He didn't need her help. He was fine on his own. Old words, old scripts. But they had served him well for years. Why give it up, just because he was doubting them now? He'd said and thought them so often that they were his truth.

Of course, he saw the point of her questions. And even if this new truth stared him in the face, the last thing he wanted was to admit it.

"You're a tricky one," Lucian said.

"Well?"

"If I needed help, then I would ask for it," Lucian said. "But only if I really needed it."

"Well, that's better than nothing."

Her face became sad and distant. Part of him wanted to scream at her that he *did* need her. But the words wouldn't come. He couldn't reprogram his mind after years of self-indoctrination.

His truths were unraveling, and he had no way to put them back in the proper boxes.

"Emma . . ." There was longing in his voice.

She looked up at him. "Yes?"

He stood and took her by the hand, and she stood with him. They faced each other there in his living room. He met her eyes, and felt himself lost. Safe, even. His heart thundered against his chest. He felt himself pulled toward her lips, her eyes slowly closing . . .

And then, she screamed.

At that moment, everything disappeared – the house, the ornaments, and Emma herself. Lucian opened his eyes to see the empty interior of his pod.

# 27

His heart racing, he immediately reached for his slate and called Emma. There was no answer.

Something was wrong.

He opened his pod and dashed out into the corridor. What had been her cabin number?

He ran to the starboard side of the ship, where he knew her to be. Was it 204, or 206?

He ended up knocking on both doors, but only 204 opened, revealing a middle-aged woman with short, brown hair. Her eyes widened immediately upon seeing him.

"Is Emma here?"

She blinked a few times, taken aback. "Why?"

He looked inside the cabin, and saw one of the pods was closed. "She might be in trouble. We need to open her pod."

"Did you do something to her?" she asked, her expression twisted with disgust. "I'll call the Captain."

"No! Just open the pod. Something's wrong."

The woman's eyes narrowed, as if she didn't believe him. Lucian lost patience and shouldered himself in. The woman let out a huff, running into the hallway and shouting for help.

Let her. He had to get to Emma.

He found the button to open the pod. Thankfully, it wasn't locked and it slid open.

To reveal Emma thrashing on her back and wailing in pain.

Lucian touched her shoulder, trying to hold her steady. She only screamed louder, the sound bloodcurdling in the cabin's dim confines. She slashed with her arm, scratching him on the neck. Lucian took a step back, tears in his eyes. How could he stop this? Might Vera know what to do?

Before he could think to get Vera, Emma's body went still. Coldness creeped across his skin. Others were shouting behind him, telling him to get off of her, as if *he* were the cause of this.

No. She couldn't be . . .

When he touched her arm, her skin was cold and clammy, and her complexion pale. There didn't seem to be any life in her. No life at all . . .

He was being pulled back. He fought against whoever was doing this, and was blind to them all. He had to get to Emma. He had to . . .

At that moment, she coughed, and her eyes fluttered open and found him.

"Lucian?"

But he was already out in the corridor and out of sight. A group of four men, two of the same male crew from before, were dragging him to the bridge.

This time, he was sure they would kill him.

———

THEY HAD BROUGHT him to the galley by now. Half or more of the ship's passengers had gathered to watch. They were shouting, arguing about what to do with him. Lucian fought to free himself, but as with Dirk and his lackeys, it was useless against so many.

"Stop! Stop right now!"

Emma broke through the crowd, stumbling as she did so.

"He didn't do anything!" she cried out. "He was just trying to help me!"

Surprisingly, people made way for her, but the two crewmen who had dragged him held on tightly.

"Lady, there's no need to defend his likes," the bald one said. "This time, he won't be a bother to anyone."

"Let him go, you idiot! I have epilepsy. He was just trying to help me."

Only when she started slapping at the crewman did the crowd let Lucian go and give him space.

Emma took Lucian by the shoulder. "What are you all looking at? Clear out!"

She led him back in the direction of her cabin. Such was her determination that no one stopped her, not even the crew.

"Are you okay?" she asked.

"Are *you* okay?

"Not really, no. At least that one wasn't so bad."

"Looked bad to me."

They finally reached her cabin, and the doors shut behind, leaving them in peace. Emma's cabinmate had gone, thankfully, and hopefully wouldn't be returning anytime soon.

"Thanks," she managed.

"I don't feel like I did anything," he said.

"It always helps to know someone is there."

She sat on her bed. She looked up at him, her eyes still fearful, as if reminiscent of the pain. Despite her brave face, Lucian knew she was still shaken.

"I can stay with you for a while," he said.

She nodded, making space for him on her bed.

"Come closer," she said.

When he pressed his body against hers, she was shaking.

She closed the door, shutting the two of them inside. As soon as they were alone, he put his arms around her.

"I hope this is okay."

She buried her face in his chest. "It's perfectly fine. It . . . feels nice to be held."

She murmured something against his chest, before turning her head to the side.

"Lucian . . ."

"Quiet, now," he said. "Just relax. Breathe."

She did as he said, seeming to calm. It took a few minutes, but her breathing slowed and her shaking ceased. Lucian thought she was asleep, but she spoke again.

"Lucian?"

"Yes?"

There was a long pause. "I'm sorry."

"For what?"

She touched him on the neck, where her scratch was still stinging.

"Don't be sorry for that. I got in a fight."

"Looks like you lost."

"Yes," he said, pulling her closer. "Maybe."

She looked up at him, smiling.

"Emma?"

"Hmm?"

"How often does that happen?"

"The seizures? As short as three days between, or as long as a month. Why?"

"I don't know. I wish we could make it go away."

"Same."

"There has to be a way to stop those seizures."

"There is. Training. Learning to stream."

How far away was that? Two weeks, at a minimum, plus the time it took to get to the Academy, get accepted, and begin lessons. And that would take time in itself, because one didn't learn to stream so easily.

"I don't know how I did it myself," Lucian said. "All I know is I got very angry, and it sort of happened on its own."

"I've been angry plenty of times. It hasn't helped."

"I don't know, then. I know nothing."

"Same."

One thing Lucian knew for sure. He didn't want her to feel an ounce of pain.

She pulled away from him, creating a bit of space. Her brown eyes watched him sadly.

"I want this as much as you do," she said. "But at the Academy, they don't allow it."

The words were like a dousing of ice water. "I'm confused."

She lowered her eyes, then nodded. "I am, too."

"We almost kissed in the sim. Or am I crazy?"

She looked up at him again. "I'm sorry for that. I'm just . . . it's hard saying all this, being close to you . . ."

"What are you so worried about, Emma?"

"Lucian, they could reject us for training if they think we're together."

He'd never thought about it that way. If that happened, then Emma would not get the training she needed. And if she couldn't train, then she would die.

"I'm being selfish," Lucian said.

"No, you're not. It's confusing. Maddening, even. And . . . I'm the one who was selfish. I just wanted you to hold me for a minute."

"That's not selfish."

"No. Maybe not."

Lucian wanted nothing more than to kiss her, then. And he knew that she wanted that. But how could they, when it could mean her death down the line?

But in the end, Emma was the one who drew forward, who

placed her lips on his. They seemed to melt into his. Their movement was desperate, wanting more than the restraint she had just been talking about.

He knew it was all but over in that moment. It didn't matter what anyone else said, what the rules were. They had to make their own path. That was his truth. But was it hers, too? That, he didn't know.

When they parted, they were both breathless. Lucian wanted more, but to make that move now felt false. Not after what she had told him.

Perhaps Emma was right. All they would be doing is torturing themselves.

"It will have to do," she said.

"It's not enough."

"No. It's not."

With a shaky hand, she opened the pod, but Lucian found he couldn't move. Emma's cabinmate was still gone, and she did not tell him to go.

In the end, it was Lucian who got out of the pod. Emma, with a force of will, let him go. Lucian stood and watched her a moment, never wanting her more than in that moment. How could they possibly make the rest of this trip together?

"Just ask me to stay, and I will," Lucian said.

Emma closed her eyes, tears coming out. "I want that more than anything. But ... we can't. We just can't."

At that moment, her pod door closed, and to Lucian, it felt as if he were being shut out forever.

# 28

LUCIAN SPENT the night tossing and turning, wondering whether what had happened was real.

It seemed a hundred times he reached for his slate to text Emma, or hear her voice, but with her shutting him out, she had made her intentions clear. He had to honor that.

He just lay there in a senseless daze, his mind muddled and unable to focus on anything but her. He hated the feeling, having to want and need someone so much. Had anyone ever had such an effect on him? It felt as if he could never be happy unless he was close to her again.

How could she do this to him? And then, he would remember. It was her life, or his infatuation.

It cleared things up, if only a little bit. The answer should have been simple, but it wasn't.

He couldn't bring himself to get out of his pod and get dinner. He just needed a few days to lay low, to think rationally again. That was how he'd gotten over Luisa. How would this be any different?

Eventually, he did force himself to go eat. He didn't even taste the food – which was just as well, since he ordered one of the options that was a part of his plan. When he returned to his pod, he tried to drown everything out with some new holos he hadn't seen yet.

He would think about reaching out for her, going back and forth on what he felt was right. But he couldn't muddy the waters anymore. Things were confusing enough as they stood.

The next morning was a little better. He still thought of her, but she no longer dominated his thoughts.

After a quick breakfast, he returned to his pod and decided to use one of Emma' extra sim pills. It was probably the most effective way to distract himself. He'd learned enough now to be fine doing it on his own.

He looked at the pill in his hand a long time before downing it. He closed his eyes, waiting for the neurological nanites to connect to his brain.

———

LUCIAN OPENED his eyes to find himself on South Shoal. He wasn't sure how he found himself here rather than the default lobby. There was still so much he didn't understand about sims that would only come from experience.

Lucian walked around the city, which was lighting up as the sun set. Despite the lack of sun, the air was warm and muggy, a welcome change from the cold, dry air of the ship.

As he walked, he allowed his thoughts to drift. Every thought worth its salt happened while walking. He couldn't walk far on the *Burung,* but here, he could walk as far as his six hours would allow. What he needed was time to think . . . and hopefully put Emma behind him for good.

Lucian wandered toward the Lincoln Mall. It floated on the ocean, a massive complex supported by antigrav masonry. Countless shops, apartments, restaurant, clubs, and bars filled its tens of floors. It appeared as it would have in real life, bursting with a plethora of humanity from all walks of life. Back home, Lucian did everything he could to avoid going here. But tonight, he liked the idea of losing himself in the crowds. There was comfort in being anonymous, unnoticed.

Lucian was riding up the escalators when he caught sight of a familiar figure. It couldn't be . . .

Vera stood watching him in her dark gray robe, her cowl thrown overhead. Her long white hair fell unfettered, and her dark eyes were intense. How had *she* gotten in here? He didn't know anything about closing servers, but something told him that such a thing would be no barrier to her.

Before he could call out, her form stole away, losing itself among the crowd.

He ran after her, catching up at a balcony with a commanding view of the dark Atlantic. Vera stood before the panorama of ocean, filled with dozens of shimmering islands. Those islands brimmed with towers and multicolored lights. Skycars shot between the islands and the mainland, while twice as many boats plied the waters.

Once Lucian stood a few meters behind her, she turned, her face visible by the lights of the mall. Every shadow and crevice on her expression seemed to hide secrets.

Emma's warnings returned to him. But under the weight of Vera's gaze, warnings meant nothing.

"How did you get in here?" Lucian asked. He hoped his voice didn't sound too accusatory.

Vera faced the ocean once again. "I'm not *here*. I don't enter these sims. I came here to find you. It's time we went over our previous lesson."

Lucian had almost forgotten about that. "How can you be in a sim if you didn't enter it?"

"Finding you is nothing to me. Psionic links don't care for distance, or even artificial simulation. The Manifold is every-where, and you would do well to remember that." She nodded toward the railing. "Stand here. I sense your trepidation. I assure you, you have nothing to fear from me."

There was nothing but to go closer. Lucian didn't like that she could read his thoughts so well.

Once he was standing by her side, she continued. "Have you thought about our conversation from last time? Have you come to terms with your identity? Have you discovered any new truths?"

Lucian shook his head. "Nothing's clear right now." He didn't go into details. Instead, he stared out at the water as he thought about what to say.

"You can't find truth without conflict. Conflict must test you, vet you, assail you. Whatever remains is truth. For the truth stands firm in the face of any onslaught. It avails you nothing if you earn your answers without blood. Without struggle. Without battle. For what would truth be then?"

"Nothing," Lucian answered.

Vera nodded her satisfaction. "Indeed."

"Which is all to say," Lucian went on, "that you can't tell me what's right and what's wrong. I have to figure it out for myself."

"I'm glad you've said that. A choice lies before you. You struggle with that choice even now. Conflict is testing you. Most people spend their lives running. It is the path of a mage, a *true* mage, to spring headlong into conflict. No easy thing, that. It goes against every fiber of our beings. Our egos thrive on faltering towers of white lies. We must be brave enough to let the storm test those lies."

Lucian remained silent.

"Living my truth has served me well," Vera continued. "We mages have a grave misfortune. If we want to live a long life, the Manifold forces us to live our truths without compromise. It is a lonely path, sometimes. And others will tell you that you're wrong. We must always face ourselves, our failings, our flaws, and temper them as we would any blade."

"How do I discover *my* truth?" Lucian asked. "Because everything feels confusing."

"That's simple," Vera said. "You must bleed."

Lucian didn't like that. He knew himself pretty well. But if Vera was right, then what he knew was a lie.

"I'm curious," Lucian said. "Why do you care about this? How does your teaching me help you?"

Vera gave the ghost of a smile. "An excellent question. One you should have asked a long time ago." She placed her hands on the railing, each gnarled and ancient. How old *was* she? He didn't dare ask. At that moment, she seemed old enough to have lived in a time before Gates, before the colonial diasporas. The thought was ridiculous. Even with current longevity treatments, no human could live beyond two hundred years.

"I sense great potential in you, Lucian. The Manifold has marked you, in a way I haven't seen in many years. In exactly *what* way . . . it has not made clear. But in time, it will make it plain. That's why I'm testing you and asking so many questions. It's meant to sharpen, not confuse." She shrugged. "Of course, my intuition could be nothing. Or it could be *everything*."

"What do you mean by that?"

"A lifetime of communing with the Manifold has taught me to trust my instincts. Instincts honed by trial and tribulation for decades. The Manifold means you to play an important role. What role that is, I can't say."

"How could you know that?"

"I *don't* know it," Vera said. "I sense it. And my senses rarely fail me." She watched him with intelligent eyes. "What is it you want, Lucian?"

How did she expect him to answer such an impossible question? Right now, he wanted off this ship. He wanted to *not* be a mage. He wanted Emma. As it stood, he could have none of them.

"I don't know. I see several paths. None of them likely."

Vera was silent for a moment, seeming to consider. "Choice is the affliction of youth. Thousands of paths spread before you. You imagine your life following each one. Every decision seems to bear the weight of a lifetime upon it. You become paralyzed with indecision. How can anyone decide, when another way might have been better?"

She'd crystallized his fears in a few sentences. "That's my problem. I see the good and the bad of every decision. It makes it impossible to choose."

"Remember that truth reveals itself in adversity. Ponder the easiest road, and be suspicious of it. For nothing is ever as easy as it seems. Something easy in the beginning incurs interest later. Choices shape and change us. They define character. Discovering oneself is a lifetime of choices. And you can't discover yourself by sitting in a room and pondering questions. That is the trouble with the Volsung Academy. They teach their students to make no choices at all. How can they ever learn if they are not allowed to make mistakes? The more courageous choice is to live your life, to make your mistakes, and live with as much honesty as you can. You may not see it, Lucian, but we mages have a gift. Our biggest enemy, in the end, is the one standing in our own shoes and staring back at us from the mirror. The easiest person to deceive is ourselves."

There was a long silence as Lucian tried to make sense of her words. They were a jumble, not seeming to connect.

"I'm deceiving myself, then," he said. "Why am I not surprised?"

"We deceive ourselves every minute of every day," Vera said. "Self-deception has a cost. The danger is when our lies become our truths, and we can no longer tell the difference."

"You say a dishonest life causes the fraying," Lucian said. "If that's true, then why are you the only mage in the galaxy who seems to think that?"

"A lifetime of experience has informed my knowledge, as it

has my instincts. Those of us mages who live to an old age have nurtured a deep-rooted truth over a lifetime. We have convinced ourselves, to our core, of who we are and what we want, and make no apologies for it. The Manifold is ultimate truth. But there is a paradox within the Manifold, because as the ultimate truth, it *defines* truth. And if we mages can manipulate the Manifold, it means we can manipulate truth." She smiled in triumph. "The greatest mystery is that there is not one truth, but many. Sometimes, truths even contradict. At the basest level of reality, where Manifold meets Shadow, things are and are not. Fervent belief is the fulcrum upon what mages define *what is*. That, we call magic."

Lucian's mind was bending by this point. "So, what are you saying?"

"That magic is belief. When we stream the Manifold, we do what should be impossible. We change reality by centering ourselves on the Fulcrum of Creation. That is how we see things without eyes. How we move things without touching them. How we trick base matter into believing it's something else. Create heat where there was only a cold void. We have only scratched the surface of what is possible. During the Mage War, the mages controlled the power of creation itself. But they were capable of so much more. Only their beliefs limited them." Vera was quiet for a long moment. "With belief, we shifted the galaxy. *That* was how close we were to winning."

There it was. What Lucian had feared, and what Emma had suspected.

She was a Free Mage.

"You *fought* with them."

Vera gave a slow nod. "I did. But that is a tale for another time. I was younger, then. Brasher. And I committed many errors I would not have today. And I have many regrets. Would knowledge have changed things?" She shrugged. "I can only wonder. Fifty years after the death of Xara Mallis, I ask myself what it was all for. Did we shift reality with our beliefs, our magic? Or did we simply not dare enough?"

Lucian was too afraid to ask anything more. Vera *was* dangerous, and he'd gotten mixed up with her. If she was a part of the war, then she was one of the few who had gotten away. Someone who had eluded bounty hunters for fifty years was someone worthy of fear. Those most loyal to Xara Mallis had died with her on Isis. If that was so, then how was Vera still alive? Perhaps she betrayed Mallis. Perhaps she had run when she saw the inevitable.

And what was the nature of Vera's regret? Starting the war, or committing the tactical errors that had ended with the Mages' defeat?

"I guess being old and experienced doesn't make you right," Lucian said.

The words slipped out of his mouth before he was even aware of them. Foolish, that. But Vera only gave her ghostly smile that gave Lucian the creeps.

"You're right," she said. "That's where we get a certain expression: *There isn't any fool like an old fool.* Am I that old fool? Sometimes. True knowledge begins with admitting you know nothing."

"Socrates," Lucian said.

Vera nodded. "What do you think that means?"

"I don't know."

*"Think,"* Vera said.

Well, if she wanted an answer, he would give one. "Nobody knows everything. If we assume we're wise, it blinds us to the truth staring us right in the face."

Vera was quiet, her face thoughtful. To Lucian, she seemed more ancient than ever.

"What do you think I'm trying to teach you?"

The answer came to him at once. "You're teaching me to teach myself."

"I couldn't have put it better myself. That said, I can teach you nothing. Despite a lifetime of learning, I can still be wrong. In that vein, this instinct I have about your future could *also* be wrong. I could run my mouth until the end of time, and it would avail you nothing. Unless you thought there was something in there worth applying. If knowledge imparted is not put to use, and does not cause self-reflection, then all is vanity."

In the following lull, he knew he had to ask the question that had been bothering him.

"Were you really part of the Free Mages, Vera?"

If that question surprised her, she gave no sign of it. "The Free Mages are defunct. I'm sure some sanctums still exist, but if so, they are a shadow of their former strength. Their teachings lost veracity at the end of the Mage War." She stared into the distance, her thoughts seeming to go back decades. "Long ago, I found power and truth in their teachings. The Academy Mages exiled us for our beliefs. Xara Mallis learned the Transcends' plan, to turn Psyche into a prison world for unorthodox mages."

So, Psyche hadn't been developed by the League at all, but by mages. Could that really be true?

"So, she shared this information. More mages flocked to her banner. They were committed not only to their own survival, but to seeking a final cure to the fraying. It was . . . a noble cause, if doomed from the start. It's not known who struck first. But the first attack led to the beginning of the war that consumed the Worlds for the next decade."

Put in that light, the Free Mages' motivations seemed more understandable. Even if they had started nobly, it didn't excuse what they became.

Vera continued. "The Free Mages emphasized developing an individual journey to discovering the Manifold, one where magic isn't limited. The Transcends, in contrast, believe in crushing your humanity to save you from the fraying. They preach an absence of feeling, so that magic is divorced from human emotional influence. It is an impossible ideal. I know, for I tried that way, once. It is the reason I warn you against studying there. I have been down that path. When I freed myself from their teachings, only then did I discover my own truth. And that truth has set me free."

"And you discovered that by joining the Free Mages?"

"Yes," Vera said. "For a time. My path diverged from theirs toward the end of the war. But I no longer walk that path, for I've forged my own." She seemed to think a moment before speaking again. "You must examine yourself, in silence and in solitude. Technology is a trap; there's a fiction that the GalNet can answer your every query. No. You must search within. *Find* your power. *Find* your will. As I've found mine. Whatever wisdom I have stems from self-reflection and quiet inner study. *That* is what the Manifold rewards: courage to live a different sort of life. A life dedicated to truth, not convenience."

It was a harsh lesson. A lesson Lucian was not ready to accept. "The Volsung Academy won't teach me any of that?"

"The problem will be the opposite," Vera said. "They *will* teach you. They will drive everything you think you know right out of your head. Then, they will replace it with everything that's theirs. There will be no room for *you*. They justify it by saying it's for the greater good of the Worlds, but who defines that greater good?" Vera watched for a reaction. "To me, it seems the Transcends are the only ones with that privilege. Their ideal pupil is a soulless husk. A non-threat. An insular, unquestioning mage that will never ignite a galaxy."

Lucian understood little of what she was talking about, but a lot of it *felt* right. But he still wasn't sure of her. Not after what she'd told him about the Free Mages.

"You've given me a lot to think about."

"That is my only wish. Reflect on it. Solitude is self-medicating. Spend more time in it, and less time on your slate and these simulations." She faced away. "This is what I leave you with."

And like that, she was gone.

Lucian stared out at the dark ocean. How many years ago had Vera gone for training at the feet of the Transcends? Such a thing was hard to imagine. Was she his age at the time, or older? Certainly, it was before the Mage War. He knew the Volsung Academy was over a century old, so it could not have been before that.

He stayed a little longer on the balcony, enjoying the Atlantic Ocean. The warm air, the smell of salt, the whir of skycars and speedboats . . . he took the image in, imprinting it into his memory.

It might be his last time to see it, if only in a false reality.

# 29

In the next few days, Lucian didn't speak to Emma, nor did he even see her. He didn't come out of his pod, except to shower, use the bathroom, or eat. But he never ran into Emma in the galley or corridors. Several times he reached for his slate to check on her, but decided against it. She had wanted space, and he still wanted to honor that.

When three days had gone by, his worry was too much. He was about to text her, when a message from her came in.

*Dirk is causing trouble.*

Great. Just what he needed. *What kind of trouble?*

*I caught a bit of it at the galley . . .*

She attached a video, which projected onto the pod's interior screen.

Dirk was standing in the galley, a bandage wrapped around his eyes. At least half the passengers were sitting at the tables, and hanging on his every word. Believer Horatia was among them.

The projection began midsentence. ". . . only a matter of time until he does it to one of you, too."

223

Kasim let out an angry shout, which only seemed to roil the crowd further.

"He attacked me," Dirk went on. "No warning. My friends tried to stop him, but he pinned them with his mind! We were powerless. He burst my eyes from the inside out!" Dirk's voice became choked. "If not for my friends, I would have died." His thin lips twitched in agitation, but then his expression hardened. He cut a pathetic figure. If things didn't get under control soon, things could get violent.

"When I learned Captain Miller set this dangerous criminal free, I couldn't believe it."

Lucian texted Emma back as the video played. *When was this?*

*Just a few minutes ago.*

Dirk blathered on and on. How mages were a bane upon the Hundred Worlds. How it was only a matter of time until someone on board woke up dead in their sleep. How even Emma herself had been attacked. The shouts of the crowd had drowned out Emma's own protests.

Watching his vitriol, Lucian's blood boiled.

After a particularly impassioned part of his rant, Dirk swelled under the attention.

"To the bridge!" he said. "Let the captain know what we think of his justice! Lock the psycho up!"

They began to chant the words, "Lock the psycho up!" over and over. After ten seconds of this, their chanting became weaker. The camera panned upward. It focused on a new figure watching from the second deck. Vera, standing in her customary gray cloak, watched the proceedings in silence. She stood like a bird of prey eyeing her domain, an effect only accentuated by her sharp nose.

Dirk seemed to know something was wrong, but he did not turn and face upward until Vera spoke.

"You are blind. Not only in your eyes, but your beliefs."

There was dead silence before Dirk recovered. "You're that creepy old woman next door to me, aren't you? What do you want?"

Vera's stare was icy as she took in the crowd. "This fool is lying to you. I saw what happened that night. He's a little boy after revenge, after he stuck his nose into business that was never his."

"She's a liar," Dirk spat. "She's friends with the mage. She *has* to be a psycho, too!"

She gave an amused smile, a smile that said she had the upper hand. Everyone watched her, as if hypnotized. She commanded an aura of respect, authority, and even fear. The sniveling Dirk couldn't match her gravitas.

"And what if I am a mage? Does my testimony bear no importance because of that? My cabin is next to yours, as you said. I not only saw what happened that night, but I heard. You and your friends hooted like jackals. You attacked a helpless young man on his way to Volsung to seek a cure for his affliction. A young mage who had done nothing to threaten or harm you. You pulled him behind your door. You beat him without mercy. He had no way of protecting himself, except, I imagine, the only way he knew how. With his mind. That is *your* foolishness. Why should any of us sympathize with a mouse who challenged a viper?"

"You *are* one of them," Kasim challenged. "I knew it!"

"Yes," Vera said. "You're a quick one, aren't you? For the rest of his life, my student will have to deal with the likes of you. Only under the greatest duress did he opt to defend himself. A harsh lesson for you . . . but sometimes, pain is the only language a fool understands. And it would seem, even now, the designation of fool is too kind a description for you."

Her student? Had Vera lied to cover for him, or did she think he had actually agreed to be her student?

"Stop this rabble-rousing at once," Vera commanded. "I

haven't the time or patience for it. I don't wish to involve myself any further. And if there *is* any more drama, you and your friends will answer to me."

With a swirl of her cloak, she stalked off, leaving the galley in silence. The video ended.

Lucian watched it again, hardly able to believe it. Vera had not only threatened Kasim and Dirk, but had revealed herself as mage. She wasn't stupid. She *couldn't* be. But neither did she seem to care.

What did it all mean? Why had she done it?

*Just finished,* Lucian sent to Emma. *I don't know what to say.*

*What's this about you being her student?*

*Let's meet up somewhere. The galley, if it's cleared out. I don't know what she meant by that.*

*I can check to see if the coast is clear.*

Five minutes later, she sent a message back.

*Meet me in the observatory. It's empty.*

Lucian hadn't been there yet, so he consulted the deck plan on his slate. Within the minute, he was out of the cabin.

———

THE OBSERVATORY WASN'T FAR, down a short corridor sternward away from the second deck cabins. Lucian walked with purpose. He didn't want anyone bothering him on the way, but the gesture proved pointless, because he didn't run into anyone.

He turned into the observatory, a small room with a view-port taking up an entire wall. Emma stood before it, her form framed by stars. Lucian's throat clenched for a moment. It was the first he'd seen her since they'd shared the pod.

There was no actual telescope in here. A small touchscreen took up one of the corners. The telescope itself must have been elsewhere, while the viewscreen was just a projection.

Emma smiled as Lucian stood at her side. Was that nervousness, or was she simply glad to see him?

"How've you been?" she asked.

Lucian shrugged. "I've had better days."

Emma sidestepped that sentence. "What did she mean by you becoming her student, Lucian?"

Lucian shook his head. "I never agreed to that. I've only been learning things from her." Her face was unreadable, reflecting the light of the stars. At her lack of response, he went on. "Either way, at least we don't have to worry about Dirk now."

"You kept that from me."

"I told you we'd talked. And we spoke again a few days ago."

"She's interested in you," Emma said. "What else have you left out?"

He tried to ignore the edge in her voice. What did she care, anyway? She was the one who had wanted more distance.

But it would be better to keep the peace. "There's been something new."

Emma listened as he told her about his and Vera's latest meeting. She only interrupted him when Lucian got to the part about the Free Mages.

"So, she *is* a Free Mage."

"*Was*," Lucian corrected. "At least, according to her."

"She's dangerous, Lucian."

"*I'm* dangerous," he said. "Remember what happened to Dirk? She revealed herself to the entire ship. Either she's very brave, or very stupid. And she's definitely not stupid . . ."

"It proves my point. It gives me chills to even think about you talking to her. Someone who was part of the Free Mages, on this very ship!"

She became distant for a moment. Lucian was unsure how to continue.

"She's taught me a few things, but I never agreed to be her student."

"Clearly, the both of you are on different pages."

"Why do you care so much? What makes you think the Transcends know what they're talking about over her? Magic isn't black and white, Emma. *We* choose how to use it. How we choose to use it influences how it manifests itself in the world."

She watched him, seemingly stunned. Lucian himself was shocked. Where had all *that* come from? It sounded like something Vera would have said.

Lucian went on stubbornly. "If Vera has answers, we'd be fools not to listen. Vera even admits the Free Mages had it wrong. And all that was fifty years ago. Are you saying she couldn't have changed in that time? Clearly, whatever she's doing is working."

Emma no longer watched him, instead staring out into space with a vacant expression. It looked as if she hadn't heard a word he'd said.

"I'm sorry, Emma," he said. "I was being too harsh."

"You can't have both, Lucian," she said. "I feel like I'm losing you."

*Losing* him? Was she changing her mind now? "What do you mean?"

"What I mean is, you can't have both. The Transcends have their way, and Vera has her own. The Loyalist mages were right, Lucian. *They* stopped the Free Mages from turning the rest of humanity into slaves. Stopped them from burning the Worlds to ashes. Shouldn't we dedicate ourselves to that?"

"I intend to. But I also intend to learn as much as I can here."

She shook her head. "Don't you see? You can't follow Vera *and* expect the Academy to be okay with it. She's already shifting your attitudes and beliefs."

He now saw what she meant. "I didn't have any to begin with. I know nothing, Emma."

"I don't, either," she said. "It's just I don't trust her. And I want *you* to trust *me*. You can only choose one side, Lucian. Which will it be?"

The question silenced him. Deep down, he knew she was right. Did Vera already think of him as her student? If he intended to go onto the Academy, he'd have to put an end to that.

A choice lay before him. He could either follow her, or continue on to Volsung.

What he didn't want to tell Emma was that he was considering Vera's offer. The Academy was the path expected of him. What made the most sense. It was the one most mages would take, given the chance.

"Well?" Emma asked. "What are you thinking?"

Lucian shook his head. "I don't know. I see your point, Emma. I do. Even if Vera might be dangerous, she also makes a lot of sense."

"I don't understand," Emma said. "Following her would not only be putting yourself at risk. It would be illegal."

Yes, there was that, too. As soon as he no longer went to the Academy, he'd be considered a rogue mage. How long would it be before Academy mages were sent to hunt him? *Would* they ever hunt him?

"The Volsung Academy can teach you properly," Emma said. "This Vera . . . we know hardly *anything* about her, but knowing she was a Free Mage should be enough." She took his hand. Despite himself, Lucian felt his resolve soften. "The answer is simple, Lucian. Come with me. Please. If you follow her, you'll be going down a dark path."

She made it sound so reasonable. Vera had wrapped her motives in mystery. Whatever Vera's story, whatever her flaws, she did have one thing going for her. She was speaking from a place of honesty and experience, at least by Lucian's estimation. Of course, it could all be some grand lie, but to what purpose? Why would someone of her stature be helping him, unless she believed he had an important role to play?

Vera knew things. And she could teach those things to Lucian. Did the Volsung Academy, or other academies like it, have a monopoly on magic instruction? The League of Worlds seemed to think so. Then again, just because something was a law didn't mean it was right. Blindly following orders could be just as dangerous.

Then again, the Volsung Academy had tradition. It had existed since the first mages emerged over a century ago. Lucian didn't doubt that they knew things. Perhaps even more than Vera. It would be impossible to say without going to the Academy himself.

But there was also no guarantee of acceptance. Vera, at least, seemed open to training him and not rejecting him. Then again, if Vera believed he was capable, didn't that mean the Transcends would think the same thing? That wasn't necessarily true, but there was a decent chance it was.

Following Vera would mean leaving Emma behind. Despite everything that had happened, that was something Lucian didn't want.

Each choice was safe in its own way, and dangerous in its own way. There were too many unknowns. Emma added another layer of complication. It was clear that *she* didn't want him to follow Vera. Why would she care, unless she felt *something* for him?

He needed to learn more. He needed to speak with Vera again, and figure this out once and for all.

# 30

LUCIAN MADE the long walk across the entire ship. His stomach fluttered once he reached Vera's cabin, right next door to Dirk's. He hesitated only a moment before knocking. He stood out there at least a minute, and almost turned around to leave, when the door finally opened.

Inside, Vera sat on the corner of her bed, seeming to have just come out of meditation.

"Yes?" she asked.

"Can we talk?"

After a moment, she gave a slow, regal nod. Lucian stepped inside, entering a space as large as his own cabin, but with only one queen-sized bed. A spacious viewport looked out on a view of the inner band of the Milky Way, a glowing stream of starlight. His stomach seemed to sink as he stepped forward, as if gravity had doubled. The air within was warm, almost balmy, laced with the aroma of incense. A leather-bound journal and an ink pen sat on a nearby desk next to several small books, though the rest of her things must have been kept in the spacious wardrobe. He'd hoped to learn a bit more about her from her things. Was she hiding them, or merely tidy?

"How might I be of service?" she asked.

It would be best to cut right to the chase. "What did you mean about me being your student?"

If that question fazed her, she didn't show it. "I suppose your friend told you something about that?"

He nodded. "I wanted to make sure we were on the same page. I agreed to learn from you, but not to be your student."

Her eyes turned cold. "I do not make a practice of teaching those who are not my students. I have *chosen* you to be my student, to let you in on secrets many mages would kill to discover. More than that, I fear we do not have a choice in the matter. The Manifold has marked you, and if the Transcends get a hold of you, it could prove disastrous."

There it was, stated with boldness that took Lucian aback. She didn't *want* him to go to Volsung, and wanted him to herself . . . whatever her reasons.

He would have to answer very carefully.

"I'm . . . honored by that. You know far more than I could ever learn myself."

She watched him, as if waiting for the other shoe to drop. "Then what is the issue?"

"I'm not sure. I guess I don't know much about you, yet. Your motives. Your plans for me. If I knew these things, the decision would be easier."

"I see. Well, I can't fault you for that." She sat straighter on the bed. "The Manifold works its fate upon us all. Despite our own inclinations, the fate of mages is written in the stars. It is far easier to accept that fate than to fight against it."

Speaking in riddles again. "What do you mean?"

"The Manifold has revealed your future to me. I see you there. You *are* my student. My Psion. The conclusion seems obvious. The Manifold meant us to meet each other aboard this ship."

How could that possibly be true? "You did that with magic?"

She gave a slow nod. "Prophecy is a tricky subject, prone to misinterpretation. I am not immune. Many mages do not believe in its efficacy. But it has its uses. I am the teacher, and you are the student. I don't know the reason yet, only that one day, it will be." Vera shrugged. "Of course, I cannot force you to do something against your will." She gave a small, almost cunning, smile. "But the Manifold can."

"I don't buy that. I hardly even know you, so why would I become your student? To be honest, your past concerns me a bit. You say you've changed, but how can I know that?"

"My involvement with the Free Mages is a closed chapter of my life," Vera said. "It is right to question me, and it is also right to not take what I say on faith. I wouldn't expect anything less. As far as *why* you would follow me, you must examine yourself for that answer. Let silence and solitude be your guide, not me. But if you want practical reasons, then they are as follows. I can train you to use the Manifold. I can teach you to listen for it, to stream its power, to keep the fraying at bay, better than any of the Transcends. For it is not they who would teach you. Not in your first years at the Academy. It would be their Talents, who are far less experienced. Besides, following the will of the Manifold is far easier than going against it. Only once have I felt a fate so marked as yours ..."

Lucian couldn't help but be curious. "Whose?"

Vera was silent for a long time, as if realizing she'd said too much. Her expression darkened. The memory could not be a happy one.

"That is a tragedy, perhaps, for another day," she said. "When you're ready."

"I'm not sure I ever *will* be," Lucian said. "It only makes me think you're hiding something."

"Be that as it may, I reserve the right to hold back lessons you are not ready for. You are a child in the ways of magic. It is for you to discover its many possibilities and configurations.

Not the darker secrets that have brought down mightier mages than you."

That only served to set fire to Lucian's curiosity, but he knew that might have been Vera's purpose.

"So, what's after this?" he asked. "Are you going to Volsung, too?"

"I aim to continue my work, whatever your decision. Work always goes on. My next ship is bound for Halia. I will tell you more, contingent upon your decision."

Lucian knew he would learn a lot with her, and travel to many interesting places. But the mere idea of it was unimaginable to him, whether Vera saw it in the future or not. *Nothing* could control his future. Not Vera, and not even the Manifold.

And leaving Emma behind felt like betrayal. There was something more there, whether she was willing to admit it or not.

"Go on to Volsung, if you feel you must," she said. "The Manifold means you for something much greater than being a Talent at the Volsung Academy. Whatever your choices, it will force you down that path. Of that, I'm sure."

"Then my choice doesn't matter, if I'm being forced down a certain path," Lucian said. "What's the point of this decision? I should just go with my gut."

"Sometimes, what seems sane and logical is anything but. Remember what I told you last time; seek silence, and listen for the Manifold. Let its truth direct you, let it hone and sharpen you. It will reveal the right path. I would encourage you to—"

"—meditate and think about it?"

She nodded. "Yes. There is still time for you to decide. We have about a week left on the voyage. You've grown, even if you haven't felt it. Something tells me that Dirk and his ilk will no longer prove any difficulty for you, even had I not stepped in. You have risen above it, have become stronger through force of will. It is but one tiny step on the path to true strength. Whatever your future path, you must stand strong." Her attention turned from him as she gazed out the cabin viewport. "Go. Think on what I've said."

He went to the door, her voice stopping him before he stepped through.

"Lucian."

He turned to look at her. She regarded him coolly.

"Just because I see your future, doesn't mean that future can't change. You can still make the wrong decision. And you can still die by those decisions."

"Why are you telling me this?"

"Because, Lucian . . . I believe you might die if you go down to Volsung. I won't know for sure until your path is set."

Lucian watched her for a moment, fighting the anxious twist in his stomach.

"I'll let you know my decision."

# 31

In the corridor, Lucian ran across the last person he expected to see. Dirk.

Dirk held out his slate, which was giving automated commands to guide him back to his cabin.

Lucian moved to the side, allowing him to pass. Dirk was none the wiser to his presence.

Suddenly, Dirk pulled to a stop, swiveling his head around. "Who's there? I heard something."

Lucian could keep walking without identifying himself. In fact, that was what he knew he should do. But something compelled him to speak.

"It's me, Dirk."

Dirk stiffened. "You? What are you doing here?"

"What? No psycho this time?"

Dirk's face blanched.

"Don't worry," Lucian said, taking a few steps forward. "I won't hurt you."

"Stay right where you are."

"I'll do what I want." Lucian looked Dirk over. What a

pathetic figure he cut. He almost felt bad for him, until he remembered having to spend ten days in the brig because of him. And until he remembered the senseless cruelty of the beatings.

"Where are your friends, Dirk? Not worth following you anymore?"

"Leave me alone. Don't make me get Captain Miller involved."

"Not until I've said my piece."

He let out a sigh. "Fine. I can hardly escape you, can I?"

Why did he get the feeling he'd just be wasting his breath? "You did it to yourself, Dirk. I don't know why you are the way you are. I just wanted you to know that, in case you're too stupid. This is all your fault."

Dirk took a step forward, clenching a useless fist. "If I had my eyes right now . . ."

"But you don't. And you never will again. Not without organ growth surgery, at least."

"Found your mouth now, have you? You wouldn't be saying this if I had my sight."

"And you would have never come after me without your dogs. Let's call it even."

He grunted. "I thought you were the noble type. Guess not. Kicking someone while they're down."

Lucian smiled. "Let's say I learned from the best. I treat my friends well, but if you wrong me, I'll never forget."

"Wonderful. Now piss off."

"Have a nice life, for whatever it's worth."

Dirk brushed past him with only a growl.

Lucian didn't know what he had expected. Having a rational conversation with Dirk was setting the bar too high.

Whatever closure he'd been hoping for, clearly it wasn't happening.

All he could do was wash his hands of it and move on with his life.

———

THE DAYS PASSED with Lucian still not knowing what to do. Neither did he see Emma. He needed time to think without the influence of either person.

He meditated as Vera had suggested. But all he could feel was anxiety and doubt pulsating deep within. He didn't trust that Vera could see his future. Emotions about Emma, worries about his mother, all intermixed, making it impossible to make a clear decision. Wherever Lucian went throughout his day, an undercurrent of anxiety moved with him, impossible to escape.

Volsung appeared in the galley viewports. It was small, yes, but every passing hour it grew larger. Seeing it grow brighter day by day only reminded Lucian of the choice he had to make. The ship was already slowing for arrival, a process which would take several days.

Vera had warned him against seeking training at the Academy. But Vera had also told him to think for himself. But how could he make a clear decision unless he saw the Academy?

There were two sides to every story. It would be unfair for Lucian to follow Vera without seeing what the Transcends had to offer. Then again, if he chose that path, he might miss out on the opportunity of a lifetime.

It was simply impossible to know.

Out the viewports, Lucian could see the blue orb of Volsung, the brightest object in space by far outside its parent star. They would be arriving tomorrow morning. In a day, he could be down on that bright dot, on his way to the Volsung Academy. Or would he be forgoing that to train with Vera, who had already shown him so much?

Well, he still hadn't learned *how* to stream magic yet. It

seemed as if Vera was trying to build a foundation strong enough to support it.

"Have you decided?"

Emma had come out of nowhere, breaking him from his thoughts as she sat at his table. Just having her so close was enough to unbalance him.

"I don't know yet."

"Well, how can I convince you?"

Even as he smiled, he felt hollow. "I don't know that, either. I can't think straight. I feel like Vera is a sure thing. I know what I'm getting. The Academy?" He shook his head. "They might reject me, for all I know."

"What does your gut tell you?"

"I don't know." He was starting to sound like a broken record. "I see the pros and cons of each decision."

"Does it have anything to do with me?"

Now, where was *that* coming from? "No. Why?"

"I don't know. Maybe I spoke too soon. Too . . . harshly."

He hated the feeling of hope building up in his chest. What did she mean by that?

She continued. "I miss you, Lucian."

Part of him wanted to hurl blame at her for that. But he couldn't do that to her. Not with the way she was looking at him.

"I've missed you, too."

"When I seized, you were there for me. I've been unfair to you. I've done a lot of thinking over the past few days. I kept telling myself I was right. And maybe I was. But whatever happened doesn't *feel* right." She watched him with her soft, brown eyes. "I'm sorry."

"No need to be sorry," he said. "I understand where you're coming from."

"Yeah," she said. "I shouldn't blame myself for not wanting to die."

"Don't say that," Lucian said. "We'll get you down there."

At that moment, Lucian felt the tension melt from his shoulders. The clouds lifted, and the path forward was clear.

The path forward was to Volsung. Maybe he was consigning himself to death, as Vera had suggested. But somehow, deep down, he knew it was the right choice.

"I'm going to Volsung."

Emma closed her eyes in relief. "I'm so glad, Lucian. I'm sorry. I never wanted to keep you at a distance. "I'm . . . just scared, I guess."

"Scared of what?"

"Of what might happen." She shifted in her seat. "I mean, aren't *you*? How could you *not* be?"

"Of course I'm afraid. But we can't live our lives in fear. And we can't control what happens, no matter how much we try."

"Maybe I was just fooling myself. I don't know if I can do it alone." She looked at him, her eyes seeming to ask for something. "I feel so much better knowing I won't have to go there alone."

"I'll be there, Emma. Right by your side. You won't have to be afraid of anything."

She smiled. "A pleasant lie."

"I'm not lying."

"I know that. It's just you believe that so fervently. The lie is not to me, but yourself."

"I don't know what you mean."

"That I won't have to be afraid of anything. There are going to be things down on that world so foreign to us. The training will be the hardest thing we ever have to go through. And I won't lie, there is the chance they judge us untrainable."

"So, I have to be crazy to come with you."

She nodded. It seemed she was willing to admit that much. "I don't know why, Lucian. But I know it's important that you come. You'll be missing something if you don't."

"There is a problem, though."

"What?"

"My account from Earth hasn't synced with this system. It might fix itself once I'm on Volsung-O, but I'm not sure."

"Do you need help?"

It wounded his pride, but Lucian made himself nod. "I need some creds to get down to the surface. I can pay you back as soon as my account syncs up."

Emma shook her head. "I can get you a shuttle ticket, no problem. Don't worry about paying back."

Lucian was about to protest, but in the end, he decided to let her help him. It was more than he would have allowed a few days ago. "Okay. Thanks."

"So, I can book you the same shuttle to Karendas, easy. I can let the Talent know you'll be coming with me at the spaceport."

"And they'd have no problem with that?"

"I'll send a message on ahead. I'm so glad it's settled. In a few days, we'll be students of the Academy!"

It was hard not to feel her excitement. Even if the future was uncertain, being committed made him feel much more at peace.

Emma retrieved her slate and projected a holo of the cylindrical Volsung Orbital. The holo showed where the *Burung* would dock, as well as the route they would take to the shuttle.

"We'll get off here and head to the shuttle airlock," she explained. "The shuttle will take us to Karendas." At her explanation, the projection switched to the planet itself. It zoomed in on a small island in a vast ocean. "We'll get off at the spaceport there, and link up with Talent Khairu. She'll take us to the docks, where we'll get on the Academy's ship. The passage across the ocean should take a few standard days. Volsung local, it'll be just over one day."

Lucian had read that a day on Volsung was fifty-four hours

and thirty minutes. He wondered how sleep schedules worked down there.

The two looked out the viewports at the approaching blue orb, a shining sapphire in the void. It was the future. A future they would be facing together.

A new world. A new gravity. And most of all, a new life.

## 32

THERE WAS one thing left to do.

Lucian went to Vera's cabin and knocked. As with last time, he had to wait a while. But eventually, the door slid open, revealing her sitting on the corner of the bed. It was as if she had sat there the entire time over the past few days without moving. For all Lucian knew, she might have.

She stared out the viewport, where Volsung hung a few million kilometers away, a bright orb of blue.

"Come in, Lucian."

Somehow, Lucian felt as if she knew his decision. Her manner was colder than usual, and she did not look at him directly.

"You've decided on Volsung."

She said it with careful neutrality, without a hint of animosity. When she turned to look at him, her expression seemed more appraising than judgmental.

"It's the right choice," he said. "I can't explain why."

"You know it to your core? Is this the direction the Manifold is leading you?"

Lucian nodded. "I don't know about that. But I'm at peace with the decision."

"It's like that, sometimes," Vera said. "The Academy will challenge you. In some ways expected, in other ways not."

"Cryptic as always."

"You must discover what those challenges are on your own. Education always begins with the learner."

"Do you think me incapable?"

"Far from it. It may be that you're not ready for the training I could provide. That shouldn't surprise me, but the Manifold is one step ahead of us. Always."

"I see the value of your insight, but for whatever reason, I'm not ready."

"You see the value?" She chuckled. "There we disagree, but I understand your perspective, limited as it is." She gave that ghost of a smile again, which made Lucian's skin go cold. "Similarly, you don't see the value of what the Transcends are offering, and yet you're going anyway."

"They have a tradition," Lucian said. "Over a century of teaching mages."

"That they do. Whether they teach magic well is another conversation entirely. But again, you will learn. If my senses are correct, your journey will not end in that place. However, I've been wrong before."

A silence lingered, which Lucian finally broke. "Well . . . thank you. I've learned a lot. I'm grateful for that."

She gave a regal nod. With that single movement, Lucian thought she had a curious sense of majesty. A quality he couldn't put into words. Once again, he found himself wondering about her past. He knew he'd only scratched the surface.

"Who are you, exactly?"

She was quiet for a moment. "Go, Lucian. You've made your choice. Now, you must live with it."

Lucian went.

———

WHEN EMMA CONFIRMED HIS TICKET, Lucian kept his eyes off her slate screen. He didn't want to see the price. It was the most money he'd let anyone spend on him other than family. Already, his mind was working out ways to pay her back if his wallet never synced. He would have to consider that later.

The *Burung* was minutes away from docking at Volsung Orbital. The blue planet dominated the viewports. Everyone was here in the galley, even Dirk, standing alone and friendless against the wall. Paul and Kasim seemed to have shown their true colors. Now that their ringleader had shown weakness, they could no longer follow him. It was a satisfying ending to Lucian.

A crewman stood next to Dirk to assist him, but Dirk's face wore a scowl while his arms were crossed. That bandage was still wrapped around his eyes. In a few minutes, Lucian wouldn't have to worry about him anymore. The thought alone was enough to make him smile.

"What's so funny?" Emma asked.

"Nothing," he said. "Just thought of something funny."

"Almost there," she said. "Are you ready?"

"Sure am."

Lucian hadn't heard anything from the captain about the incident with Dirk. The captain had warned the lawyers might get involved, but he didn't have time for that. Lucian couldn't get off this ship and down to the surface fast enough.

Outside the viewports, there wasn't a hint of land in sight – only boundless blue ocean and white cloud cover. Volsung was an ocean world; in the Godsdeep, it went down to a depth of over twenty kilometers. As the planet rotated, a band of gray storm clouds over the planet's tropics flashed with lightning. Probably one of the planet's famous super hurricanes.

Every passing minute, Volsung loomed ever larger. Lucian had his luggage ready. Emma only had a heavy backpack, which she seemed to have no trouble toting around. He wondered if she'd be able to handle it in Volsung's higher gravity. Grav-lag was a real concern, and it affected some more than others.

Emma looked at an incoming message on her slate. "That's Talent Khairu. She says she's docked the boat."

Emma swiped out a reply in under two seconds.

"Look," she said, pointing out the viewports.

Green islands and archipelagos spotted the cerulean surface below. On the horizon, a new, larger landmass was coming into view.

"Looks like the Ostkontinent," she said. "And if I don't miss my guess, all those thousands of little islands are the Pillars of Poseidon."

"The Wonder of the Galaxy," Lucian said. They'd all seen the commercials.

"Volsung also rotates the opposite direction of Earth," Emma said. "Sun rises in the west and sets in the east."

Lucian knew that, too, but he let Emma chirp the facts at him. She seemed excited about it.

"We'll be landing at Karendas. It's on an island almost right in the center of the Ocean of Storms. It's on the equator, so it will probably be warm. Probably not too different from Miami." Emma watched him, to see if this fact had any impact on him. "The Volsung Academy is actually far north of Karendas, almost as far as the northern ice cap. But the closest spaceport is at Karendas."

Lucian took in the news without a word. He was feeling anxious now, especially when something materialized against the planet's surface.

"There it is," Emma said. "Volsung-O."

The orbital was not the size of Sol Citadel – not even close – but Lucian knew it was quite impressive in its own right. It was a long, spinning O'Neill cylinder, two kilometers long. Basically, a giant soda can if far more technically advanced. From what he'd read, Volsung-O was home to ten thousand people. It was also the waypoint for any ships in the system. Being the only habitable world in the system, Volsung was the main hub.

Though the orbital was two kilometers long, it looked tiny indeed against the blue planet.

"We need to get to the shuttle fast," Emma said. "It leaves in an hour."

Emma readjusted her backpack as the *Burung* closed into the station, looming larger in the viewport. Lucian could now discern individual ports and bays at the cylinder's end. Various ships and shuttles zoomed about, docking and departing. As with Sol Citadel, he couldn't help but gawk.

Seeming to notice his reaction, Emma smiled. "One day, I'll show you L5. Your jaw will hit the deck."

"Prepare for docking," came the captain's voice from the intercom.

The passengers clamored for the door. Even as they crowded each other, they had left a sizable space around Lucian and Emma, for which Lucian was thankful.

Lucian scanned the crowd for Vera, but there was no sign. There was a final sliver of doubt as he questioned his decision. But there was no more time to think about it. The ship had stopped. Lucian felt a light vibration through the deck, followed by the click of the airlock. For the first time in four weeks, that lock opened, letting in a rush of cold air.

People surged through, like the breaking of a dam.

Lucian joined the flow. After one month, the main part of the journey was over.

# 33

THEY HALF WALKED, half ran, through the bustling orbital. The interstellar terminal was a swarm of people jostling in every direction. Despite the copious amount of space and many decks, this end of the cylinder was so *crowded*. Emma and Lucian could hardly push through the teeming mass. They had less than half an hour to make it to the gate.

They were moving too fast to make out many details, but Lucian could see that this was definitely an older orbital that hadn't been kept up with. The decks were dirty, and many of the fluorescents flickered while a good half of them were out. Groups of rough-looking men gathered in the dark corners, watching passers-by who walked speedily between their destinations. All of the stores and entrances were barred or covered with grills. Security guards bearing shock batons stood vigil over many of the entrances.

The sooner they got to the gate, the better.

The end of the wide cylinder faced out onto the large, blue orb of Volsung, where countless vessels orbited between the habitat and planet. Lucian saw anything from small personal craft to large interstellar freighters. Several of those freighters even had antiquated rotation rings. Modern freighters were flat, with power plants efficient enough to generate their own AG.

They ran past boarding tunnels as they rushed toward the planetside shuttle bays. Tickers above revealed destinations Lucian would likely never see: Mulciber, Kasturi, Pontus, Nessus, Freyr, Arion, Hephaestus.

The crowds thinned a bit as they made their way farther from the interstellar hangars. Lucian was beginning to doubt Emma's slate was steering them right. Emma seemed blind to everything but the holographic arrow pointing the way. Lucian, however, was focused on a pack of four men who seemed to be edging closer to them.

"Keep moving, Emma," he said.

"Another five minutes," she said.

That was when the leader of the group pounced. The young man couldn't have been more than Lucian's age, but his three lackeys moved with him toward Emma, probably with eyes on her bag. Her nice clothing had made her a target.

Lucian sprang into action, dropping his bag to better fight, placing himself between her and the approaching men. Two of the assailants peeled off from the group and grabbed his isolated luggage. Lucian watched helplessly as the thieves made off with almost everything he owned.

But there was no time to mourn the loss. The lead attacker rammed into him, causing him to spill to the deck. The other threw a few punches, which Lucian held up his hands against. It was two against one, while Emma screamed and dug for something in her bag.

"Go, Emma!" Lucian said. "I'll hold them off."

A punch landed on Lucian's jaw. He grunted in pain, even as he was tackled again by the second assailant. The original attacker peeled off of Lucian, going after Emma.

"No!"

Lucian pushed his own attacker off, something easy to do in

the lower gravity of the station. The attacker's arms and legs were thin, a sure sign he'd grown up in lower gravity without the benefit of muscle treatments. Lucian was more than a match for him just by virtue of growing up on Earth.

Lucian stood, and focused on the primary attacker, who was bearing down on Emma. She was still digging in her bag, looking for something.

Lucian wouldn't reach her in time. "Emma, look out!"

But as soon as the gangly youth reached her, she ripped something from her bag and slammed it into the thief's gut with a determined expression. A shock baton. She pressed the trigger and streams of electricity sizzled against the assailant's torso, making him go inert and collapse to the deck, quivering.

The other attacker ran, and there was no sign of the other two, who had made off with Lucian's bag. He now had nothing more than the clothes on his back and the slate in his pocket, along with the small backpack he carried, which only had a change of clothes and a bottle of water.

And there wasn't time to go chasing after them.

"You okay?" Lucian asked.

She managed a nod. "Yeah. I'm glad I packed that thing."

"Well, I just lost everything," Lucian said, looking in the direction the thieves had run.

"Not everything," she said. "We still have our lives."

"They weren't interested in killing us. Just our stuff." He nodded. "Thanks. That was some quick thinking. Maybe you should wear that baton on your belt."

"I could've gotten it out faster had I not buried it under all my clothes," she said. "Oh well. We should get moving. We have five minutes to get to the gate."

Lucian ran after Emma.

"There it is," Emma said, pointing ahead.

A long queue was lining up outside a door. The shuttle, a sleek, silvery craft, was already connected to the airlock. That airlock was already opening. There were people here, so they should be safe as they boarded.

"Just in time," Emma said. "Your pass should be on your slate."

Lucian saw the incoming notification. "Got it."

"Great. We can't get off this station fast enough!"

Lucian watched a droid take Emma's luggage, securing it inside a metal crate. That crate would float out into space and be magnetically sealed within the cargo hold.

There were no issues when the boarding attendant scanned his ticket. Despite everything that had just happened, Lucian felt excitement mounting. He couldn't think about the fortune he'd have to find to replace everything he'd lost.

He was about to go down to the surface of a new world.

———

GRAVITY INTENSIFIED as the shuttle burned through Volsung's atmosphere. Even the inertial dampeners couldn't completely take the edge off.

The portholes revealed a few clouds stretching across an endless, cerulean expanse. The Ocean of Storms was not true to its namesake, at least on this portion of the planet.

Before the shuttle reached the first layer of thin, wispy clouds, it slowed and leveled out. Two distant, green islands came into view. Lucian noticed the leftmost island held hundreds of silvery skyscrapers. The city gleamed in the bright afternoon sun. While those towers looked small from up here, it was only because of the shuttle's altitude.

A long, white line connected the two islands, and it took Lucian a moment to realize what it was: a bridge. There were a few buildings on the island to the right. A few cargo ships plied the pure blue waters, looking like toys from up here.

The shuttle glided over the city to begin touching down.

Tall, tropical trees intermixed with the bustling cityscape. The city looked bright, modern, and sleek. As Emma had mentioned, it might have been a smaller Miami, aside from the mountain it was built on.

"I thought Volsung was a cold world," he said. "Looks more like Honolulu than Oslo down there."

"I told you it was warmer on the equator," she said.

The shuttle lowered itself vertically in the middle of the city. Towers rose on all sides, looming over the shuttle. Lucian expected the landing pad to be outside the city. The underside thrusters ran an even burn to allow a slow, steady descent. About ten meters from the ground, a crane arm grappled the shuttle. The arm lowered the shuttle the rest of the way, allowing the thrusters to power off.

The shuttle touched down on the gray tarmac. For the first time in Lucian's life, he would breathe the air of a new world.

# 34

THAT AIR WAS hot and humid.

It blasted Lucian as soon as the shuttle's airlock opened. The air pressure seemed higher here than back on Earth. Or, Lucian thought, he was just used to the lower pressure of space-ships. Either way, the gravity felt heavy, even if he knew it was a bit less than Earth's. And the air pressure made his ears ring. On the bright side, he didn't have a bag to tote around.

The yellow sun shone down bright and hot. It, too, was less luminous than Sol, but it might as well have been twice as bright. His eyes weren't used to it.

"She's already texting me," Emma said, shading her eyes as they strode across the shuttle pad to the terminal.

"Khairu?"

She nodded. "Says she's out front."

The spaceport's interior was cooler, but still warm. This concourse was not as busy as Volsung-O's, but it still hummed with life. And it didn't look as if they'd get jumped any second.

The Karendas spaceport didn't seem big. After Emma picked up her luggage, they went down a long escalator to the wide-open entrance.

"Do you need some help with that pack?" Lucian asked.

"I've got it."

Lucian stood back as she huffed and puffed carrying her bag under the heavier gravity. Well, if she wanted to be stubborn, he would let her.

Outside, a line of ground cars had parked themselves, loading and unloading their passengers. Above the street was a Lev station, with a new train about to leave.

Though the upper tiers of the spaceport shaded the street, it was still hot. Stifling, even. Emma fanned herself with her slate, which had become wide and thin to accommodate the action.

"It's so *hot* here," she said.

"Nothing like L5."

She shook her head, and sighed. "I can't wait until we get farther north." She pointed. "I think that's her."

Lucian followed Emma along the sidewalk. She was walking toward a young woman of average height, light brown skin, and dark brown hair cut short. The woman wore a gray cloak like Vera's, though it was lighter in shade, and she wore a yellow sash over her left shoulder. That cloak must have been oppressive in this heat. She had a pretty, heart-shaped face, but there was a serious intensity to her stare that put Lucian on guard.

Talent Khairu's brown eyes betrayed no emotion as she nodded to Emma in greeting. "Welcome to Volsung, Emma Almaty. We don't have much time before the boat needs to set out, so we should hurry." Khairu took Emma's backpack and put it in the car beside her. The Academy Talent didn't seem to notice Lucian at all. He hung back, unsure of where he stood. She should have been expecting him, but so far, she wasn't acting like it.

"Talent Khairu," Emma said, with a bit of trepidation, "this is Lucian Abrantes. He's the mage on board I told you about."

Lucian came forward and put out his hand. "Nice to meet you, Talent Khairu."

Her eyes went to his hand, and then to his eyes. She looked back at Emma.

"I'll tell you what I said before," she said in a calm, but firm, voice. "My instructions are to bring you alone to the Transcends. He may come, but whatever they decide to do with him is out of my hands."

"That doesn't seem encouraging," Lucian said.

Emma's cheeks colored. She'd made it sound as if there would be no trouble at all.

Lucian fumbled for what to say. "I apologize if I'm an inconvenience. I'm already here, though. My baggage got stolen, and I have nowhere else to go."

"As long as you've paid your harbor fees, we'll have no quarrels."

"It's paid," Emma said.

Talent Khairu eyed Lucian. "Volsung is a dangerous place. Mages aren't allowed in Karendas for long. If things happen, don't expect much in the way of justice. Our boat needs to be gone in the next couple of hours. Traffic in the city can be bad, so we need to go now."

All three hopped in the car, and within a moment, it was self-navigating the busy, winding streets.

That first meeting hadn't gone as Lucian had expected, but now that he was on world, he hoped things would get better.

———

THE CAR RIDE was silent as they rolled away from the spaceport, joining the flow of traffic down a tree-lined avenue. The canopies were verdant green, and there were many blooming red flowers. So many, in fact, that the blossoms floated in droves onto the street below. They had stained the street blood red with their pigment.

The car drove down a canyon of skyscrapers, many connected by foot bridges. Tropical greenery grew on the sides of the edifices. Everything was new and pristine. Lucian didn't see so much as a crumpled food wrapper on the sidewalks. Most of the people wore light suits designed for the tropical heat, and the mood was busy and professional.

Swinging from the vines hanging above the cars were scaly, four-limbed creatures. Their green, reptilian skin and curled tails made them a strange cross between an iguana and a monkey. There were dozens, all letting out the same grating hoot. The cacophony echoed off the sides of buildings, only amplifying the sound. One of the creatures hung by its curled tail, staring right at them in their car. A meter-long tongue shot out from its mouth.

Emma watched with widened eyes as the road took a turn down a steep hill. Karendas was a mountain covered by trees and buildings. The car swerved into a tunnel, which exited onto a street running alongside a cliff. The sheer drop on the other side fell several hundred meters toward the blue ocean below. The ocean's surface was smooth, almost glassy. Volsung had no moon, meaning there were no significant tides, so any waves would come from the weather. A few more islands rose in the distance, though they were too small for habitation.

"It's beautiful here," Emma said.

"Beautiful," Khairu acknowledged, "but dangerous."

"How do you mean?"

"The storms will kill you faster than the cold."

That cold, at least here in Karendas, seemed a distant thing.

The car rolled down the street, navigating a series of switchbacks to the harbor below. The harbor extended as far as the long white bridge connecting the two main islands. That larger, southern island rose in front of them, green and vibrant, but with fewer buildings. Looking back, Lucian could see the towers of the city rising high above them. A layer of clouds obscured the mountain's peak.

Khairu leaned back in the driver's seat, content to let the car do the driving. Lucian had questions, but Khairu didn't seem to be in the mood for conversation.

The car rolled to a stop at the front of a marina filled with personal-sized vessels. The three of them got out, and Emma grabbed her backpack. The car drove itself off. Lucian and Emma followed Khairu down toward the dock.

That was when a deep male voice boomed from behind them.

"Hey, psychos!"

Lucian turned to see three rough-looking men standing next to a large truck. The one who shouted wore a superior smirk.

"Hope a storm takes you all," he said. The other two ruffians guffawed.

"Go ahead," Khairu instructed. "I'll deal with them. Ours is the sailboat at the very end. Name of *Lightsail*."

The two of them walked down the dock as Khairu dealt with the men. Once a safe distance away, they turned around to watch.

"Shouldn't we help?" Lucian asked.

Khairu's hand was on some sort of weapon she had hidden beneath her robes. At this distance, Lucian couldn't hear a word she was saying.

"Let's get to the boat," Emma said.

It didn't take long for the men to disperse. Whatever Khairu had said, or threatened, it seemed to have done the trick. The weapon was never revealed.

Khairu jogged down the dock to join them. Once she'd caught up, Emma asked, "Does that happen a lot?"

Khairu shook her head. "Some people around here know

the *Lightsail*. Just tough guys who learn they're not so tough." She looked at Emma. "The path of a mage isn't an easy one. The Academy is thousands of klicks from here. We don't have to deal with their kind there."

Though Khairu only seemed to be in her mid-twenties, she spoke with a gravitas that belied her age.

They finally stood in front of the vessel, a long and sleek sailboat. It bobbed on the smooth ocean surface. Lucian judged it was large enough to hold up to twenty or thirty people. The hull might have even been real wood, which Lucian had read was more expensive on Volsung.

He and Emma boarded, while Khairu untied the line. The boat drifted away from the dock as she hopped on deck.

"Follow me to the helm."

Inside the bridge, Khairu pressed a few buttons. A moment later, the deck thrummed as an electric motor kicked on. The boat immediately embarked.

As the ship picked up speed, the motor cut out as both sails unfurled and caught the wind, filling on a starboard tack.

Lucian watched as the island, and its city of towers, crawled into the distance.

# 35

As *Lightsail* plied the smooth waters, more of the island revealed itself. Steep, sheer, and green, it looked like paradise. The water was clear cerulean, and Lucian could see quite deep. Schools of fish swarmed around multicolored reefs. Humanity had not had time to put a dent in their numbers.

"There's some cabins aft," Khairu said, once they were far away from the shore. "Get some sleep, if you want."

Emma and Lucian left the bridge, going down the main corridor. There were only three doors on either side, all open to the hallway. One led to a wardroom, another to a galley, and another a lav. The next doors were all cabins.

Lucian claimed the one on the end. The single light switch lit an old-fashioned bulb that fought to illuminate the small space. There were four bunks, so Lucian took one of the bottom ones.

After depositing their bags, he and Emma returned to the helm to find Khairu no longer there. Instead, she stood at the bow, holding whatever weapon she had hidden at the harbor.

It was a thin spear, which had to be incredibly lightweight, judging by the speed with which Khairu handled it. With that spear she simply . . . *danced.* There was no other way to describe it. As Lucian watched her practiced movements, it was as if she were fighting an imaginary army. His breath caught when light shimmered along the length of that spear. Emma gasped when streams of electricity flickered up and down the weapon. Khairu never slowed her movements. She knelt, leapt, sliced, and stabbed, flowing like water. The spear crackled with each sudden movement, brimming with electric charge that shot from the spear's pointed tip.

It was all they could do to stand and watch in silence. Khairu's movements seemed to make the spear build up energy. After fifteen seconds or so, a fork of lightning would lance from its tip, extending one to five meters.

"What is it?" Lucian asked.

Emma stood quiet for a moment, seeming completely rapt. "I . . . think it's a shockspear. Mages used them in the war. Their electric charge can pierce energy shields, and it's powered by . . ." She swallowed. "Well, the mage."

Khairu did a few more graceful spins, though her movements were now slowing.

"Are we going to learn that?" Lucian asked.

Emma didn't answer for a moment. "I don't know." She gasped when Khairu jumped onto the railing of the boat, lifting a leg and balancing. This was with the water getting choppier and breaking on the bow.

Emma and Lucian rushed from the bridge. But Khairu did a graceful backflip, falling slower than she should have. It was hard to tell whether that was Volsung's lower gravity or . . . something else.

The electricity dissipated as the spear shrunk into itself, no larger than a wand. She placed it inside her robes.

"How did you do that?" Emma asked. "That was amazing!"

"Practice," Khairu said. "And patience. If you're accepted, you can learn, too."

Lucian wondered if Khairu was trying to show off. She went right back into a training routine, this time with no electricity. He and Emma might as well have not been there.

She practiced like that for hours, long after Emma and Lucian had gone inside to get relief from the hot sun.

"This day has been so long," Lucian said. "It's still as bright as when we left Karendas."

"I know. I'm so exhausted. But I'll try to make it to this evening. That's about ten hours from now."

It had gotten windier, too. Gusts slammed the side of the boat, though the skies were still clear. It made the boat practically fly across the water.

"I wonder what a storm would be like out here," Emma said.

"I don't want to find out."

"You'd think that because this world is cooler, it would be less stormy. Well, Volsung's ocean is *vast*, and there's nothing to break up those storms as they race around the world. Usually, that doesn't happen until they hit the Ostkontinent. And the Vestkontinent is so flat that they blow right over it. By the time they're said and done, they dwarf any cyclone Earth has ever produced."

"You've done your research."

"You never know when knowledge might come in handy."

Hurricanes on Earth had long been a thing of the past. Even with global warming, solar shades could cool a developing storm long before it became dangerous. A hurricane hadn't made landfall in more than a century. Even the floating cities of the Caribbean hadn't seen one in as long.

Despite being one of the First Worlds, Volsung didn't have the infrastructure of Earth. Nowhere even close. While humanity had done much to tame the planet, the people of Earth had a head start. Infrastructure would come in time, but for now, Volsung was dangerous and wild. A lot of the luxuries

Lucian took for granted didn't exist here. There wasn't even a planetwide GalNet network. As soon as they were a few hundred kilometers out to sea, his slate would be useless. He took a look at it to see no message from his mother.

Emma went to take a nap, despite her earlier dedication to stay up until evening, which was still hours away. Lucian wondered how people slept here. On planets like Mars, with a day only thirty minutes longer than Earth, the change was easy. But here, staying awake all day would be impossible.

Lucian went to the stern to watch the sailboat's wake. Karendas was long out of sight by now. It was shocking how fast the ship was going. The ship's many sails caught wind from every angle, adjusting with every deviation.

Lucian wanted to stay up, too, but he realized he was fighting a losing battle. When he passed Emma's cabin, she was already sprawled out and snoring. He went to his own cabin, lay down, and closed his eyes.

Within moments, he was fast asleep.

———

WHEN LUCIAN WOKE UP, he headed out to the stern in time to see the sun sinking below the eastern horizon. The blood red drop cast the ocean's surface a fiery hue. It took the sun over half an hour to sink under the horizon in full. Despite the lack of sunlight, the surface of the water was still glowing.

Something was *shimmering* down there, creating its own light. Lucian could see to the bottom – the water couldn't have been more than ten meters deep. The wind had calmed, producing a still surface broken only by the wake of the boat.

A proliferation of life swarmed below. In every direction stretched kilometers upon kilometers of glowing, multicolored reefs. Among them schools of fish shone with luminescence. Electric eels teemed among coral towers. The reef, at points, even poked above the water in small atolls. This would have been dangerous, but the vessel knew to weave around them.

As night fell, the entire scene glowed with ethereal beauty. Beneath the surface of this alien ocean, Volsung's true heart thrummed. Lucian could almost feel its power.

He stood out here alone for another quarter of an hour, enjoying the silence and fresh, salt-laden air.

At the sound of footsteps, Lucian turned to see Khairu, the tail of her gray cloak thrown by the breeze.

"Take care of any last business," she said. "We're about to lose GalNet signal."

With that, she turned to leave.

Lucian opened his slate to see no new messages. His message from Volsung-O had hours yet to reach his mother in Alpha Centauri. He realized that by the time she responded, he would never receive her message. The thought made his throat clench. Tears formed in his eyes, but they were dried by the wind before they could be shed.

*This might be my last message for a while,* he began. *Where I'm going, I'm not sure they have much in the way of technology. There will be no GalNet signal out there. I'm on a ship right now, and should be arriving at the Volsung Academy in a few standard days. At times, I didn't think I would make it, but I'm almost there. I hope things are okay with you. It's been a long trip, and something tells me it's only going to get longer.*

*I wish I had the data to send you a vid, too. It's beautiful here.* Lucian realized he might not have much time to say anything more. *Let's hope that you can come out here soon. Thank you for everything. You said you weren't the best mother, but don't believe that. Without you, I wouldn't have made it this far. I love you. And .. . stay alive.*

Lucian couldn't risk the time to refine the message any further. At any moment, he would lose signal. He sent it off, and it confirmed within a few seconds. A few days from now, that message would arrive on her slate in Alpha Centauri.

He only hoped it wouldn't be the last.

The rest of the day was only visible as a rosy glow on the eastern horizon. Within the hour, that too would be completely gone.

Lucian went to the galley to rummage for food, finding some biscuits and fish dip. It wasn't much, and not what he'd usually eat, but it was something.

Afterward, he went straight back to bed, careful not to wake Emma as he passed her cabin. She was still sleeping on her back. Khairu slept in the cabin opposite, her shockspear half a meter from her hand. Even though she was asleep, Lucian had the feeling she was quite aware of her surroundings.

Lucian crawled into his own bunk. The lapping of water and the creak of the ship's wooden hull lulled him to sleep.

# 36

WHEN LUCIAN WOKE UP, it was still dark. When he checked his slate for the time, it read 44:12.

That threw him for a loop. He'd slept around twelve hours. It was still dark outside the portholes, and would be for hours yet.

Lucian stumbled to the galley and found some microwave meals in the freezer. He warmed one up, some fish over rice with a spicy red sauce. It was different, but not terrible. He supposed fish was the main meat on this world, for obvious reasons.

He ate, and from the bridge could see both Emma and Khairu near the bow, illumined by the glowing sea. Once finished, Lucian washed his plate and headed to the stern, not wanting to interrupt.

The night was halfway over, but there was still no sign of dawn in the west. The reefs from the evening before were gone, replaced by deeper water. The wind was cooler here. They should be far north of Karendas by now. He'd never felt so far from everyone, and everything. Looking up at the foreign constellations, he didn't even know which star held Earth.

What was he doing here? How could he be a mage? Even after everything, it felt unreal. What if he came all this way, only for the Transcends to reject him? The opportunity to follow Vera had long passed. She was well on her way to Halia by now.

He'd risked everything to be here. Had he made a mistake?

"There you are."

Emma joined him at the railing. They watched the sailboat churn a glowing trail that stretched to the horizon. Since coming out here, they hadn't seen a sign of any other ship, or even a plane. Volsung was an empty world compared to Earth. It was as if the whole planet were their own.

"You okay?"

It took Lucian a while to answer. "I'm trying to convince myself I haven't made a huge mistake."

She was quiet for a moment. "Do you *feel* like you have?"

"If I'm not accepted here, I don't have a fallback plan. It's all or nothing."

"They'll accept you. I don't know *how* I know, but I know. You're exactly where you're supposed to be."

He gave a bitter laugh. "I wish I had your confidence."

"Well, why are you doubting things?"

"I don't know," he said. "Khairu seems a bit cold to me. Like I'm a waste of space. What if the Transcends feel the same way?"

"Well, she's a bit uptight. I wouldn't take it too hard."

Who *were* these Transcends, anyway? The name implied they'd transcended something, but what could that be? Lucian didn't voice that thought. It didn't bode well if he were questioning the ones in charge of judging him.

Emma continued. "Look. We mages have an intuitive sense of how things should be, unlike others. We see things before they happen. We envision possibilities that would never cross the minds of others. I have that intuition about you, that this is where you're meant to be."

"Vera said the same," Lucian said. "Except she had the intuition that I was going to follow her."

"What did she say, exactly?"

"That the Manifold meant me to be her student."

Emma's expression seemed troubled. "Well, you're here. Doesn't that prove her wrong?"

It was hard to argue with that. But it still felt as if something were missing.

"I don't know," Emma said doubtfully. "I don't trust her. I'm struggling, too. I sent one last message out to my parents. If the training is what they're saying, I won't get to talk to them for a while."

Silence followed these words. There was nothing but the sound of the ship plying through the water and the rush of cool wind. However far they had come, they were clearly out of the equatorial regions by now.

"It helps knowing I'm not alone, though," she said. "And I'm glad you came."

"Have you been talking to Khairu?"

"A little. She's hard to read. But I want to learn."

"Getting a head start on training, then?"

"That's the idea."

"Well, at least you're sure you have a place here. Why else would the Transcends bother to fetch you?" He shook his head. "Me, though? I can't be so sure."

"It won't matter," Emma said. "You'll be fine."

"I wish I knew what would happen. If I had that, well, then I would know what comes next. Learn how to be a mage, become a Talent, follow orders. Easy, right?"

Emma laughed. "You have a sense of humor about it, at least. When I get an intuition, it's never wrong." She took his silence as an invitation to explain herself further. "I can't explain it. It's like, when I see you there's some sort of aura. Not a physical one, but something I'm pulled toward." Even in the darkness, Lucian could see her cheeks reddening. "No, not like . . . *that.*" The color deepened, betraying her feelings even further.

Lucian couldn't help but laugh. "Are you still trying to pretend like there's nothing between us?"

She huffed. "I'm *not* pretending! You're too much. Actually, we should talk about that. Where we're going, they won't look kindly on . . . I don't know. Whatever *this* is."

She gestured toward the space between her and Lucian. That space, Lucian had noticed, had somehow shrunk during their conversation. As if conscious of that, Emma shifted her position a step away.

"You need me," Lucian said. "And yet, you're pretending you don't."

"Lucian . . ." She started to say something, but then stopped.

"I care about you, Emma. I know we're not *supposed* to. I don't want to ruin things. Still, what I feel scares me." He clung to the railing, and kept his eyes on the passing ocean. Saying all of this was hard, but it needed to be said. He hated the feeling of being vulnerable. And waiting. "The last thing I want is to jeopardize our chances at the Academy. If you think we should step back, then that's what we should do."

She was quiet for a long time. Too long. Had he said something wrong?

"Is that what you want, Lucian?"

They were the last words he expected to hear. "What does what I want matter?"

He could feel her eyes on him. Somehow, they were standing close again, close enough for their shoulders to touch. The sensation was warm and welcome. It was also painful, knowing that it couldn't last.

She stepped aside, to give space again. "Confusion is the

last thing I need right now." She heaved a sigh. "You were honest, so I should be, too." She smiled, but her eyes were sad. "It's a bit . . . unfortunate. It could've been something, I guess. We've got bigger priorities now." She took his hand. That touch was friendly, not romantic. "I'm sorry." She squeezed his hand then, a shade too long.

"What do you want, Emma?"

She didn't remove her hand, nor did Lucian pull his own away.

"You asked me the same question," Lucian went on. "Why would you even ask that, if not to find out what I felt for you?"

She looked down at the deck. Tears had formed in her eyes. She had no answer, other than caressing his hand gently. It was as if she didn't say it out loud, it wasn't real.

"If only," she said, a hint of disappointment in her voice.

It took effort, but Lucian let go. He pulled his hand away. Her body seemed to freeze with that action.

He hated doing that. It felt . . . wrong. So, he reached out and took her hand again. When he did, her posture thawed, and her face turned to his. They stood close. She was so beautiful in the starlight. Looking into her eyes, words no longer mattered. Expectations no longer mattered.

They moved with inescapable gravity. Lucian couldn't push her away.

His lips touched hers, and they kissed. It was soft at first, until she kissed him back with great need and intensity. They kissed until all pretense was gone and the truth stood revealed under the starlit sky of Volsung.

When they parted, Lucian held her close, letting her head fall under his chin. He felt her tears warm against his neck. He wanted to remember this moment forever, for when she pulled away again.

She took a shuddering breath. "I'm sorry."

"It doesn't matter anymore. We couldn't have stopped it even if we wanted."

She nodded against him. "I know."

At last, they stood apart, holding each other's hands a moment before letting go.

"Still a couple of days left," Emma said, wiping her face clean of tears. "Couple more days till . . ."

She trailed off, resting her head on his chest, right where his heart was still pounding.

"Lucian . . . if I can't get training, I'll *die*."

Those words hit him like a punch.

"I . . . don't regret what happened," she went on. "But this has to be the last time."

He nodded, though it pained him to do so.

"We should head up front," she said. "Wait five minutes and follow."

When she was gone, Lucian looked back out over the ocean, his heart reeling.

## 37

HOURS LATER, when the sun came up, they were still training. Khairu took them through a breathing exercise. She said it would strip away all emotions, prejudices, and ego. If there was anything that could sober Lucian after his encounter with Emma, it was this. It was hard to keep from falling asleep.

"Imagine a white, shining light, a light that purges you of anything you think you are," Khairu intoned. "Imagine it so much that you *become* that light."

Lucian found it hard to form the image. It kept slipping away, like sand through cracks. His concentration wavered as the water grew choppier. His stomach started doing flips.

Even as a light shower started to fall, Khairu did not call off the meditation. Lucian almost quit right there, but again, he knew showing dedication was important. No matter the circumstances.

He opened one eye a bit, to see both Khairu and Emma sitting on the deck, in clear meditative bliss. How could they *do* this? Why couldn't they move inside the bridge?

When he was about to give up and go inside, Lucian heard

someone stand. He opened his eyes to see Khairu staring off toward the west.

"That's enough for this morning," she said. Her hair was dripping, while water ran rivulets down her brown face. "A storm is coming."

Following this announcement, both Emma and Lucian looked out to the west. A thick layer of dark clouds was covering the sun. In fact, the clouds covered the whole *horizon*. A rumble of thunder sounded in the distance. The water was even more tumultuous, its former cerulean now slate gray.

After Lucian dried off and changed clothes, he joined the two women on the bridge. The boat was rolling good now, up and down hills of water under a bilious gray sky streaked with lightning. Lucian's stomach lurched with the ship's every motion. Rain fell in thick sheets.

"Will we be okay?" Emma called, over the sounds of the gale.

Khairu seemed unconcerned. "A morning storm. This is nothing."

Despite her words, the rain fell harder, as the hilly waves became mountainous. Lucian had to strap himself down to a chair. He heaved a couple of times, but nothing came up. Emma, after a couple of minutes, also had to strap herself in. In contrast, Khairu was well-balanced, predicting movement before it happened. Lightning streaked across the sky, sometimes striking a rod extending from the mainmast.

After a few minutes of this, Lucian wondered how Khairu could be so unconcerned. The winds were at least hurricane force.

"Are we almost out?" Lucian shouted.

Khairu stood at the helm, intent upon the direction of the ship. She read the display, which showed angry bands of red extending in all directions.

"The only way out is through it," she answered.

For hours, they pushed through. Lucian thought they might drown, especially as water slapped across the deck. Those torrents could have easily carried any of them away. Water even rolled into the bridge a few times, though only a few centimeters deep. The boat plowed on, to the top of crests, only to crash into the roiling valleys beneath. Only for the waves to lift it up again.

Finally, the Ocean of Storms was living up to its name. If Khairu seemed so unconcerned by this, Lucian wondered at what point she *would* be.

In time, the winds slackened, and the waves lowered. It felt as if they had spent all day in the storm. But when the clouds finally broke, Volsung's bright sun had only crawled halfway up the western sky.

It would be a long day yet.

———

ONCE LUCIAN'S stomach had settled enough, he ate a small meal and took a long nap. When he woke up, it was close to 27:00 . . . noon on Volsung. His circadian rhythm was completely confused now.

He found Emma and Khairu sitting in the small wardroom, eating a simple meal of rice, fish, and greens. When Lucian filled his plate, he thought this might be a bit harder to get down. The cuisine here would be hard to get used to.

He joined them and listened to their conversation.

"The Manifold is what we use to describe the force that's behind visible reality," Khairu explained. "The Manifold, in a sense, *is* reality. What we call reality, you can think of as a shadow. What the Transcends call the Shadow World."

So far, nothing was contradicting with what Vera had already taught him.

"All we can see, smell, taste, touch, or hear is but a reflection of the truth, and that truth is the Manifold. Mages are those wakened to the fact that we exist on *both* planes. This one, the shadow, and the Manifold, the reality that casts that shadow."

"And we can change the Manifold?" Emma asked.

Khairu nodded. "Yes, but it's not easy." Emma hung on her every word. "You see, we've taken for granted that this reality is the only one. Those who can sense the true reality, the Manifold, are what we call mages. The fraying occurs because our feeble minds cannot comprehend both. At least, that's the current theory. The training builds awareness of the Manifold. You can only do that by letting go of preconceived notions that keep you from accepting its truth. Worldly attachments, romantic love, greed, cognitive dissonance. They've designed the training to help you move beyond such limitations. In so doing, you can keep the fraying at bay. Part of the process, yes, involves changing the Manifold. What we call *magic*. We use magic to aid the Transcends' mission in bringing peace to the Worlds."

"How long does the training take?" Emma asked. "Will my seizures stop?"

"Length of training depends on aptitude, and the mage's willingness to follow teachings." Khairu looked at Lucian before returning her attention to Emma. "The key is letting go of all the things holding you back. Emotional attachment can trigger the Manifold to overwhelm a mage who isn't ready. Your seizures will stop once you've learned to stream magic using what's called a Focus."

"What's that?" Lucian asked.

Khairu's expression hardened. "A Focus is a simple mental image that's easy for the mage to hold onto. It acts as an anchor for one's magical stream. You can think of it as a spring, and the magic has to go somewhere. We will teach you to direct the

Manifold's stream outward, not inward. That is the source of your seizures."

"But some mages are unteachable," Lucian said. "Right?"

Khairu looked at him, her face stern. "Most are not teachable, if I'm to be honest. The path to becoming an Academy mage is most difficult. To embark on a path that eschews all worldly attachments, to seek the very death of ego . . . all of this is an almost impossible task. We are human, and to be human is to be imperfect. That's why we wish to train a mage as early as possible. The further developed they are, the more difficult it is to teach them new ways."

"In what circumstances would the Transcends accept someone who's been a mage a little longer?" Emma asked.

"I cannot answer that," Khairu said. "It is a question for the Transcends. We should reach the island by late evening."

"So, about a standard day from now," Lucian said.

"You said earlier that everyone exists in both realms, the Manifold and the Shadow," Emma said. "What determines those who are mages, and those who aren't?"

"*That* is a mystery," Khairu said. "And completely arbitrary, as far as we can see. After over a century of research, we don't know what causes some people to awaken, and others to remain asleep. And we know little of the Manifold itself. It has *always* existed, as far as we know, and was most likely created as a byproduct of the Big Bang. Some say it was the instigating force. What we do know comes from the writings of fallen Transcends. These brave mages subjected themselves to the fraying to delve the Manifold." She paused, as if in respect to those fallen masters. "One thing is clear: there *is* a Manifold, and it controls *our* reality. The mages are its stewards, but the why of it remains a mystery." She paused, as if in thought. "Of course, being aware of the Manifold comes with a cost, and that cost is the fraying, if magic is used irresponsibly. Without training, the fraying dooms mages to a horrible fate. Most of our Transcends are in their sixties or even older, and show no signs of fraying. Our teachings are the only way a mage can stream magic without hastening their demise."

Lucian thought of Vera. The awareness that there were other paths led him to be skeptical of that statement. And yet despite that, this was the path he'd chosen. He would have to learn to accept it as the correct way. If the Transcends sensed any doubt, it worsened his odds for acceptance.

And Khairu herself seemed to sense that skepticism, because she was looking at him now. "You must rid yourself of all your preconceived notions. Are both of you ready?"

Lucian nodded. "I'm ready to learn more."

"So am I," Emma echoed.

Khairu looked at Lucian, then Emma, and nodded. "The days ahead will be difficult, and the path is dangerous. But it is the only path. And ours is a way of peace, with a method honed over decades." She looked at each of them. "You are both in the right place."

# 38

LUCIAN SLEPT once the waters had calmed. When he awoke, Volsung's evening light was filtering through the porthole. It was as red as it had been yesterday. Footsteps tromped on the deck above.

Lucian checked his slate for the time. 40:00. If they weren't close to the Academy by now, they would be soon.

He showered, put on clean clothes, and went upstairs to the bridge. There, he found Khairu at the helm, steering, while Emma stood beside her. Through the screen, Lucian could see a mountain with a flattened top rising from the choppy water.

"Is that it?" he asked, joining Emma's side.

"Transcend Mount," Khairu said. "We should make landfall within the hour. Compose yourself."

Emma gave Lucian a sidelong look and a small shrug before turning her attention back to the island ahead.

Transcend Mount was tall and sheer. Most of it was gray, though the lower reaches were dense with forest. The eastern sun had dipped below its flat top, upon which stood some shadowy buildings and towers. The rocky beach far below contained a single wooden dock.

The sailboat plowed ahead on a starboard tack, making steady progress. On the western horizon, the first stars and planets appeared in the darkening sky.

By the time they were mooring, the ship was in the island's shadow. It was cool, here. Volsung's short summer was drawing to a close. Lucian had never been to such a remote place his entire life. Aside from the few buildings at the top, there was no sign of habitation.

They left the boat tied to the dock, and it rolled in the surf as they approached the gray, rocky beach ahead. There was a narrow trail leading up the mountainside, lit by oil lamps every few meters. Lucian didn't understand the primitive technology. A fusion reactor small enough to fit on the sailboat could power everything on this island.

If there *was* no power here, it had to have been a deliberate choice. Lucian's slate could charge from sunlight, but something told him that wouldn't matter. There was no GalNet out here, and he had no doubt the Transcends would forbid the use of his slate.

In many ways, living here would be like going back in time a millennium.

As they walked up the narrow trail, Lucian realized they had to have *some* form of power. Exposed as it was, how could this place shield itself from debris cast by Volsung's mighty storms? The one earlier had been frightening, but nowhere near this planet's destructive potential.

They made their way up in silence, surrounded by trees that were a strange mixture of local and Terran. Volsung's biosphere was mixed. Any Earthlike world, over time, became blended, sometimes with disastrous ecological consequences. Pines and aspen intermixed with local trees with thin white trunks and hanging vines. Various chortles and clicks emanated from the stringy undergrowth. Over the water,

Lucian spied several dozen globules floating over the dark surface. They looked like airborne jellyfish.

Yes, he definitely wasn't on Earth anymore.

By the time they were halfway up, Lucian was short of breath. He hadn't had to do anything strenuous in this gravity yet. Emma was also huffing and puffing from beside him, but neither called for a break. Khairu set a fast pace, and didn't seem worried about leaving them behind. Emma let him carry her pack once they were halfway up.

They continued without pause, until they were three-quarters of the way up. It was then that Lucian saw Khairu tense. Something was wrong.

"What is it?" Emma asked, after a few deep breaths.

Khairu waited another moment, looking out to the water. "Another storm. This one'll be bad. A real storm."

Lucian looked off into the distance. The western sky was clear as far as he could see, but he didn't want to question her. The storm could be coming from the other side.

"As bad as yesterday?" Emma asked.

Khairu shook her head. "No. Worse."

"What do we do?" Lucian asked.

"Hurry," she said. "They might have to put up the shield tonight."

Khairu picked up the pace.

The trail only got steeper the higher they went, becoming stairs toward the top. Looking down at the shoreline, there were more floating globes glowing in the night. There must have been hundreds of them. Even if Lucian wanted to ask about them, he was too short of breath.

Khairu didn't seem fazed in the least. She was still breathing through her nose.

After another agonizing ten minutes, the trail leveled off after a final switchback. From up here, Lucian could see kilometers toward the western horizon. It seemed a little closer than it should have, just enough to bother him.

Emma had stopped, but she wasn't looking at the water below. She was looking ahead at a stone complex. Its massive blocks were beaten and worn by constant erosion. A colossal stone building hulked before them, at least fifty meters tall. Narrow slits lined its massive face. Lucian figured they were windows, but they were open to the air. Besides this monstrosity, there were connecting halls, corridors, and towers. The bottom part of the complex was covered by a pinkish lichen. Lucian counted six towers, rising high above the Academy itself.

This place was a veritable fortress. How had it been built? By whom? It looked far older than two centuries, the length of time humans had been on this world. But it was too well-preserved to be ruins left behind by the Builders.

Lucian had little time to ponder these questions. Here at the flat top of the island, the wind was blowing hard. The sky beyond was a dark mass. Flashes of lightning illuminated the Academy's decrepit exterior, giving it a menacing air.

Khairu was running now, and despite his exhaustion, Lucian ran, too. The first cold drops of rain fell right as they reached the open threshold.

After a month of travel, they had finally made it to the Volsung Academy.

———

THE ACADEMY OPENED into a large antechamber, a circle with a high dome supported by pillars. Lucian guessed the cavernous space might be a hundred paces across. Outside those pillars, many torches blazed, and a large central brazier cast its own light. Despite all the fires, it was insufficient to push back the darkness. Shadows cloaked the top of the dome.

Lucian could see three corridors leading deeper into the Academy. One went left, one right, and one straight ahead. The stonework below was worn smooth, without so much as a speck of dust.

This complex belonged deep in the jungles of Central America like a long-lost Mayan ruin. Heaviness and gloom pervaded all, an atmosphere only amplified by the torrents of rainfall outside. Cold gusts of wind swept inward, carrying with it not only raindrops, but pellets of hail.

"Follow me," Khairu said.

She led them deeper within, and stood for a moment by the central brazier to warm and dry herself. Emma and Lucian followed her example. The two shared a nervous glance, the silence too heavy to break.

After a minute, and without a word, Khairu continued on. Lucian returned Emma's pack.

They passed no one as they walked deeper into the Academy. From its size, Lucian had expected hundreds of mages to be here. But it felt as if they were the only ones.

"Where is everyone?" Emma asked, her voice echoing.

"Night meditation," Khairu said. "You may speak if you must, but it's discouraged."

Emma and Lucian kept quiet.

At last, Khairu brought them into another chamber, not as big as the entry hall, but still large in its own right. It was lit by various sconces and braziers blazing with flames. Shadows danced along the walls. A long row of stone seats, eight in all, lined the opposite wall. They were like thrones, but each was the same size. There were also two torches on either side of the seats, none of which were lit.

There they stood, and waited. For what, Lucian didn't know. He was hungry and wanted a shower. If this place even *had* those.

Minutes dragged on in silence. Then an hour. Lucian's

clothes were damp, and the air cold. His thoughts raced. He wondered if all this was a huge mistake. It was difficult to hold onto any one thought for long. His mind only reached for another. He could hear the winds of the storm wailing outside. That the storm's sound could reach this deep within the Academy was a testament to its power.

Finally, after what felt like an eternity, footsteps approached from outside the chamber. Three figures in colored robes – Blue, Gray, and White – seemed to float through the archway. They entered this inner sanctum with an aura of power. Those in the gray and blue were elderly men, each with wrinkled faces. The blue-robed one had dark skin and close-cropped hair. The one in gray had snowy white hair and a narrow, sorrowful face.

The last person, in the white robes, was a stooped old woman. She had narrow shoulders, a bony frame, along with a sharp nose set in a wrinkled face. A long, white braid fell over her shoulder.

When those dark eyes found Lucian's, seeming to know him to the core, he couldn't believe it. His skin went cold.

It was Vera.

# 39

LUCIAN TRIED to hide his shock, but as Vera's eyes bored into his, there was no doubt. The Transcends took their seats. As they did, the sconces lit on their either side. The flames burned the same color as their robes, lending brightness to the room. The two old men weighed Lucian with their eyes. A heavy silence followed, broken only by Khairu bending on one knee while lowering her face. Lucian wondered whether he should do the same, but Emma remained standing, and seemed to be as shocked as him. She gawked at Vera, who sat on the far right throne.

"Your Eminences," Khairu said. "Before the Spectrum of Transcends, I bring two foundling mages for consideration. The first is Emma Almaty, from L5, Sol System. The details and reasons for her coming, I'm sure you're aware of." She paused, and pursed her lips. "The other is Lucian Abrantes, whom she met aboard the ship by coincidence. He is from Earth."

"There is no coincidence," the gray-robed Transcend intoned. "All is in accordance to the will of the Manifold."

Khairu seemed to not have a response for a long moment. "Very much so, Transcend Gray. Emma told me his powers manifested on board the ship in a somewhat . . . *violent* . . . incident."

Lucian looked at Emma. When had she told Khairu *that*? As he felt the sting of betrayal, Emma kept her eyes forward, her cheeks coloring.

Emma would have *had* to tell her. Khairu would have wanted proof that he was a mage. It could explain Khairu's coldness toward him.

"We'll let the foundling give an account of himself," Transcend Blue said in a neutral tone.

Vera watched, her dark eyes gleaming by the light of the fires. How had she gotten here so fast? Why had she been on the ship in the first place? And what was she doing here? Lucian had too many questions racing through his mind, one after another.

"We will begin with Emma Almaty," Transcend Gray said. "But first, some introductions would be in order. As I'm sure you know by now, I'm Transcend Gray."

The black man spoke next. "Transcend Blue."

Vera gave a small smile, her scratchy voice sending a chill down Lucian's spine. "Transcend White."

Something in her tone suggested that White was the highest rank possible. If there was anyone he needed to impress, it was her.

Transcend Gray spoke first. "Emma, the letter sent to us by your parents intrigued us."

Emma's back straightened, as if she were a private in the Fleet being addressed by the admiral.

"Your convulsions are an affliction known to us. It's called the Wreaking, and if caught early enough, we can correct it. It is a sign of great magical potential." He eyed her with a discerning air. "But without our training, you will fray and die."

"Then you must train her," Lucian said, unable to help himself.

Khairu shot him a venomous glare, while the stares of Transcends Gray and Blue were icy. Vera, Transcend White, watched him with an almost amused expression.

"Are you ready, Emma?" Transcend Blue asked, as if Lucian had not spoken at all.

"I am," Emma said, lowering her head.

"That is good," the elderly Transcend Gray said. "The path is difficult. Harder than even the Wreaking. Even with perfect training, the Manifold has its own plan. It is the Manifold, and not us, that must accept you."

"I understand," Emma said.

"The Manifold is dangerous," Transcend Blue warned. "It is not a tool that serves us. We are tools that serve *it*. It can sense dark intent. Having an attitude of death to self and service to others is paramount. It is the mage's lot to promote the values of peace, knowledge, and harmony. As soon as a mage loses that path, they lose themselves." Transcend Gray looked at Emma with great solemnity. "Do you understand what this means, Emma?"

There was a moment's pause. "I don't understand it fully, but I get the general idea."

"Though we three are Transcends, even we are not perfect," Transcend Blue explained. "The path to understanding is a lifetime in the making. Opening oneself to the Manifold is not about power. It is about *giving* power to ideals greater than oneself. That is the first lesson any mage should learn."

"She misses home," Vera said, in her gravelly voice. "She misses her father, her mother, the gardens of her family's estate. She misses her friends, she misses music, and she misses the false worlds she loved more than her own."

A long silence hung in the chamber following this pronouncement. Transcends Gray and Blue seemed to consider Vera's words.

"She is too old in the Manifold," Vera said, at last. "I sense the Manifold has stirred within her since childhood, even if it hadn't manifested. And she has formed ... difficult attachments to the things of this world. That will be hard to remedy. If we take her for training, these will prove to be of the greatest difficulty to root out."

"I'm ready," Emma said, almost with defiance. Some of her former animosity toward Vera was coming out. But she didn't dare ask her reasons for the deception.

"Are you ready for salvation from yourself, Emma?" Vera challenged. "Many would say death, even by Manifoldic Wreaking, is an easier path than the one that lies before you. There will be many times you doubt yourself in the days ahead. Many dark nights where you regret your decision to train with us. Often, the object you seek brings you the most pain."

"I came here to be a mage. I'm ready to give up everything. To dedicate myself to a higher calling."

"Are you?" Vera asked. "We will see."

Vera's sharp words seemed to deflate Emma, who looked down at the floor.

"And what of the other one?" Transcend Gray asked. "This . . . Lucian Abrantes."

Vera met Lucian's eyes. If Lucian hadn't known better, he would have said that look communicated that she *didn't* know him. A quick glance at Emma revealed that she was also confused.

"Lucian," Vera said. "Your acceptance within these halls would be more miraculous than Emma's. I sense great conflict within you. I sense also that your powers are recently emerged."

"Yes," Lucian said, surprising himself at the steadiness of his voice. "I've known about a month."

"As I thought," she said. "It's remarkable that two foundlings would chance to meet on the way here. As Transcend Gray said, that is no coincidence." Vera looked at him, her gaze sharp and focused. "Describe what happened on board the liner."

Lucian knew what she wanted him to talk about. And he didn't relish having to repeat himself. It felt pointless, but it could be that she was asking for the benefit of the other Transcends. He'd have to hold back his criticism for now. There was too much at stake.

"There was this group of Fleet recruits. They had it out for me the minute I set foot on that ship. They discovered what I was, and attacked me."

Vera nodded for him to continue. He felt ridiculous, telling her a story she already knew, but he wasn't ready to call her out. Not yet. He was curious about why she was hiding the truth, but he also wanted to play the game.

That meant he had to humor her, at least for now.

"They started attacking me right there," Lucian said. "Punches. Kicks. It was merciless." He watched all the Transcends; their collective gaze didn't seem to miss a single detail. "I didn't mean to lash out at them. It sort of happened. Like an instinct."

"Magic, you mean," Transcend Blue said.

Lucian nodded. "I don't know how it happened, but their leader, Dirk, started bleeding from his eyes. He turned out okay, but the captain threw me in the holding cell for ten days. Since then, I haven't touched magic at all. I came here to train. I need to learn to control this power inside me. And not hurt others in the process."

Lucian stopped telling the story. If they wanted to know more, they'd ask questions. But the length of their silence was grating on him, making him feel as if he hadn't explained himself well enough.

"If it were not for the sincerity in your voice," Transcend Blue finally said, "I'd be hard-pressed to believe you. What you did was no easy thing, especially for one untrained. To manipulate matter in such a manner, without any prior training . . . is remarkable, I must admit."

"Binding," Transcend Gray said. "Or Psionics, perhaps."

Transcend Blue held up a cautionary hand. "This is not praise, child, so do not take it as such. It might mean you've gone too far down the path. It's obvious you've trained yourself in some way. Once trained, it's difficult for a foundling to accept a new way." He shook his head. "I'm afraid that I cannot accept you for training."

Those words knocked the wind out of him. He opened his mouth, but no words came out.

"We should deliberate this more in private," Vera said. "Talent Khairu, please take them to some beds in the guest wing. I wish to keep them isolated for now."

Khairu inclined her head. "As you command, Transcend White."

She gestured for the young mages to follow her. Like that, the audience with the Transcends was over.

# 40

THEY FOLLOWED Khairu down the dark, empty corridors. Lucian's thoughts were reeling with the encounter. At this point, he didn't know what to make of it.

It wasn't long before they reached a heavy wooden door, which Khairu pushed open with a creak. A dark bare stone room stood revealed, containing a chest of drawers, a couple of candles, and a small bed. The bed came with a rough-looking blanket.

"These are your quarters, Lucian."

He looked back at Emma, who watched him with widened eyes. They might have time to talk about it later, but they couldn't do so here, in front of Khairu.

When Khairu left, Lucian closed the door and got out his slate to provide light. The room was so small he felt as if he were back in his prison cell. For such a large academy, he thought it would have a bigger room.

Lucian sat on the bed, wondering what to do, when a timid knock broke him from his thoughts. When he answered it, Emma stepped inside and shut the door behind her.

"About what happened on the ship," she said, without

preamble. "Khairu asked me how I knew you were a mage, and I didn't want to lie about it."

"Don't worry about it," Lucian said. "You should've just told me."

She sighed. "I know. I should have. I thought you would be mad." Her expression was apologetic. "I'm sorry. I messed up."

"Vera is more important," Lucian said, sitting on the bed. "Did you see that?"

Emma sat next to him. "I know! How could she have gotten here before us?"

"Maybe she came on a separate vessel. I'm wondering why she'd lie about it. That doesn't seem like something a Transcend would do. And on the ship, she said their teachings were a joke." He shook his head. "It doesn't make sense."

From Emma's silence, Lucian could tell she was stumped, too.

Lucian wanted to call Vera out on it. That would lock him out of consideration, but hadn't Vera preached honesty? What if all this were some elaborate test? That didn't seem too likely, either.

It was time to test her on her own word. Lucian had to be true to himself, whatever the consequences. Maybe that would only get him rejected, but if so, then at least he could hold his head high.

But what was the point of holding his head high? He *needed* to be accepted here. If he wasn't . . .

The Transcends were deliberating, even now. What would they decide?

"What do we do?" Emma asked.

Lucian closed his eyes, trying to imagine a future in this place. A future next to Emma, but not *with* her. A future of dying to himself, of divorcing himself from feeling. All to be able to control his connection to magic, and not die in the process.

It seemed like a bleak future. But were madness and death really a better alternative?

Finally, he responded to Emma. "We have to take it one day at a time."

"Where does someone even get food in this place?" Emma asked. "I'm *starving*."

Footsteps approached the door. There was a soft knock before it creaked open to reveal Khairu. From the way she stood in her gray cloak, Lucian thought she was going to scold them for being together.

Instead, though, she cleared her throat. "It's time."

It hadn't even been half an hour since the audience. That meant the decision was rather easy. It was hard to tell if that was good or bad.

There was only one way to find out. They followed Khairu through the dark halls of the Academy.

————

THE THREE TRANSCENDS sat on their stone chairs, not having moved since Emma and Lucian left.

"Emma Almaty," Transcend Blue said. "We accept you into our ranks, and raise you to the rank of Novice."

Emma's face had gone pale, and the offer didn't seem to make her relieved.

"Thank you," she said, her voice tremulous in the vast chamber.

As one, the Transcends' gazes fell upon Lucian. "Lucian Abrantes," Transcend Blue continued. "We have chosen to not accept you for training."

Emma looked on in shock, but the expression was gone with a clearing of Khairu's throat. Vera's eyes watched and weighed him, seeking a reaction.

"I understand your reasoning," he said, after swallowing the lump in his throat. "I expected it. Only, I don't have money to get back to Karendas."

"There's no need to worry about that," Transcend Blue said, his voice ominous.

The Transcends' silence was icy. They watched, unwilling or unable to offer more. Lucian had given everything for this opportunity. Now what?

The Manifold, it seemed, had spoken. It was his fate to die.

Transcends Blue and Gray shared a look before returning their attention to Lucian. The way they were staring made Lucian feel as if they were holding something back.

"You can stay here for the meantime," Vera decided, finally. "We'll make arrangements."

The last thing Lucian wanted was to be stuck in a place he wasn't wanted. But what else could he do?

"The storm precludes travel, in any case," Transcend Gray said. "I expect a few more days before it passes."

Lucian couldn't bring himself to ask the most obvious question. Maybe it was pride. After spending a couple of hours here, he'd seen enough.

"Your Eminences," Emma said. "I don't mean to question your judgment, but . . ."

"Then don't," Vera said, her voice cracking like a whip.

Lucian's eyes went to Vera. Her dark eyes bored into his, seeming to pierce straight to his soul. It took every bit of will he had to question her, and still, it only came out as a single word.

"Why?"

"I sense confusion within you, child," she said. "Speak now."

Transcends Blue and Gray looked at her, in mild surprise. Lucian got the sense that someone like him was beneath her notice.

"I don't understand," he began. "Why are you acting like we've never met before? As if . . . you don't even *remember* me?"

Vera stiffened, almost recoiled, at the words. "Whatever do you mean?"

"Why . . . you were on the ship," he said, fumbling. From her hard, dangerous stare, it was almost enough to make him feel as if *he* were the crazy one. As if he'd imagined it all. "You talked to me about the Manifold. About the fraying. About . . . finding my path. And now, you're acting like you've never seen me before. Is it punishment for choosing not to follow you, or something else?"

All three Transcends stared at him, their expressions unreadable. Vera's eyes smoldered like hot coals. Her face was a neutral mask of suppressed anger. It was terrible to look at.

At the same time, he couldn't break his gaze away. She *owed* him an answer, Transcend or not. She had gone against her own word, and needed to be held accountable for that. Even if he had chosen not to follow her, that had been *his* decision. It wasn't worthy of this punishment.

Finally, Vera relented, turning her head aside to speak. "Please, Transcends. Leave us a moment. Something extraordinary has happened."

There was a brief flash of surprise on their faces. And then they nodded, stood, and withdrew from the chamber. The colored fires on their either side burned out. Following their example, Khairu and Emma followed. Emma passed him, her expression worried, while Khairu seemed to be appraising him anew.

Once they were gone, the stone door slid shut.

Now, it was only Lucian and Vera.

## 41

VERA AND LUCIAN faced each other in the chamber, which was silent save for the flickering fires. Shadows danced like things alive in the fiery darkness.

"There's only one thing that makes sense," Vera said. "As unlikely as it might be."

"What do you mean?" Lucian could hardly control his anger. "Why would you talk to me on the ship, then pretend not to know me?"

"Let me clear your confusion," Vera said. "I sense you're telling the truth. And if that's so, you never met me. You must have met my twin sister."

The revelation was like a dousing of ice water. Vera had a *twin*, and that twin was none other than a Transcend here at the Academy. Looking her over, there was nothing in their appearance that suggested any difference. The only difference Lucian could see was Transcend White had a braid, while Vera wore her hair freely.

But it was the only explanation that made any sense. Despite their physical similarities, Lucian could sense a difference. Something about Transcend White's bearing seemed even colder than Vera's. Which was saying something, because Vera was cold.

Lucian cleared his throat. "Forgive me. She looks exactly like you."

"Yes, I'm aware of that," Transcend White said. "So, you spoke with her?"

Lucian nodded. "Several times, but the talks were long. She saw what I was, and shared some of her knowledge."

Her attention seemed to sharpen, and Lucian could almost hear the gears spinning in her head. "What knowledge?"

Under White's steely gaze, Lucian found it hard to even remember. "Things about the Manifold. Things about the fraying . . ." He shrugged. "It's hard to remember everything . . ." He trailed off, going blank. The way she was staring made him nervous.

"Compose yourself, child," Transcend White said. "This is important. You mean to tell me that you, Emma, and my sister were *all* on board the same vessel?"

Her tone stated that such a thing should have been impossible.

"It seems that way, your Eminence." It felt strange to call her that, but both Khairu and Emma had done the same. In Lucian's head, she still looked like Vera.

Her long, claw-like hands clamped on the stone armrests of her seat. Her expression became distant and thoughtful. Lucian had questions of his own, so when White hadn't said anything for a while, he took his chance.

"Is she dangerous?"

Transcend White's attention returned to him. "I want to know what she told you. I want to know everything."

He could hardly refuse. She had the same knack as her sister of gleaning every little detail, that much he could see.

So, he started talking. He began from the moment he first met Vera, to her philosophical musings about the Manifold and life. He spoke for what seemed a good half hour, only hesitating toward the end.

Transcend White watched him a moment. "Go on."

"She . . . requested I become her student."

To admit that seemed a betrayal to Vera, but all the same, Lucian felt the words being pulled from him.

Once done, he drew a deep breath, realizing he'd hardly stopped to breathe. He'd summarized everything that could be of interest to Transcend White.

Transcend White looked off to the side, her brow furrowed in thought. There she sat, ruminating, for what had to be a good quarter of an hour. In fact, it seemed she'd forgotten Lucian was even there. But he didn't dare interrupt her. He stood, his anxiety mounting every passing moment.

At last, Transcend White broke from her stillness like a statue coming to life.

"You are very fortunate to be here, Lucian Abrantes." She regarded him coolly. "My sister is a dangerous mage, and you're lucky to have escaped with your life. A powerful Transcend she once was, until she gave herself to the Free Mages to pursue power and her own selfish ends. Had you agreed to her offer, you would have been lost forever. Not only to us, but to yourself. You would have failed all who know, love, and depend on you." She looked at him, her gaze intensifying. "I've made a crucial error, something I don't often do. I misjudged you. What you did was no easy thing, refusing an offer that would have tempted many mages. Tell me: what made you choose to come here, when it seemed so unsure? Many would have taken the easier path. And it's not every day one receives a chance to learn from the most powerful mage in the galaxy."

When she said that, all Lucian could feel was stunned. When he found his tongue again, his reason had to have sounded pathetic. "I didn't know that. I guess she kept that to herself."

"Indeed? Count yourself lucky, then." She straightened in her seat. "I detect no falsehood in your tale. And you have no reason to lie. I also sense you have a good friend in Emma. Though you never said so, I detected shades of her influence in your words. Without her, you would have gone down a different path. It was only by accepting her help, and trusting her judgment, that tipped the scales enough." She regarded him seriously. "As it stands, it behooves us to train you, Lucian. We have no other choice, even if it defies the conventions of our Academy."

"Why?" he asked. "What's changed?"

"Everything, perhaps," Transcend White said. "And perhaps nothing. One thing is sure: whatever is of interest to my sister, is of interest to me."

There was still one thing Transcend White wasn't considering. "What if I *don't* accept?"

The corners of Transcend White's lips upturned into a small, mysterious smile. That smile reminded Lucian very much of her sister.

"What a strange question. Most who come here undergo a journey at great personal cost. Some come from many Gates away, traveling for well over a year. The Volsung Academy is the most prestigious mage training facility in the League of Worlds. If we accept your refusal, it would be the first such case in a century of our existence."

Lucian was quiet as he thought about those words. Refusal wasn't even an option. He had no other choice. After what Transcend White suggested, he was thinking he'd passed up an opportunity with Vera he was too ignorant to see.

"What about your sister is so dangerous?" Lucian asked. "I get she's a powerful mage. I may be speaking out of turn here, but many of the things she said made a lot of sense. Not everything. But some of the things."

"Her appeal is the one of the easier path," Transcend White

said. "Things that make sense to the untrained, animalistic human mind. To give in to the desire for power, to twist the Manifold into something self-serving, is a perversion. A perversion that has tempted many mages over the years, to their destruction."

These things made little sense to Lucian. Vera had argued that the Academy was the easier path. He still wasn't sure who was right.

"One thing is sure," Transcend White continued. "You will die without training. And the training offered by my sister would have led to a fate worse than death." Lucian got the feeling that she was about to tell him something more, before thinking better of it. "The only choice, as I see it, is to take you on here. Acceptance on your part would be ideal, but the boat can't leave for several days yet."

"I see your point."

"Yours is a stubborn mind. It may even be impossible to train you. But I fear we have no choice. You, or me." Transcend White stood, and looked down upon him. "But all the same . . . we must try."

At some unspoken signal, the door to the chamber opened. Transcends Blue and Gray returned, along with Talent Khairu. Of Emma, there was no sign.

"Lead him to the Novice Wing," Transcend White said, to Khairu. "And confiscate his belongings." Before Lucian could say anything in protest, Transcend White continued. "I invoke my executive privilege as Transcend White. Lucian Abrantes is to be entered into our ranks as a Novice."

Her dark eyes focused on him. Those eyes so like Vera's, but not like hers. And like Vera's, they seemed to hold secrets, and plans of their own.

"His training begins tomorrow."

# EPILOGUE

*FIND THE ASPECTS . . . bring them to me . . .*

The voice whispered in the darkness. Lucian fought to free himself from this nightmare, but he was paralyzed. His heart thundered. It felt at any moment, the tiger's jaws would find him.

*Promise me . . . promise me . . .*

*Who are you?* Lucian asked. *What do you want with me?*

*You promised. Find the Orbs. Bring them to me . . .*

*Let me go. Let me out!*

*Promise me.*

Lucian wrestled with the dark voice. He knew, beyond the shadow of a doubt, he would never wake up if he continued to refuse.

*I don't know what the Aspects are. What are the Orbs?*

*You will know,* the voice said. *You will know when you see. Promise me. You must promise me . . .*

Lucian fought with the voice for a long time. Time stretched, and darkness deepened. He didn't know how long he waited as the darkness pressed into him, as if he were at the bottom of the Godsdeep.

Seven shining lights. Red, Orange, Yellow, Green, Blue, Violet, and Gray. They were arranged in a Septagon, one light for each corner. And at the center . . . a shape too bewildering to behold. Something about it was . . . wrong. Corrupted. It expanded within his mind, taking root there like an unwanted weed.

*Promise me . . .*

All Lucian wanted was to forget that voice. But the voice wouldn't allow that.

*Promise me . . .*

Claustrophobia. Panic. Suffocation.

*Promise me . . .*

He had to get out of here. He would do anything. Say anything. Accept anything.

*. . . I promise.*

The voice relented and allowed Lucian to sleep.

Starsea would rise again.

## THE END OF BOOK ONE

*The Starsea Cycle* continues in Book Two,
THE ORB OF BINDING

Lucian has achieved the improbable with his acceptance into the prestigious Volsung Academy. Now, he must do something even more difficult: survive it.

As a Novice, he must learn the fundamentals of magic while navigating Academy politics. Lucian must not only pass the grueling Trials, but survive other mages' mechanizations. But doing that is difficult when he's being left behind.

But one day, Lucian makes a breakthrough that puts *him* on top.

He's about to learn that being good is far more dangerous than being unexceptional. Expulsion is an ever-looming threat, and with it, Lucian risks losing the only place in the Worlds he can call home...

# ABOUT THE AUTHOR

Kyle West is the author of a number of sci-fi and fantasy series: *The Starsea Cycle, The Wasteland Chronicles,* and *The Xenoworld Saga.*

His goal is to write as many entertaining books as possible, with interesting worlds and characters that hopefully give his readers a break from the mundane.

He lives in South Florida with his lovely wife, son, and two insanely spoiled cats. He enjoys hearing from his fans, and invites them to connect with him through his Facebook page, website, or newsletter.

kylewestwriter.com
kylewestwriter@gmail.com

For information on new releases, please sign up for my newsletter.

 facebook.com/kylewestwriter

# ALSO BY KYLE WEST

### THE STARSEA CYCLE

*The Mages of Starsea*

*The Orb of Binding*

*The Rifts of Psyche*

### THE WASTELAND CHRONICLES

*Apocalypse*

*Origins*

*Evolution*

*Revelation*

*Darkness*

*Extinction*

*Xenofall*

*Lost Angel (Prequel)*

### THE XENOWORLD SAGA

*Prophecy*

*Bastion*

*Beacon*

*Sanctum*

*Kingdom*

*Dissolution*

*Aberration*